# HERE COMES TROUBLE

Young adult novels by Kate Hattemer

*The Land of 10,000 Madonnas*
*The Vigilante Poets of Selwyn Academy*

# HERE COMES TROUBLE

## KATE HATTEMER

Alfred A. Knopf
New York

Text copyright © 2018 by Kate Hattemer

Jacket art copyright © 2018 by Marie Thorhauge

All rights reserved. Published in the United States by Alfred A. Knopf, an imprint of Random House Children's Books, a division of Penguin Random House LLC, New York.

Knopf, Borzoi Books, and the colophon are registered trademarks of Penguin Random House LLC.

Visit us on the Web! rhcbooks.com

Educators and librarians, for a variety of teaching tools, visit us at RHTeachersLibrarians.com

*Library of Congress Cataloging-in-Publication Data*
Names: Hattemer, Kate, author.
Title: Here comes trouble / Kate Hattemer.
Description: First edition. | New York : Alfred A. Knopf | Summary: Soren is famous for his pranks, but with his best friend gone and well-behaved cousin Flynn visiting for a year, he tries to mend his ways.
Identifiers: LCCN 2017028599 (print) | LCCN 2017040461 (ebook) | ISBN 978-1-5247-1846-6 (trade) | ISBN 978-1-5247-1847-3 (lib. bdg.) | ISBN 978-1-5247-1848-0 (ebook)
Subjects: | CYAC: Practical jokes—Fiction. | Schools—Fiction. | Family life—Fiction. | Cousins—Fiction. | Behavior—Fiction.
Classification: LCC PZ7.H2847 (ebook) | LCC PZ7.H2847 Her 2018 (print) | DDC [Fic]—dc23

The text of this book is set in 12-point Chaparral Pro.

Printed in the United States of America

May 2018

10 9 8 7 6 5 4 3 2 1

First Edition

for Henry

# CHAPTER ONE

OUR MISSION: to see out the window without anyone seeing us.

Difficult, sure, given the whole windows-made-of-glass thing. But Ruth and I have had a lot of experience with spy work, and we instantly saw the potential in the long white curtains. She swaddled herself in one and I took the other. We couldn't move, and we couldn't retaliate when our brother, Ivan, who's two and terrible, hit us with his Barbie. But we would get the first look at any car coming down our street.

"They better get here soon," said Ruth. "I feel like a mummy."

"Mummies can't feel," I told her. Ruth is only in fourth grade, and sometimes her lack of education shows. As her big brother, I feel it's my duty to enlighten her. "Their brains have been siphoned out—ah-*choo!*"

"Don't tell Dad how dusty these curtains are," said Ruth. "He'll make us vacuum."

"Ah-*choo!*" I wiped my nose on the fabric. "What if I'm sneezing and I miss the car? I'm keeping my eyes open next time."

"No! Soren! No!" The white column that was Ruth swayed in panic. "If you keep your eyes open when you sneeze, they explode out of your head."

"No way."

"I read it in a book."

"I don't believe it."

"Fine," said Ruth. "Try. See if I care." She stared dourly out the window. "See if *I'll* pick up your bloody eyes from the floor. See if *I'll* put them on ice while we wait for the ambulance. See if—"

"Okay! Okay! I'll—ah-ah-ah-*choo!*"

I'd closed my eyes.

"*Thank* you," said Ruth.

It wasn't fun, being burrito-wrapped in a curtain that was rapidly coming to resemble the inside of a tissue, but I needed to get a look at Flynn before he got a look at me. A newcomer is big news when you live in a tiny town. And I mean *tiny:* there's not a single person in Camelot who doesn't know me, my parents, and how old I was when I last wet the bed.

(Too old.)

You see, Flynn's mom, our aunt Linnea, is an artist. She won a prize where she gets to study in Paris for a year, and she doesn't have to work in a restaurant, too, the way she does in New York. It was a big deal. Probably a bigger deal, though, was that our cousin Flynn was coming to live with us for the entire school year. It was the most exciting thing to happen in Camelot since Mr. Flick's pig made it to the Sweet Sixteen of the Northern Minnesota Hog Farmers N-C-Double-Oink March Madness Tournament.

"My new best friend is about to get here," I said to Ruth, "and I don't even know what he looks like."

Flynn and I hadn't seen each other since we were Ivan's age, nine years ago. I had no memories of the visit, but Mom sure did. "You didn't get along," she'd said. "You had entirely different senses of fun."

"What do you mean?"

"Flynn was calm. He would sit in a corner and page through books, even though he couldn't read. His favorite toy was a child-sized yoga mat."

"He did yoga?"

"He'd be in downward dog," said Mom, "and you'd be sprinting circles around him, *whumpa-whumpa*-ing, pretending you were a helicopter."

"I bet Flynn's more fun now."

"People are different, Soren. People have fun in different ways."

She'd kept talking, but I'd tuned out. The thing was, Flynn couldn't have been coming at a better time. Alex, my best friend and partner in crime, had moved away at the beginning of the summer, and I was lonely without her. Ruth and I were pals—we'd really bonded since Ivan was born; nothing like a common enemy—and I had other friends at school. But a *best* friend is different. A best friend is your default. Your other half. If you've had a best friend and then not had one, whether because of moves or new schools or betrayals, you know. You know how much it stinks.

"There!" squealed Ruth.

I peered out the window. Ruth did the same. Even Ivan attempted a pull-up to boost himself above the windowsill.

Dad's Honda crawled down the street and stopped in front of our house. Our eyes were trained on the passenger door.

It slowly opened.

A bowling shoe emerged.

An argyle sock.

A cuffed pair of—

"Are those *skinny jeans*?" said Ruth.

Then the other leg, and then the torso: a purple plaid shirt, a black bandanna tied in a jaunty, cowboy-like V.

Longish brown hair, topped by—

"Is that a *beret*?" said Ruth.

And under the beret, a face that looked way too much like mine—

"Is that *Flynn*?" said Ruth.

That was Flynn.

FLYNN HAD TWO pieces of luggage: a messenger bag and a trunk. He handled the messenger bag. Dad heaved the trunk up the walk to the house, his lips pursed into the face that I privately call *if I weren't a dad, I'd be cursing right now.*

Flynn followed, his mouth moving fast. Dad dropped the trunk on the porch and crumpled against a pillar, wiping the sweat off his shiny bald head. As Flynn reached for the doorknob, Ruth and I jumped to get untangled from the curtains.

"Greetings!" Flynn called into the house.

Ruth and I looked at each other.

"You have dust on your forehead," I told her.

"Well, there's *something* hanging from your nose," she told me.

We wiped our faces on our curtains.

"Are we good?" I said.

"We're good."

I'd expected some kid in gym shorts and a ratty T-shirt. Someone like Alex.

Someone like me.

We went into the entry hall.

"Flynn," said Dad, panting slightly and gripping his lower back, "you remember your cousins. Soren and Ruth."

Flynn extended his hand with a dramatic windmilling move. "Delighted."

"Um," I said, gingerly shaking his hand, "me too."

"Absolutely *delighted.*"

"Same," said Ruth.

We stood there. I kicked my left shoe with my right. Ruth fiddled with her pigtail. Dad, who is oblivious to awkwardness, and in fact creates it whenever possible (do not, under any circumstances, allow this man to chaperone your school dance), said, "A family reunion! What a day, what a day!"

Ivan charged into the entry hall, still wielding the Barbie.

"And this," said Dad, "is—"

Ivan crashed into Flynn's legs.

"—Ivan."

"The Terrible," Ruth and I added in unison.

Dad scooped him up. Ivan hates being restrained— strollers, car seats, cribs, he sees them all as the prisons they are—so he started howling. "Oh, shush," Dad said crabbily. "I'm not letting you maul your cousin on his first day."

Flynn flinched. "Don't worry," I told him. "Ivan's relatively harmless. He'll throw food, sure, and toys, especially pointy ones, and he's got really good aim, which is weird, since he'll run right into a wall if there's nothing in his path, but he's not that bad. . . ."

"Lies," whispered Ruth.

"Well?" Dad asked Ivan. "Do you promise not to attack Flynn?"

"WON'T!" hollered Ivan.

Personally, I'd have asked Ivan to specify: Won't attack, or won't promise? But Dad, a hopeless optimist, set him down. Ivan growled in satisfaction.

"Well, well, well, Flynn!" Dad said. "We'll have dinner when your aunt Lucinda gets home, but what would you like to do now?"

"Ruth and I can give you a tour!" I said.

We'd practiced that morning. I was the tour guide, and she was Flynn. She kept saying things like "Wowzers!" And "We don't have chicken coops in New York!" And "How amazing is it that you have a pet piglet?"

It had made us both even *more* excited for his arrival.

"I don't know," said Flynn. "How extensive is this tour?"

"Very," I assured him. "The house, the garage, the chicken coop, the vegetable garden, the tree platform, the clubhouse, the dock, the pigpen—"

"You keep pigs?"

"One piglet," said Ruth. "One adorable, roly-poly piglet."

When our neighbor Mr. Flick had offered us Jim Bob, the runt of the litter, the idea was that he'd live a typical piggy life: gain four hundred pounds, turn into sausage. Then Ruth had gotten attached. She'd rather eat her own arm than a Jim Bob patty.

Her expression had gone all hazy and lovestruck. "One darling pork dumpling, cuddleable, snuggleable—"

Flynn shifted from foot to foot. "I'm not sure about touching a live pig."

"Let's go introduce you two!" said Ruth.

He glanced up at Dad. "It's just, I've been traveling all day. . . ."

Dad jumped in. "Come on into the kitchen. We'll relax, catch up, get reacquainted. May I offer you a Coke?"

RUTH, IVAN, AND I will do anything for Coke. We never get it except for holidays. So we followed Dad into the

7

kitchen like ants following a sugar trail, which I guess we kind of were.

"You pour and we'll choose," I told Ruth. She got down four glasses, and I monitored her to make sure she wasn't pulling the ol' ice cube trick. (You put less ice in your own glass so you get more drink. Ruth is known for it.) "You can have first choice," I told Flynn, like the gracious host I am.

"Actually," he said, "I don't consume corn syrup."

"You mean—"

"I don't want any. Thanks, though."

Ruth, shocked and appalled, stared at Flynn. I must have looked the same way, because Dad said, "*Children!* Manners! Do we stare at our guests?"

"But he doesn't want Coke," Ruth told Dad.

"A healthy choice!" said Dad, clapping Flynn on the back. "Maybe we should *all* cut out corn syrup."

Ruth and I shot each other identical looks of dismay.

"I'll stir up some lemonade instead," said Dad.

"Actually," said Flynn, "I don't consume any sugar. No white sugar, no brown sugar, no corn syrup, no rice syrup, no dextrose, no sucrose, no evaporated cane juice—"

"What's left?" said Ruth.

"I used to eat honey, but then I became concerned for bee welfare. Uncle Jon, may I use the kettle?"

Dad, clearly gobsmacked, gave a nod.

"Would anyone like a hot cup of Japanese green tea?" Flynn rustled around in his messenger bag and pulled out a bag of brown twigs. "It's sourced directly from Mount Fuji."

"DIRT!" cried Ivan. "STICKS!" He beamed—he's used to receiving massive amounts of positive reinforcement every time he uses a word other than *no, won't,* or *don't*—but nobody paid him any attention. We were watching Flynn measure twigs into a tiny strainer.

"I get this at a specialty store called Sereni-Tea," he said. "Back in Brooklyn, of course. I can walk there by myself."

"We're allowed to walk around Camelot by ourselves too," said Ruth.

"It's next door to Spinster, my favorite record shop. And down the street is L'Éléphant—they sell vintage luggage; that's where I got my trunk. Ooh, water's boiling!"

He poured the water into the strainer and set an hourglass on the counter. The sand trickled down. "It steeps for five minutes."

"Couldn't you use the microwave timer?" I said.

"I like to keep the tea ceremony pure."

"I have a feeling this family will learn a lot from you," said Dad.

Flynn smiled in a way that reminded me of this angel ornament we have. Ruth and I call him Little Angel Two-Shoes, and every Christmas Eve we have a secret contest that involves beaning him in the head with peanuts.

The last grains of sand slipped through the hourglass. Flynn crouched to photograph the tea. "Who wants a sip?" he said.

He looked so eager. Round eyes, raised eyebrows, a hopeful smile. He looked from Ruth to Ivan, and I thought,

Fat chance in *those* quarters. They were sucking down Coke like they were being paid by the ounce.

"I'll try it," I said.

I lifted the cup. The steam hit my nose. I nearly heaved. I had to set it down so I could swallow the saliva filling my mouth. The tea smelled, no joke, like a barfy toilet.

But I couldn't back out now.

I took a sip.

*"BLECH!"*

A warm mouthful of Japanese green tea, sourced directly from Mount Fuji, splattered across the kitchen.

"Soren!" said Dad, wiping droplets from his face.

"Gross!" said Ruth, rubbing her eyes.

"BLECH!" said Ivan in imitation, spitting out a glob of Coke and drool.

I sprinted to the sink and stuck my mouth under the faucet.

"Want me to brew you a full cup?" said Flynn.

"That tasted like pig pee!"

"Manners!" said Dad.

"How do you know what pig pee tastes like?" said Ruth.

"Disastrous game of truth-or-dare—let's not get into it. Flynn, you *drink* that?"

"I think it's good."

But for the first time since he'd arrived, he sounded hesitant.

"It's dead-on pig pee," I said. "Come out to Jim Bob's pen and I'll prove it."

"Unacceptable," said Dad. "Soren, apologize to your guest."

"Sorry, Flynn," I said, "but it's got that *tang*, you know?"

"To your room, young man!" said Dad.

"I don't *have* a room anymore," I reminded him.

"Soren Ebenezer Skaar. *Immediately.*"

I whirled around and left.

"Please excuse us, Flynn," I heard Dad say as I stomped up the stairs. "Soren needs to work on his manners."

"I listen to an etiquette podcast I could recommend to him," Flynn said. "Maybe it would help."

# CHAPTER TWO

"COCK-A-DOO-ARGH-ACK-ECK-EH!"

I was released from solitary confinement just as Martha, our rooster, decided it was dawn.

"COCK-A-DOO-ARGH-ACK-ECK-EH!"

He starts out with your standard crow, but then he switches to a terrifying hacking noise. It's like he's puking. Or dying. "Good afternoon, Martha," I called, giving the coop a wide berth.

He snarled at me. His wives pecked at invisible bugs. When he was a chick, he looked like our most adoring great-aunt, all fluffy-haired and wrinkly-ankled, so we named him Martha. Then he turned out to be a scrawny old rooster and she stopped being so adoring. Oops.

I dug around in the garage and found the old soccer ball I use for shooting on the woodpile. I shot—*thwop*—and the ball bounded back. The woodpile's almost as good as a friend. Alex and I used to spend a lot of time out here on the driveway, kicking around and plotting our next prank.

*Thwop.*

It had been sunny earlier, but now clouds were blowing in. Ruth came outside. "Where's Flynn?" I said.

"Taking a nap."

"Voluntarily?"

"He said he wants to be rested for the first day of school tomorrow."

"Oh. Weird."

I passed to her. She did a nice trap and passed back. "Will you tell me?" she said. "Please?"

"Tell you what?"

"I'll keep it a secret. I promise."

"I don't know what you're talking about."

"Tomorrow's the first day of school, Soren." She gave me a significant look. "The *first* day of *school.*"

"Do you have to rub it in?"

"Just tell me what you're planning! I'm old enough now. I won't spill to Mom and Dad."

I hit my pass too hard. It went wide, and I had to jog to the chicken coop to get it. When I came back, I said, "Nothing."

"Come on, Soren. What are you going to do?"

"Nothing. I told you. Nothing."

"But you always have an epic prank for the first day of school!"

"Well, not this year."

It had been a tradition, the epic welcome-back prank. Alex and I used to spend all summer planning. We'd had our share of failures (when the thousand live crickets we'd bought online had escaped in her bedroom a week early), but people still talked about our successes (when the trophies for the Kick-Off Kickball Game had been found mysteriously encased in Jell-O).

But now that she'd moved three hundred miles south . . .

"I might have retired from pranking," I told Ruth.

"Yeah, right," she said. "I saw what you put in the saltshaker last week."

"That wasn't a prank. That was a modest joke. How am I supposed to pull off an epic prank without Alex?"

"I could help," she said.

"You're only nine."

"You pulled off Tapegate when you were nine!"

I smiled despite myself. We'd replaced all the toilet paper at school with rolls of duct tape. "Everyone got stranded," I said reminiscently.

"Not Connor Carraway," said Ruth. "He wiped."

The sky had gone a yellowish gray, and we heard a clap of thunder. "Kids!" Dad yelled out the window. "Tarp the chicken coop before it rains, would you?"

Ruth and I groaned. Our coop's sort of ramshackle. It doesn't have a real roof, just a wire grate. You probably think throwing a tarp doesn't sound too bad, but that's because you haven't met Martha.

The thunder clapped again, a lot louder. "Don't dilly-dally!" yelled Dad.

Ruth shot me a dark look. "Let's get this over with."

We got the tarp from the garage. The chickens, sensing the coming rain, had huddled on the roosts and in the nesting boxes, but Martha was eyeing us. "COCK-A-DOO-ARGH-ACK-ECK-EH!" he screeched.

"He saw the tarp," said Ruth.

I felt a drop of rain on my cheek. As bad as it is to tarp the coop, it's worse to clean it once it's gotten wet. The bedding gets all mildewy, and the chicken poop liquefies and makes paste with the dirt. "Hurry," I said.

We stretched the tarp between us. It was really raining now, drops hitting the packed dirt so hard they spattered up on the rebound.

"Ready?"

We approached the coop. This is the part that's terrifying. Martha *hates* being tarped. So when he sees it coming, he hurls himself against the wire walls of the coop.

And yeah, the walls are going to hold. (Probably.) But if a twenty-pound rooster with ferocious claws and a pointy beak and a high-decibel crow is hurling himself at you, you're going to want to fling yourself out of danger.

The part of your brain that's evolved for survival doesn't think much of chicken wire, is what I'm saying.

"One," we chanted. "Two. Three—"

Martha attacked just as the tarp was sailing toward the coop. Ruth dove to the ground. The tarp got all wadded up. "Sorry," she said.

"I was about to go down myself," I admitted.

"It's a simple task, kids!" yelled Dad. "Just get it done!"

"I'd like to see Dad face down Martha," I grumbled. Our parents don't believe us about how mean he is.

"One," said Ruth after we'd gotten into position. "Two. Three—"

"AHHH!" I launched myself to the ground. I couldn't help it. He'd flown right at me.

"Think about chicken fingers," said Ruth, who looked as pale and shaken as I felt.

"How did we end up with a rooster who's claustrophobic *and* a psychopath?" I said.

"We *dominate* you, Martha!" Ruth shouted into the coop. "We have your kind for *dinner!*"

"One. Two. *Three!*"

We threw the tarp. It landed. We could hear Martha freaking out inside—flapping his wings, pitching himself against the walls, and cock-a-doodle-vomiting while his poor wives clucked—but we were safe. "Come on," said Ruth. We ran through the pouring rain to the house.

# CHAPTER THREE

"WHAT A NIGHT!" said Dad over dubious-looking plates of eggplant, couscous, and something stringy and orange. The storm was wailing outside. We had the lights on in the kitchen. Every so often the rain was interrupted by the roar of thunder, the snap of branches, and the distant, haunted screeches of Martha. "We've got a lot to celebrate!"

"A lot to *mourn*," Ruth corrected him. "School starts tomorrow."

"Yes, school starts tomorrow!" said Dad in exactly the opposite tone. "And this morning, Ivan went to music group and didn't hit anyone with his tambourine!"

"DID!" Ivan insisted.

"Well, only me."

"Progress," said Mom, patting Ivan on the head. "Good boy."

"But most importantly," said Dad, "we're welcoming our dear nephew and cousin to Camelot!" He raised his glass. "To Flynn's year studying 'abroad'!"

"And to my gracious hosts!" said Flynn. They clinked glasses. "This reminds me."

He stood.

"I just started playing the banjo." He whipped it out from under his chair.

"Very cool!" said Dad.

"And as a small gesture of appreciation to you—you're so generous, taking me into the bosom of your family—"

I gagged. The combination of eggplant and the word *bosom* was just too much. Flynn waited till I was done coughing.

"—I wrote you a song on the plane. It's to the tune of 'O Little Town of Bethlehem.' I'm a huge fan of using religious songs for more inclusive purposes." He strummed a chord. "May I?"

"Of course, Flynn!" said Mom. "We're honored!"

Another chord, and he began.

> "O tiny town of Camelot,
> Thy fields have lured me in.
> This city mouse has found a house
> With country mice, his kin!
> I'm already enchanted
> By rustic, homespun charm.
> My city grit, my jaded wit,
> Are sweetened on thy farm."

"We don't live on a farm," said Ruth.

"Shush," said Dad.

*"O peewee town of Camelot,*
*Where all is sky and tree,*
*No subway trains mar these great plains,*
*There's nothing to do but be.*
*How quaint the prairie seemeth,*
*When I think of whence I roam,*
*Yet earthy scents and dirt-cheap rents*
*Make this my home, sweet home!"*

He strummed one final chord and looked up eagerly. "What do you think?"

IF I WERE starting at a new school, I'd be nervous. So after dinner, after Dad told Flynn to skip the dishes, after Ruth and I did the dishes, after we got into a splash fight over the dishes, after we got yelled at for getting water on the floor, after we mopped, I went to his room. Which, until yesterday, had been my room. Now I was sharing with Ruth and Ivan.

I did a double take when I walked in the door. "You rearranged the furniture," I said.

"Do you like it?"

"It's different."

"Thank you."

I didn't really mean it as a compliment, just a comment. He'd put the bed at a diagonal, and the room seemed off-kilter. It reminded me of these Mondrian paintings we'd learned about in art. They're white with lines and blocks, but they aren't symmetrical at all, and though I'm not a neat freak—kind of the opposite, actually—it bothers me.

Flynn was arranging mason jars on the windowsill. "I like to keep these filled with seasonal plants," he told me. "Lilies in the summer, goldenrod in the fall, et cetera."

"I guess that's goldenrod?"

"Your dad took me out to pick it after dinner. You don't know the plants in your own garden?"

Flowers have petals. Weeds are ugly. Don't step in poison ivy. That's about the extent of my plant knowledge. "Why are you doing all this decorating, anyway?"

"I'm very sensitive to my surroundings. My mom says so."

I plopped down on the diagonal bed. "This angle would make me seasick."

"Good thing I'm sleeping here, not you."

It was weird hearing that about my room, but I guessed I'd get used to it. I'd have to. "Listen, about tomorrow," I said. "We're in the same class, so stick with me. I'll introduce you to all the teachers."

"I can introduce myself."

"Sure, but they teach fifth grade too, so I know them really well already."

"In Brooklyn, we start middle school in sixth grade."

"Well," I said, kind of annoyed at his interruptions, "Camelot's not big enough for a middle school. So we have K to six and seven to twelve. Any other questions?" He shook his head. "Okay. Teachers. Ms. Madigan is math. If you raise your hand for the bathroom, she acts all disappointed, so what you've got to do is make a thoughtful comment and *then* ask to go. Ms. Hutchins is science, and she's super intense about lab safety, so I know it'll be tempting, but if we do anything with acid, do *not* pretend to drink—"

"I'm good with teachers," said Flynn. "Adults like me."

"Still, I wouldn't suggest fake-chugging acid in front of Ms. H."

"I've been going to school in New York. I think I'll be able to handle it here."

"But you don't even know where the cafeteria is!" I wasn't halfway through the fundamentals of survival at Camelot Elementary School. "You don't know where detention is!"

"I'm not planning to get detention."

"Yeah, that's what I always say too," I said grimly. "You don't even know which teachers *give* detention. Or which stall doesn't flush, or which water fountain tastes like blood. You don't know what we do at recess!"

"You have recess?"

"You don't?"

"It's considered passé."

I didn't need to ask him what *passé* meant. If he'd let me finish my teacher intros, he'd have known our Language Arts teacher was obsessed with context clues. "I'd quit school if we didn't have recess," I said. "We play pickup soccer. Do you play soccer?"

"I'm on a club team. Well, I *was* on a club team. At home."

"Really?" I said, excited. "That's perfect! I'll draft you for my side."

He had to be good, if he played club. Maybe *really* good. And Billiam Flick wouldn't know how good, and my team would win. And Flynn and I could play on the driveway every day after school, and sometimes maybe we'd get Mom or Dad to take us down to the high school so we could shoot on a real goal. He could show me tricks he'd learned from club, and I could show him tricks I'd learned from YouTube, and I'd have someone to play with all the time. Someone who weighed more than fifty-four pounds, unlike my sister. Someone whose idea of "defense" wasn't smearing the ball with deer poop, unlike my brother.

Someone who lived in Camelot. Unlike Alex.

This school year wasn't going to be so bad after all.

"It's still light out," I said. "Let's go kick around on the driveway!"

"I don't know," said Flynn. "I'm tired. Tomorrow's a big day."

"Oh."

"Hey, um," he said, twiddling a goldenrod stalk, "what are the other kids in our class like?"

"Normal. Well, mostly normal. Some of them. Sometimes."

He twiddled more. Finally, he said, "Do you think I'll have friends?"

"You'll have me."

"Is that it?"

"There haven't been any new kids since the Andrezejczak triplets came in first grade. Everyone's going to be very, very interested in you."

I wouldn't have guessed he was the shy, retiring type, not after what he'd done to that Christmas carol, but he looked terrified.

"Soren!" Mom yelled. "The shower's unoccupied! Now's your chance!"

"What if I don't need to shower?"

"Not an option!"

"But I don't smell!"

I could hear Mom laughing from two floors away. Flynn followed me to the door. "The bus ride tomorrow morning—can I sit with you?"

Maybe he *was* nervous. Or maybe he just wanted to sing me a song. *We three kids of Camelot are / On the bus we travel afar.* "Sure," I said. "You can even have the window if you want. Full disclosure, though: I get carsick on the aisle."

# CHAPTER FOUR

CAMELOT ELEMENTARY SCHOOL is a big redbrick building. It has round towers at each corner, and it looks like a castle, except with a playground instead of a moat.

Flynn's banjo case knocked against the seats as we walked off the bus. I hitched up my backpack and gave my hair a quick rub. Mom likes to lick her palm and smooth it down before I leave the house, and this morning I hadn't dodged quickly enough.

"Move faster," Ruth grumbled from behind us. "Some of us have friends we want to see."

I took a deep breath and stepped into the playground, which was already teeming. Ruth shot off.

"Where are *your* friends?" said Flynn.

"Um," I said, "I'm looking."

There was Ruth's pack of fourth-grade girls, already playing double Dutch. There were the cool kids, who all wear the same socks. There were the tetherballers and the monkey-barrers and the climb-the-firepolers and the fun-sized replicas of human beings known as kindergartners.

24

But where was—

Oh.

Ever since kindergarten, I'd gotten off the bus and looked for Alex. I guess I was so used to it that I'd . . . I'd forgotten.

"Come on," I said to Flynn. Over by the flagpole, I saw guys from my grade: Jéronimo Luna and Freddy Firkins and Marsupial Jones. We play recess soccer together. I go to their birthday parties, and they come to mine.

They're fine.

They aren't Alex.

But they're fine.

They were in a tight bunch, examining something in Freddy's palm. I joined them. Flynn hung back. "What's in there?" I said.

"Mexican jumping beans!" said Freddy. "My uncle gave them to me!"

I craned in. Six brown beans were sitting on his palm. I opened my mouth to ask what was so special about them, and then one of them jumped. It jumped half an inch, right before our eyes.

"Are they mechanical?" I said.

"They've got moth larvas inside," said Jéro.

Another jumped, and another. It was so weird. Just when you thought they were normal dried beans, they'd twitch.

"Wow," I said, imagining the possibilities. "You know how Ms. Hutchins always has that big salad for lunch?"

"So?" said Soup. (His mom is a naturalist; that's how he got named Marsupial. But everyone calls him Soup.)

"So I've got the perfect plan," I said. "We'll send Flynn to the teachers' lounge. If anyone asks, he got lost looking for the bathroom. He opens the fridge, finds her salad, dumps in the beans, and no one's the wiser."

They stared at me. Flynn had edged closer when he heard his name, and he was the first to speak.

"Isn't there a sign on the door of the teachers' lounge? Wouldn't I know it's not the bathroom?"

"You're not going to get in trouble on your first day at Camelot. Oh, hey, everyone, this is Flynn. My cousin. Flynn, meet Jéro, Freddy, and Soup."

They nodded.

"Back to the plan," I said. "Flynn? Try first period, because that way if you're redirected, we'll have three more chances before lunch—"

"I'm not feeding my beans to Ms. Hutchins," said Freddy.

"She wouldn't eat them. She'd be *about* to eat them. They'd be on her fork, and then . . ." I gave a sudden, twitchy hop in my best impression of a Mexican jumping bean. "Imagine her face!"

"I like my beans," said Freddy. "I want to see the moths hatch."

"They're pets," said Soup.

"Would you put a dog in Ms. Hutchins's salad?" said Jéro.

"Besides," said Flynn, "I think I can find the bathroom."

"You're all missing the point," I said.

Alex would have understood. Alex would have called my

26

idea and raised it. Who *knew* what would have happened? Things tended to spiral out of control when Alex and I worked together.

How would I ever prank again without her?

*PHWEEET! PHWEEET!*

Mrs. Andersen whistled on her knuckles to call us inside.

"HELLO, HELLO!" said Ms. Hutchins. She's our homeroom teacher and our science teacher, so we have her for seventy minutes first thing in the morning. I like Ms. Hutchins. She's pretty chill, except when it comes to veganism and science. "I hope you all had a wonderful summer." She smiled, pretending she'd missed us the way they make teachers do. "Who did something exciting?"

"I went to Washington, D.C.," said Jeremiah Johnson.

"I went to the mall in Duluth," said Goldie Grandin.

"I got Mexican jumping beans," said Freddy, spoiling the prank once and for all.

"I got chicken pox," said Tabitha Andrezejczak.

"Chicken pox is extinct," said Jéro.

"Not for me," Tabitha said proudly.

"I always knew you were a mutant," I whispered.

Tabitha rolled her eyes and whispered back, "Nothing's as mutant as your face, Soren Skaar."

"Soren!" said Ms. Hutchins. I jumped. "I believe something exciting happened to *you* this summer!"

"Uh . . ."

My summer: Kicking a ball against the woodpile. Playing

27

Settlers of Catan with Ruth. Seeing what Ivan would and wouldn't eat. Rereading Harry Potter, all sad because the Fred to my George had moved away.

What was Ms. Hutchins talking about?

"Would you introduce our new student?" she said.

Oh!

Flynn was perched on the edge of his seat, his feet tucked up on the rung. "Yeah," I said, "so that's my cousin."

"Soren! Where's our Minnesota politeness? Let's hear a real introduction!"

I coughed. "Ladies and gentlemen, please allow me to present *the* Flynn Skaar, straight outta Brooklyn." That got a laugh, even though Alex would have said it was overused. "Flynn likes . . ." Uh-oh. What *did* he like? "He likes banjo, green tea, soccer, and—"

"Science!" said Flynn. "I love science!"

Ms. Hutchins beamed. "Flynn," she said, "why don't you tell us a bit—"

He was already on his feet. Here was something else Flynn liked: an audience. "Hello, everyone!" he said. "I'm thrilled to be here in Camelot for my sixth-grade year! I hail from New York, and I'd be happy to answer any questions you might have about life in the city."

The class was staring, openmouthed. So much for him acting nervous last night.

"Soren's right, I'm currently a banjo-tea-soccer kind of dude, but my passions change a lot. Let me give you my usernames so you can keep up."

We aren't allowed to have phones or iPods or anything in school, but he spelled them out, and Goldie wrote them down. And if Goldie does something, other girls do it too.

"Long story short," said Flynn, "Adidas over Nike, pita chips over potato chips, Yankees over Mets. That about sums it up! That's me!"

He popped into his seat. "I like pita chips too," Goldie whispered.

"Well, *I* like the Yankees," said Freddy.

"You do not," I reminded him. When they'd swept the Twins last year, Freddy had bought a Baby Ruth bar just to smash it to a pooplike pulp on his driveway. "You hate the Yankees."

Nobody paid attention to me. "Pinstripers, unite!" said Flynn, giving Freddy a high five. He turned to Goldie. "Potato chips are just too greasy, right?"

Goldie and Freddy looked extremely pleased with themselves. Everyone else looked jealous.

"The grease is the good part," I said. I was ignored.

Luckily, nobody was paying attention to Ms. Hutchins, either, and she had a lot more power. "Class!" she called, clapping her hands. "Class! Quiet, please! No video announcements today since we'll have an assembly later, so let's dive into our course material. This is our sixth-grade theme!" She gestured to the banner strung above the whiteboard: THINK LIKE A SCIENTIST! "Who can tell us what that might mean?"

Dead silence.

Finally, Soup raised his hand. "Do we get to wear safety goggles this year?"

"We'll see," said Ms. Hutchins wearily. "Anyone? What does it mean to think like a scientist?"

"Follow the scientific method," said Emily Garcia. "Ask questions, gather background information . . ."

"Absolutely." Ms. Hutchins turned to the whiteboard. "Let's start with a quick review of the scientific method. And yes, you should be writing this down."

It was going to be a long year.

# CHAPTER FIVE

WE WERE WELCOMED home by Martha. "COCK-A-DOO-ARGH-ACK-ECK-EH!"

"Is that normal?" said Flynn.

"For Martha, yes," I said. "For roosters, no."

"I've got to visit Jim Bob," said Ruth. "He's been missing me all day. Want to come meet him, Flynn?"

"The hog?"

"The American Yorkshire piglet," she corrected him. "He'll love you! He's so friendly."

"I don't like pigs," said Flynn.

"You've never met a pig like Jim Bob."

He hesitated.

"Are you scared?" I said.

"No!"

"Come on!" said Ruth. "I'll let you feed him his bottle!" She grabbed Flynn's hand and began dragging him to the pigpen. He looked at me the way a shipwrecked rat looks at a piece of floating timber.

"Flynn probably needs a snack," I told Ruth. "I'm starving."

"Me too," said Flynn, shaking himself free.

"Your loss!" said Ruth.

We turned toward the house. "I was a bit scared of Jim Bob before I met him," I said. "Because you should see his mom, Mr. Flick's prize sow. Her name's Hercules Mulligan and she weighs six hundred pounds and snorts like a rhino."

"Stop," Flynn moaned.

"But Jim Bob's nothing like that." I considered the facts of life as I opened the kitchen door. "Well, not yet."

In the kitchen, Ivan was banging a spoon on his high-chair tray. Dad was reading a seed catalog, which he threw down upon our entrance. "Soren! Flynn! All hail the conquering students! How was school? Tell me all about it!"

After a day at home with Ivan, Dad gets way too excited about humans who can talk in full sentences. "It was fine, thanks, Uncle Jon," said Flynn.

"Details!" cried Dad.

"Our classes were good. But I think I've already learned a lot of the stuff we're doing in science."

"Flynn won Scientificopardy!" I said.

"Bless you!" said Dad.

"No, Scientificopardy! A review game Ms. Hutchins invented. *Jeopardy!* plus fifth-grade science, minus prize money."

"Well, well, well!" said Dad. "Congratulations!"

"The questions weren't that hard," Flynn said modestly.

Maybe not for him. *I* found them hard. Over the summer, I'd forgotten everything I'd ever learned about igneous versus sedentary-or-whatever rocks. I couldn't name a single parasite besides Ivan, and I knew King Philip Came Over, but for what, who the heck knew? But Flynn had nailed every one.

"And guess who's my lab partner?" said Flynn.

"Who?" asked Dad.

"Hint: she assigned them alphabetically by last name."

"And that means . . ."

"Dad," I said, "me and Flynn have the same last name."

"Oh!" Light dawned. "The Skaar Science Squad! Eh? How's *that* for a team nickname?"

"Love it," said Flynn at the same time as I said, "Yeah, I don't think so."

"Lucky Soren," said Dad. "Partnered with the champion of Scienti-Scientifo-Scientisto—er, the review game! So what else happened? Outside of the science classroom?"

"We had auditions for music groups," said Flynn, patting his banjo. "Mr. Brandoon was very impressed, he said, but I guess there aren't banjo parts in band music, so I have to do Intermediate Choir."

"I got Intermediate Band," I said from inside the refrigerator, where I was digging for after-school sandwich ingredients. I play the trombone. Badly.

"I'm going to ask Mr. Brandoon if the choir and band can work together to perform one of my original songs." Flynn strummed a chord. *"Roosters we have heard on high / Sweetly crowing o'er the plains."*

"Maybe for the holiday concert!" said Dad.

"My goal is to have a full concept album by the end of the year. *O Strum, All Ye Faithful*, I think I'll call it. What do you think?"

"I can't wait to hear the whole thing," Dad said. "Ivan! Play with Gloria or eat your tomato soup! Not both!"

"SWIM!" yelled Ivan.

Dad, sighing, took away the soup, but not before Ivan had dipped in his favorite Barbie headfirst. I lidded my sandwich. "This is a work of art," I said.

"Soren," said Dad, "offer your cousin half your sandwich."

"I think it has corn syrup."

"Offer," said Dad through gritted teeth.

I had just taken a massive bite. "Ouldoo ikaffuh myand-itch?"

"Huh?" said Flynn.

I stuck my jaw forward and, feeling like a rattlesnake who'd done well for himself, swallowed. "Would you like half of my sandwich?"

"That's okay." He eyed it. "I've lost my appetite."

I didn't see the problem, myself. Peanut butter, banana, marshmallow, and pickle on sourdough. Every major food group was represented.

"PLAY!" yelled Ivan.

"I'll play with you," said Flynn. "Hi, Barbie!"

"BARBIE NOT BARBIE!"

Flynn didn't even know what the Barbie's name was. "He calls her Gloria," I said. "After the baby sister in the Frances books. Right, Ivan?"

"IVAN NOT BABY!"

"Uh, you missed the point, dude."

Flynn leaned in. "Hi, Gloria!"

"He likes to throw her," I said. "I'd be careful if I were you." Ivan glowered at me.

"Will you play with me, Gloria?" said Flynn.

Ivan regarded him suspiciously.

"Glo-Glo-Gloria!" said Flynn. "Will you take me on a tractor ride?"

We don't even own a tractor.

"Will you give me a farmland tour?"

Ivan giggled.

"I can play too," I told Ivan. "Gloria! Want to go for another swim in the tomato soup?" I tugged at the Barbie's leg, but Ivan only grasped her more firmly. "Come on, Ivan. Give her to me. Swim time, Glo!"

"NO!"

I yanked. Ivan yanked back.

"Fine." I returned to my sandwich.

"Oh!" said Flynn. "Soren—watch out—"

I glanced up just in time to see Ivan's eyes narrow and his arm rear back in a windup. Gloria winged through the air. She spun toward me, limbs akimbo, drops of soup pinwheeling from her hair—

She hit me right in the eye socket.

"Gloria!" said Flynn, all fake shocked. "Who taught you to fly?"

And Ivan, that little traitor, he giggled. Again.

# CHAPTER SIX

OVER THE COURSE of the next week, my black eye went from black to purple to blue to orange to green. "*What* happened?" said Jéro at lunch on Tuesday.

"I told you. I got kicked." I hadn't mentioned that a Barbie had done the kicking. "But you should have seen the other guy."

I'd broken off Gloria's leg.

When we got freed from the cafeteria, we all milled out to the—well, I won't say *field,* but it's a field*ish* thing, 90 percent dirt, 10 percent scrappy weeds that try so hard but get stomped down every day at 11:35 a.m. Recess soccer's fun, though sort of stressful because there's no ref. That means when there's a dispute, whoever yells the loudest wins.

We rotate captains. That day it was me and Billiam Flick. He said, "I'll take Freddy."

"Hmm," I said. I tried to look like I was deciding, even though I already knew. "I'll take . . . hmm . . . Flynn."

"*Him?*" said Billiam.

After a week of school, I'd finally convinced Flynn to make his recess soccer debut. Nothing he'd done so far would make anyone think he'd be good at soccer. He'd worn a lot of skinny jeans and swirly shirts and caps, and he'd won another review game, Who Wants to Be a Scientistionaire?

"Him," I repeated.

"O-*kay*," said Billiam, skeptical. "I'll take Randall."

"Goldie," I said. She jogged over and low-fived Flynn. They were friends now.

We picked the rest of the teams, and I took the kickoff. I tipped it back to Jéro, who dribbled a couple of yards and paused, looking up for the pass. Freddy and Randall converged.

"Look at Soup!" I yelled.

Jéro passed. Soup thinks he can dribble, but Kiyana stole the ball from him in about half a second. She took it up the line. Then, in a streak of paisley, appeared Flynn.

I don't know how he did it. One second Kiyana was whizzing up the wing; the next, Flynn was whizzing in the opposite direction. He dodged Randall, and he dodged Freddy, and he glanced up even while he kept moving full tilt ahead. Poppy Moore was posted in the center. He crossed the ball to her. All she had to do was stick out a foot. The ball ricocheted into the goal.

I blinked.

"Goal!" shouted Goldie.

"Goal?" said Poppy. "I—I—scored?"

"You *scored*!" yelled Flynn.

"I *scored*!"

Usually she spends the whole game braiding clover.

"Get back in position," I called. "No time for celebration."

Billiam kicked off with a long pass to Jack. Jack tried to get it to Randall, but again Flynn intercepted. He dribbled around Randall like Randall was a cone—they do kind of look the same—and he crossed a high floater to Soup, who'd been keeping pace down the field. Soup leapt and headed it into the dead center of the goal.

"Brilliant!" cried Flynn.

Next he assisted Goldie, then Jéro, then me. We gave up one on a penalty kick after Poppy accidentally handballed, but we were still winning 5–1.

*PHWEEET!* That was the two-minute warning. Billiam kicked a clod of weeds. "Let's quit now."

"We're playing to the end," I said.

Jack tapped it to Freddy. Flynn, with a burst of speed, was on him. He had the ball. He took off toward their goal, the ball staying on his toes like it was glued there. Billiam approached. With a flick of his foot, Flynn megged him. Billiam tripped over his own feet and crashed to the ground. Flynn didn't even look back. Randall and Jack were advancing, but Flynn threaded the needle between them.

"Yeah, Flynn!" yelled Jéro.

He reached the grassy spot near the goal. In a last, desperate attempt to stop him, Freddy went for the slide tackle. Flynn wasn't fazed. He jumped over Freddy, caught the ball on the other side, and casually slotted it into the corner of the goal.

"FLYNNIE!" cried Goldie in glee.

"I've never seen moves like that in real life," said Soup.

"He's related to *you*?" Billiam said to me.

*PHWEEET! PHWEEET!*

My team gathered around Flynn. *Both* teams gathered around Flynn. They were beaming. They tugged at his sleeve and slapped him on the back. That's what you want to do when you see something amazing. You want to touch it. If you see a cupcake frosted like a Lego or a caterpillar that looks like a squishy string of beads, you want to reach out and touch it with your very own hand. Touching it makes it real.

We tromped back inside, pushing sweaty reefs of hair off our foreheads, jangling into a line for the water fountain. Everyone was happy and excited but me. I hung to the back.

# CHAPTER SEVEN

"HE'S REALLY GOOD," I told Alex when we video-chatted that night. It was the first time we'd talked since school started. "He's way better than the rest of us. Which could be bad, but he's not a ball hog."

"At my new school there's not enough playground space for soccer," said Alex. "Everyone just hangs out by the fence."

"There aren't monkey bars or anything?"

"Well, there are, but sixth graders are too old."

"That's a school rule?"

"No. That's just what everyone says."

It sounded awful. "Do you miss us?" I said. "I mean, Camelot?"

Alex scowled. Our Internet was being slow, so she got all jerky whenever she moved. "Well, obviously."

"Oh. Sorry."

"My new school's a lot bigger. There's like three hundred sixth graders. I only know a few people."

"Weird." I knew all the kids at Camelot. I knew their birthdays. "Do you have any friends?"

"Kind of." She adjusted her screen. Her face turned into a pixelated mess. "Mostly people don't even know my name. I'm just the new kid. But there's this nice girl who's in my reading group. Her braid's so long she can sit on it."

Seemed to me that could cause trouble on the toilet. "Cool."

"I'm going to see if she wants to be my new pranking partner."

That made me feel weird. It wasn't like I wanted Alex to be alone, but I didn't want to be replaced *that* fast. "What are you guys going to do?"

"Probably we'll start with some good old-fashioned Post-it-ing."

"Classic." We'd done it to Ms. Hutchins last year. What you do: You take a couple of packs of Post-its and you cover the teacher's whole desk, like it's a fish and the Post-its are scales. Cover the chair, too, if you have enough. And the lamp. Everything. It looks hilarious. Even Ms. Hutchins had laughed. "That's nice that you get to do all of our old pranks over again."

"It's the only good thing about moving." She pushed her glasses up her nose. She'd gotten new ones, purple and thick-framed. "I'd be really bummed out if it weren't for that."

I almost told her I wished she'd move back—like, I *really* wished that, all the time—but I figured (a) she knew and (b) it wasn't like she got any choice in the matter. So instead I said, "Everyone'll know your name as soon as you do a prank."

She straightened and smiled. "True."

"I think I'm retired from pranking, myself."

"What? Soren! No!"

"It's no fun without you. And too hard."

"Have you even tried anything?"

"I need a new team first," I said. "Or at least a new partner."

She frowned, her eyebrows blundering down in slow motion. Stupid Internet. "Who? One of the soccer guys?"

I remembered how Freddy and Soup and Jéro had reacted to my idea with the Mexican jumping beans. "I don't think so. No."

"The Andrezejczak triplets?"

"I don't know."

"They like making trouble. And they live next door to you."

"But they're mostly friends with each other." Not to mention, they were intimidating. They moved in a pack and had their own language made up of eyebrow raises and weird acronyms. It was common knowledge that you didn't want to find yourself on their bad side. Get one Andrezejczak, get gotten by all three.

"Well, you should find a new partner. You're not going to feel like yourself unless you're pranking." She was being so encouraging. It was the total opposite of my automatic jealousy of Nice Butt-Braid Girl. "What about your cousin?" she said.

"Flynn?"

"Could he be your new partner?"

"Soren!" yelled Mom from the other room. "Time to get off the computer!"

"You said I could have it till eight!"

"Flynn needs it for homework," she called. "You know the rule."

This is the rule, which is terrible: whenever someone needs to do homework, they can kick you off immediately. What Ruth does, she does five minutes of online math and then switches to a game, and unless you stay to watch over her shoulder you don't even know.

"But we don't have any computer homework!" I yelled.

"At my new school," Alex said from the screen, "we always have computer homework."

Flynn appeared in the doorway. "I want to type my Language Arts answers," he told me.

"Mom! He could just write them! I'm talking to Alex!"

"It's the rule, Soren!" called Mom.

"I like to go above and beyond," said Flynn. "Typing is more professional."

"You know that question you just asked?" I said to Alex. *What about your cousin? Could he be your new partner?* "The answer is no." I x-ed out of the chat and left the computer, and the room, without meeting Flynn's eyes.

WHEN WE WERE in third grade, Alex and I were caught planting plastic ants all over the teachers' lounge. Mean Ms. Rue was the one who discovered us, and it turned out

43

she had an ant phobia. We got dragged, actually dragged, to Principal Leary's office.

Want to know what kind of friend Alex was? "It was all me, Principal Leary," she said. "My idea, my ants. Soren was in there because he was trying to stop me."

I started to protest. She pinched me under the desk. "I take all the blame," she said.

Later, she didn't even let me thank her. "It was the sensible move," she said. "*One* of us should have a clean record."

"I'll pay you back someday," I said, but we were never caught again, so I never had the chance. Now I probably never would.

That was Alex. My best friend. Nobody would ever replace her. Nobody would come close.

# CHAPTER EIGHT

"GUYS! GUYS! SIXTH GRADERS!" Ms. Hutchins is nice, so nobody's on best behavior in her class. "Sit down, Kiyana! Marsupial, now is not the time to hop around the room!"

She finally got everyone settled. Fanning her armpits, she said, "What's our theme for the year, class?"

"'Think Like a Scientist,'" read Emily and Poppy from the banner above the board.

"Precisely!" said Ms. Hutchins. "And to practice the scientific method, we're going to do a class experiment where we'll all investigate this question."

She clicked on the projector.

DO PLANTS GROW TALLER WITH WATER OR WITH COKE?

We got with our lab partners to make hypotheses. "What's our background information?" said Flynn.

Finally. Something I knew more about than he did. "Once I saw Ms. Hutchins and her wife at the grocery, and they were buying fifteen pounds of kale. Plus a bag of carrots so big Mr. Karlssen was keeping it with the livestock feed."

"So?"

"They *juice*."

"And?"

"Ms. H is a vegan foodie health nut. There's no way she'd have her class do an experiment that makes Coke look good."

"That's your background information?"

"Mark my words. The plants that get water are going to do way better. Look at her desk! Just look!" Among the bazillion photos of her dog and her wife, Ms. Hutchins had two huge metal water bottles. One said FOR THE PLANET and the other said BECAUSE PLASTIC WILL KILL US ALL.

"A pure scientific experiment," Flynn began, "is unbiased, not going for one outcome or another. . . ."

I snorted. "So you want to hypothesize that Coke is better for plants?"

"Well," said Flynn, backpedaling, "all that acid in soda, it can't be good for their roots."

"Great. We agree." I grabbed our worksheet and wrote, *Hypothesis: Coke will kill the plants, but water will make them grow big and tall.*

"When you're done, guys," yelled Ms. Hutchins above the din, "come fetch your seedlings!"

The baby bean plants were growing in cardboard egg cartons. Each lab group got two to repot in cottage-cheese containers. The classroom became pleasantly chaotic. Dirt was flying everywhere. Flynn labeled masking-tape strips *COKE* and *WATER*. He had cool handwriting. He even gave the letters little feet, like a font on the computer. "Decision time," I said. "Which plant do we doom with Coke? And which plant gets to thrive with water?"

"Technically, we shouldn't know which is which," said Flynn.

Soup poked me with his ruler. "What'd you guys put for your hypothesis?"

"Duh," I said. "Water."

"We put Coke," said Jéro, his partner.

"Coke had better win," said Soup. "Then my mom'll have to let me drink pop all the time."

"Um, humans aren't plants," said Flynn.

"Yeah?" said Soup.

"So you can't take a plant-based experiment and apply the results to humans. By that logic, we'd do best if we stood around in dirt, facing the sun."

"Plenty of people spend recess that way," I said.

"Take your initial measurements!" Ms. Hutchins shouted. "Be precise!"

Everyone hunkered down over their plants. Flynn and Soup and Jéro could think what they wanted, but I *knew* Ms. Hutchins, and right now, that was way more important than knowing about sugar or acid or photosynthesis. She'd never do an experiment that made Coke look healthy, and she wouldn't care that it was just plant-based, either. We'd probably have to write a whole paragraph on the prompt "If Coke can kill a hardy bean plant, what do you think it can do to you?"

Unless.

Unless the experiment somehow turned out the other way.

"Soren!"

I jumped. My eyes had gone out of focus. Flynn gave me a strange look. "I said your name like six times!"

"Sorry. Daydreaming, I guess."

"Here." He handed me a beaker. He'd just returned from the fluid station with our two-ounce allotments of Coke and water. "Let's feed these guys."

"Wait," I said quietly. "Wait."

HERE'S HOW IT would have gone with Alex.

Me: "Wait. Wait. I have an idea."

Alex: "Oh. *Oh!*"

I wouldn't have even had to explain. It was an obvious prank. Simple and brilliant. We'd sneak into the classroom and sabotage the plants. We'd make the Coke plants grow, feed them water and fertilizer. We'd slowly kill the water plants. Pinch their stems.

I could imagine the whole thing: getting all nervous and excited and heart-poundy while we sabotaged, trying not to laugh in class when we heard things like "I don't know why my water plant is dying so fast!" and "Wow, Ms. H, plants really like Coke, huh?"

It would have been amazing.

I GUESS I was tricked by how amazing it *would* have been, because even though I 100 percent knew it wouldn't work, I tried it out on Flynn.

"Sabotage?" he said. *"Sabotage?"*

"Keep your voice down, okay?"

"But—Soren—this is *science*!"

"Shush!"

Ms. Hutchins was roaming the room like a hungry vulture, on high alert for illegal activity. "Milton DeVoe!" she yelled. "That Coke is for your bean plant, not for you!"

Flynn waited for her to pass. There were blotchy pink splotches on his cheeks. He gestured at the banner. "Think like a *scientist,* Soren. Science is about truth! What would happen if scientists faked experiments?"

"Never mind," I said.

"Medicine! Engineering! Food! Technology! We wouldn't be able to rely on anything! The modern world is built on trust in science—"

The splotches were getting worse. "I get it," I said quickly. I didn't want Ms. Hutchins to catch wind. "It was a bad idea."

"You can say that again."

"It was a bad idea."

Flynn groaned. But even that only cheered me up a bit. What I was thinking as I counted leaves: How had everything changed so fast? I used to have a best friend who'd have happily killed plants with me, but she was gone. As far as my life was concerned, she was a bunch of choppy pixels on a screen I wasn't even allowed to use very often. She was off in Minneapolis with a new pranking partner, and me? I was here. I was here with Flynn.

# CHAPTER NINE

IF YOU'RE A bug, the last thing you want to do is fly past a hungry frog. Well, that was me walking through the kitchen on block-party day. Mom flicked out her long tongue and I was stuck.

"You can either peel the oranges or open the cans of pineapple," said Mom. "But you have to do one."

"Pineapple." At least opening cans involves a cool gadget. Peeling oranges is death to my thumbnails. "What are you making?"

"What are *we* making. Jell-O salad. A lot of it."

Jell-O salad, in case you don't know, is the best salad, because there's nothing green in it (unless you're making lime). It's basically a lot of canned fruit suspended in Jell-O—like those insects that got caught in amber at the end of the dinosaurs—that you douse with whipped cream. "Did you get Reddi-wip? Can I do the spraying?"

"If we ever get to that point," said Mom, who was boiling three pots of water. "I've never made Jell-O salad for a hundred. But how much harder can it be than making it for ten?"

"Probably ten times harder."

"Thanks, Soren. Very helpful. Hey, where's your cousin?"

"No clue," I said morosely.

"What's all this?" Mom always picks up on tone. Sometimes it's nice, like if you want some attention and your other parent is busy keeping your baby brother from eating a matchbook. Sometimes it's annoying. "Something on your mind?"

"Nope."

"School okay?"

"Yep."

"You've done your homework for the weekend?"

"Of course . . ."

She turned on the faucet to run cold water.

". . . not," I whispered.

She turned off the tap. "How's school treating Flynn?"

"He loves it," I said. "And it loves him."

"Good. Here. Stir." She dumped in the boiling water, and I stirred in the powder. We were making the Jell-O in the biggest pot we had. It was practically a cauldron. When Ruth and I played Baba Yaga with Ivan, we made him sit in it so we could pretend to cook him. "This year must feel very different to you."

"Yeah. Even though I have the same teachers."

"Sometimes when things stay the same, the big picture feels even more different."

How did she know? "Maybe."

"Is Alex planning a visit soon?"

"I don't think so. Because of her mom's job." Mrs. Harris cuts hair. Here in Camelot she'd worked in a salon, but the reason they'd moved to Minneapolis was so she could start her own business giving haircuts in people's homes. It was called Ubercut. There was an app and everything.

"Right," said Mom. "It's hard to take time off when you're just starting. Have you talked much with Alex?"

"We *were* talking. But the computer got snatched. We haven't been online at the same time since." I gave the Jell-O water one last stir while Mom ripped open a huge bag of ice. "It'd be a whole lot easier to keep in touch," I added, "if I had a phone."

"Not a chance, whippersnapper. Nice try."

"Flynn has a phone."

"That's his mother's decision. *Your* mother says no."

"*Mo-om . . .*"

"You see that contraption on the counter over there? Black? With the buttons? Specially engineered to fit from ear to mouth?"

"*Mo-om.*"

"Free to use, anytime you want."

"That's not a *real* phone."

You'd think Mom would be pro-technology, given that she designs websites for a living. She tossed in the ice. The Jell-O water sloshed and overflowed. "Darn it," she said, grabbing the spoon. "That'll be sticky. Listen. Soren. Your whole life doesn't have to change just because Alex moved. I'd bet you she's still doing the things she likes to do down in Minneapolis. And you can keep doing what you like to do up here."

What Mom didn't get was that to do the things I liked to do, I needed Alex. I couldn't pull off a massive prank alone. I couldn't even pull off a micro prank alone. And nobody wanted to work with me. Look how fast Flynn had shot me down on the first day of the plant experiment.

"It's okay to be sad. Someone's gone who was a big part of your life, and now your life's different. That's tough, honey."

Things had been weird the past few months. I guess tough. Nothing was wrong, but nothing was that fun, either. Like a Pop-Tart with no frosting or sprinkles. Better than nothing, but.

"Give me back that spoon," I said. "I can stir."

"First," said Mom, "come here."

She squished me in to her. It made me feel like a little kid again. Mom doesn't touch us much. Which I appreciate, honestly, because so often as a kid you just get prodded, patted and petted and poked, so it's nice to have someone who gets that even though I've got a mini body, it's still *my* body.

But the occasional Mom hug is gold. It always makes me cry. And the other great thing about being hugged really tight is that you can wipe your eyes and/or nose on the person's shirt and they never even know.

"Okay," she said. "That's enough. Stir."

CAUTION

# CHAPTER TEN

WE LIVE ON a dead-end street, not a block, but we've been having this party for as long as I can remember. It's a good time. Some adults grill, and some get competitive with desserts, and there's a bike-decorating contest and a watermelon-seed-spitting contest, both of which Ruth dominates, and there's chalk and bubbles and cornhole and Bruce Springsteen. The grown-ups are too busy chatting to keep track of how much pop you're drinking, and the food is amazing. Last year Mrs. Andrezejczak made this thing that was like s'mores in a casserole dish, all these layers of chocolate pudding and graham crackers and marshmallows. I had so much that I threw up in Mr. Flick's pigpen, and then his pigs ate it, but, frankly, it was so good I didn't blame them. And it's not like it was all that digested.

"Oooh!" squealed everyone when Ruth showed up with Jim Bob. "He's *so* cute!" Some of the boys tried to hold back, the ones who care about being tough and not-so-secretly think boys are better than girls, but you could tell they wanted to ooh and aah too.

Jim Bob was lying stomach-up in Ivan's old stroller, and Ruth had dressed him in baby clothes: a ruffled bonnet with holes for his ears and a onesie that said *iPood* under the Apple logo. He looked highly pleased with himself.

"Can I hold him?" asked Goldie.

"Sure." Ruth hauled him out of the stroller.

"How much does he weigh?"

"Eight pounds," said Ruth, chucking him under the chin. "Still a wunt, aren't woo, my wittle sparewib?"

"I *need* a picture." With her spare hand, Goldie wriggled her phone out of her back pocket and handed it to Flynn. "Smile, Jim Bob!"

"Stunning," Flynn pronounced. "Give that a classic filter and you won't believe the number of likes you'll get."

Flynn was as popular as Jim Bob, and he didn't even have to wear an *iPood* onesie to get there. He'd made friends. Real friends. He'd gone over to Goldie's after school on Friday, and they'd eaten pita chips, he'd said, and watched this old movie called *Clueless.*

"I want a picture too!" said Kiyana.

"I already called next!" said Evelyn.

*The ladies-in-waiting follow Queen Goldie*—that's what Alex used to say. So Flynn was automatically friends with Kiyana and Evelyn and Tori. *And* all the boys liked him. He made them look so good at soccer that he was impossible not to like.

"I'll be the official photographer," said Flynn. "And if you don't have a phone, I'll get them on mine and send them to you."

Flynn was fine. Flynn was great. I just didn't need to line up to get my photo taken with Jim Bob. I lived with Jim Bob. We could do an uncle-nephew picture anytime. I dropped back and sat on an overturned recycling bin. "Are we even going to play Spud this year?" I wondered.

"Why would we want to do that?" said Olivia, the smallest Andrezejczak triplet. She's randomly two inches shorter, even though they're supposedly identical. That's because Lila and Tabitha were stealing her food back in the womb.

"Because we always play Spud at the block party? Because it's fun?" said Tabitha. "Round them up, Lila."

Lila's lips were drawn. "They're busy. We'll wait."

Me and the Andrezejczak triplets were the only ones not into the photo shoot. "Maybe we're getting too old for Spud," I said. I got the feeling the *Vocabulary Workshop* book calls *melancholy*. The block party would be over soon, over for a whole other year, and it wasn't even that fun anyway. It was like a banana-flavored Tootsie Roll. Gross but also too small.

"They'll want to play soon," said Lila.

"The only thing they want to do is take pictures with Flynn," I said.

"They just have to get the newcomer out of their systems," said Lila.

"I wish I could get the newcomer out of *my* system," I said without thinking.

"That's mean," Lila told me, but Tabitha looked interested.

"I thought Flynn was a good guy."

"He *is* a good guy." I wished I could take back what I'd said. "I meant Jim Bob."

"Oh," said Lila. "Yeah, I bet it's no fun to have to shovel out his pen."

"Exactly," I said. But Tabitha gave me a laser-like look, one of those beady-eyed beams of observation straight out of an alien movie, the kind that does a quick brain probe and knows just what you're thinking and why. That's the thing about Tabitha: she's an alien. Just kidding. The thing about Tabitha is that she notices. Everything.

"Flynnie!" cried Goldie, so loud that I looked over. "Your turn for a pig pic!"

"That's okay," said Flynn.

"You *have* to! It'll be *such* a great photo!" She thrust out Jim Bob. Flynn shied away. Jim Bob squawked.

"Whoa!" said Ruth. "Support his neck!"

"I don't want to hold him right now," said Flynn.

"But when else would you use the pig emoji?" said Goldie. "It's your turn!"

"I just don't want to."

He was turning red, a blush that trickled all the way down the collar of his black V-neck shirt. I decided to save him. And myself.

"Hey, everyone!" I yelled. "Who wants to play Spud?"

"Me!" said Tabitha.

"I call captain!" said Billiam.

"You can't *call* captain!" said Jéro.

In the hubbub, Ruth returned Jim Bob to his stroller. "I'm taking him home," she told me. "He needs a rest."

"Good idea," I said. "You're not bringing him back, right?"

"Nah," said Ruth. "Enough excitement for one day." She tucked a baby blanket around his head so only his snout and eyes showed. "Right, my wittle bacon bit?"

"Soren!" called Tabitha. "You just got picked! You're on Billiam's team!"

I ran back over. Flynn poked me. *Thanks,* he mouthed.

"Huh?" I said. "Come on. Do you know how to play Spud?"

# CHAPTER ELEVEN

THE BELL RANG. Ms. Hutchins pulled down the projector screen. We have announcements in homeroom, and a few years back they switched to a live video broadcast. It was supposed to be a great technological innovation, but all it really means is that we have a daily betting pool on Principal Leary's necktie.

Today it was patterned with tiny pencils. "Good morning, students and teachers," he said from behind his desk. "Lots of announcements this Friday morning. The Safety Patrol will meet after school in Mr. Doyle's room. . . ."

Jéro flipped through his records. He wants to be a bookie when he grows up, so he runs the Video Announcements Necktie Betting Pool. You propose your bet to him ("Red on Tuesday," "New tie any day this week," "Three consecutive days of stripes"), and he calculates odds and keeps a massive spreadsheet with the running totals.

". . . anyone interested in playing basketball this winter should see Coach Compton for a training schedule. . . ."

I hadn't made any bets yet this year, so I wasn't too invested. But it's always fun to watch my classmates' faces as they win or lose fortunes. Chloe Ting looked really upset. She's the worst gambler in the class, and I think she's addicted, too. Meanwhile, Milton DeVoe was bouncing lightly in his seat, looking pleased with himself.

". . . and the Rubik's Fanatiks will meet during lunch in Ms. Rodney's room for a special cube-greasing event," Principal Leary said. "WD-40 will be provided."

He set down the paper. "One final note regarding behavior in the lunchroom." I sighed and tuned out. I know *how* to behave in the lunchroom, even if actually behaving in the lunchroom is sometimes a different story.

Alex and I never got to do this prank we'd imagined, where we'd hack into the school network and interrupt Principal Leary's announcements with some other video. We hadn't decided what we'd show: she wanted a call to revolution; I wanted baby pandas on a slide. We hadn't figured out how to hack the network, either, but the Internet has instructions for everything.

I sank down in my seat. I'd never pull it off without her.

"Food is to be eaten, *not* thrown," said Principal Leary. I probably couldn't even pull off a food fight without her. I looked around the classroom. Chloe was frantically sorting a pile of nickels and pennies. Jéro was scribbling odds on his bookie notepad. Flynn was patting his hair, which he'd gelled this morning, I'd noticed, and Goldie, Kiyana, Evelyn, Olivia, and Tori were all sneaking looks at Flynn. Everyone else looked bored.

Nobody else looked like they missed Alex.

That, I thought, was the weirdest part of this year. It was like I was the only one who'd noticed she'd left.

"Bus your tray when you're done eating," said Principal Leary. I'd heard this lecture so many times I could mouth along. "And check around your seat for debris," we both said, him out loud, me with just my lips.

I'd never make it through a year like this.

Something had to change.

*Your whole life doesn't have to change just because Alex moved,* Mom had said. *Keep doing what you like to do.*

Fine, I thought. I would.

AFTER SCHOOL, WHILE Flynn and Ruth were still stuffing their faces with Dad's special stovetop pepper popcorn, I went to the computer. Alex was online. "Hey," I said, feeling a rush of relief even to see her face. "*Hey. So.*"

"What's up?" she said. She was eating a granola bar.

"I have to prank. I have to."

"I knew you'd get there," she said. "It's like pooping. You can only hold off the urge for so long."

I kind of wanted to keep exploring the comparison—school was obviously the toilet, but what was the toilet paper? What made it smell? Did Alex and I have prankarrhea?—but I had more important things on my mind. "I had an idea in science," I told Alex. "Help me figure out how it'll work?"

Alex set down her granola bar. "Gladly," she said.

It felt like riding a bike on the first warm-enough day in

the spring. Back at it, and it was just as good as ever. I told her my plan. "You need detention," said Alex.

"Right!" Detention means you have to clean white-boards. "Brilliant."

"You'll be alone in the classroom—"

"Left to my own devices—"

"Do something bad enough that you get detention twice a week," she said. "For, say, three weeks. It's got to be pretty bad, but don't accidentally get suspended."

"Good point."

She gave a happy sigh. "This is awesome."

"Yeah, I just wish—"

I shut up, but not fast enough. We both knew what I was going to say. It killed the mood. It reminded us that this was *actually* like riding a bike on a random warm day in February, when a blizzard's on the way.

"How's *your* prank?" I said.

"Oh," she said, "fine. I guess. You know the girl in my reading group?"

"Ol' Butt-Braid?"

"Yeah, her. *Sophia*. I told her about it, but she didn't even get excited. She was just like, 'Oh! Goodness gracious! I can't risk getting in trouble!'"

"She actually said that?"

"Pretty much. Not those words, but you know."

"Weird."

"No, I like her. But I'm not pranking with her." Alex started crumbling the half-eaten granola bar.

"Go it alone."

"I don't know if it's worth it."

"You've got a great idea. It'll kick off the year."

"I don't know."

"Just do it. You've got the Post-it notes already, right? Sneak in during recess. I believe in you."

"Maybe."

"You can't hold it in. Remember? You said so yourself. Like pooping."

That got a small smile.

"It's unhealthy to hold it in," I said. "You'll get a stomach-ache."

"True," said Alex. "Constipation kills."

# CHAPTER TWELVE

THE SETTING: A lunchroom in the basement of a school in Camelot, Minnesota. There's a hot-food line, tables, garbage cans, and signs Student Council made that say, in big bubbly pink letters, *Throw Out Your Trash or Else* You're *Trash!* It smells like ketchup and sweat.

THE TIME: 11:22 a.m. Smack-dab in the middle of fifth- and sixth-grade lunch.

THE ENEMY: Mrs. Andersen roams the room, and Principal Leary stands at the doors with his arms crossed. The rest of the teachers are at the faculty table, highly distracted by their conversation, which is probably about something super fascinating like, I don't know, mortgages.

THE HERO: Soren Skaar sits at a sixth-grade table. He—

I—

—said, "Hey, is anyone not going to drink their milk?"

"You can have mine," said Freddy, tossing me his pouch. We used to have milk cartons, but they switched to pouches to save money and room on garbage. You just poke in your straw and suck it down. It was weird at first—you felt like a

64

hummingbird stabbing its long beak into a flower—but we got used to it.

"Thanks." I punctured Freddy's pouch with his straw. I'd already set up mine.

"What are you doing?" asked Soup.

"Nothing."

"Is this . . ." His eyes lit up. "Does this have something to do with *Alex*?"

I told you. She's legendary.

"I don't know what you're doing, dude," said Soup, "but I know I'm a fan. Here. Take mine."

"Thanks."

I set up Soup's pouch right next to Freddy's. Now was the moment. Principal Leary and Mrs. Andersen were far enough away that I'd have some time before I got tackled, but close enough that they'd know it was me. Three weeks of Tuesday/Thursday detention, that was my goal.

I positioned the first straw.

Three.

Two.

One.

With the flat of my hand, I squished the milk pouch.

*Thwsssst!*

There was a faint whistling sound. A stream of chocolate milk shot out and arced through the air. My mouth fell open. I'd wanted to do this since day one of milk pouches, but Alex and I had a strict rule: we were never bad for bad's sake. We were bad only in service of the greater good.

"Ew!" squeaked Billiam from the other table. "Hey!"

"Whoever's doing that, *stop!*" cried Kiyana.

"There's milk on my shirt!" yelled Jeremiah, plucking it from his chest.

"THERE'S MILK," yelled Goldie at the top of her lungs, "ON MY *FISH STICKS!*"

*That* got everyone's attention.

The boys at my table were pointing and laughing, but I didn't let myself get distracted. Calmly, coolly, I squashed the next bag. The milk shot out. "AHHH!" yelled Poppy and Emily, leaping out of the way.

"SOREN!" bellowed Principal Leary. He and Mrs. Andersen were advancing upon me, but it was hard for them to get through all the chairs and legs that blocked the aisle as kids dove for safety. "STOP THAT!"

Three weeks of detention, I reminded myself.

Not one week. Not two weeks. Three.

I locked eyes with Principal Leary, and I squished the last bag.

The arc of milk wasn't pointed at him, but it crossed the path he'd have to take. There was no way around it. Mrs. Andersen hung back, but Principal Leary gritted his teeth and sprinted through the milk stream just like you'd sprint through a sprinkler. When he got through, he had a dribbled streak of brown across his white shirt.

"It's washable," I told him. "I checked."

"Soren," he said, panting from either sprinting or rage, "go to my office. *Now.*"

# CHAPTER THIRTEEN

I HELD MY breath as we walked in the kitchen door after school. So far, everything had gone perfectly. I'd gotten my three weeks of detention, and I'd cleaned up the lunchroom during recess. I was just hoping Principal Leary hadn't called home.

Dad spun around from the stove. I was braced for him to tell me to report to their bedroom for a serious conversation, young man, do not pass Go, do not collect an after-school snack, but instead he said, "Hello, schoolchildren!" Phew. Normal. "Hello, rational speakers of English! I am *so* pleased to see you!"

"Hey," we said.

The whole room reeked of play dough. You know how. Like French fries except off. Dad was cooking up a new batch in the wok.

"PLAY WITH PLAY DOUGH!" Ivan shouted from the table.

"Ooh!" said Flynn, settling down next to him. "What color do I get?"

"FINNIE GET BLUE!"

"What do I get?" asked Ruth.

"ROOFIE GET RED!"

"What about Sorie?" I asked him.

Ivan eyed me, absentmindedly massaging a glob of purple play dough into his left eyebrow. Finally he said, "SORIE NO GET!" He cackled.

"Fine. I don't even want to play." I went over to the stove. "Hey, Dad," I said quietly. "I signed up to help Ms. Babbitt with sets for the winter play."

"Wonderful!" said Dad. "Thrilled to see you taking an interest in the theater!"

"Er, right," I said, shifting from foot to foot.

"Backstage, though? I wouldn't have expected a Skaar to shy from the spotlight."

"I love the spotlight," said Flynn from the table.

"We know," I muttered. Dad gave me a lips-pursed, head-tilted look, the one that tells you you're on thin ice.

"So," I said, looking at my feet, "I'll need to stay after school Tuesdays and Thursdays."

"Okay."

"For the next three weeks."

Before he was a stay-at-home dad, Dad was a lawyer. He says all his lawyerly skills are permanently encrusted beneath a layer of diapers and carpools and vomit and *Hop on Pop,* but sometimes they peek out. "Three weeks?" he said, eyebrows rising. "And then never again?"

Oops. I hadn't thought of how weird that'd sound. "She

wants to get most of the building done before the rehears-als really get going, so the actors won't be in danger. . . . Hammers, you know. . . ."

I've never been good at lying under pressure. Alex and I used to practice, but the practice hadn't helped. I still babbled.

Ivan saved me. "IVAN NEED BROWN!" he shouted.

"Just a sec, Soren," said Dad. The best four words in the world. "Ivan, you want me to dye the new batch *brown*? Are you sure? What about a nice, autumnal orange?"

"BROWN!" insisted Ivan.

"You could make autumn leaves! Or pumpkins!"

"IVAN NEED BROWN!"

"Fine," sighed Dad. "Soren, help. What primary colors make brown?"

"All of them," I said. "Just dump them in." If I've learned anything from art class, it's how to make ugly colors.

When we'd kneaded the new batch smooth and let it cool, I took it over to Ivan. I peered at their projects: Ruth was making a set of mini fruits; Flynn was making a dude playing a banjo; Ivan was making a mess. "Is that a self-portrait?" I asked Flynn.

"I'm thinking it has good potential for my album cover."

"Ah."

"You should make something, Soren," said Ruth.

"Am I allowed?" I asked Ivan.

"SOREN SIT!" he yelled.

"Really?" I was touched. My baby brother wanted my

company. Flynn was okay and all, but I guess it just wasn't the same without me.

"SIT!" Ivan said.

"I'm going to make a model of Lionel Messi," I said, pulling out the chair.

I sat.

Something squished.

Ivan cackled.

I jumped up and felt my rear end. It was damp with a huge clod of play dough, which, I saw as I attempted to peel it off, was from the new batch. A rich, fruity brown.

*"Ivan!"*

Ruth and Flynn howled with laughter. Ivan joyously banged a spoon. I scraped brown play dough off the seat of my pants.

"Did I get it all?" I asked Ruth.

"Spin. . . ."

As my butt passed Ivan, he yelled, "FEE SEES!"

"What?"

"SOREN FEE SEES!"

"What? You see fees? Fee sees? Who is Fee?"

"Oh," said Dad, abashed. "I'm sorry, Soren. I taught him that word today."

"Fee? Like an admission fee?"

"We were discussing polite language, but I'm not sure anything sank in except that one word. . . ."

"What word?"

"FEE SEES!"

"Um," Dad said delicately, "I believe he's saying *feces*."

Ruth and Flynn resumed howling, but even louder. "I'm leaving," I said.

"IVAN LIKE FEE SEES!"

"Ivan *is* a fee sees," I muttered.

I could hear them laughing all the way up the stairs.

# CHAPTER FOURTEEN

MR. JACKSON, JANITOR and very nice guy, looks exactly like Andrew Jackson, the guy on the twenty-dollar bill. Hairdo and all.

He (the alive one) gave me a bucket of rags and a spray bottle of whiteboard cleanser. "Now," he said, "you do not want to ingest this board cleanser. Pure acetone. It'll eat you from the inside."

"I'm not going to drink whiteboard cleanser, Mr. Jackson."

"That's what they all say," he said darkly, "but I've been in this business for a few years. I knew a kid once—No-Hit Norman, they called him, best pitcher Camelot Elementary ever had. But he got thirsty cleaning the board, and instead of visiting the water fountain . . ." Mr. Jackson shuddered. "No-Guts Norman, that's how he was known ever after. He was a shell of his former self. Literally."

"Got it, Mr. Jackson."

"If it were up to me, the most dangerous thing you kids

would hold would be a No. 2 pencil. Not that No. 2 pencils can't cause serious damage. Are you old enough to recall Perfect Pamela? No? On track for sixth-grade valedictorian, quite a student—until, that is, she became Perforated Pamela. . . ."

If I didn't start now, I'd never get to Ms. Hutchins's classroom. "I'll be extremely careful, Mr. Jackson," I assured him as I headed off down the hallway.

"And you watch out for those rags!" he called after me. "The stories I could tell you about rags!"

I gave him a wave as I turned the corner into the kindergarten zone. The teachers were gone, their rooms dim and dustily quiet. I worked my way up the classrooms, youngest to oldest, cleaning the boards as fast as I could.

Finally, I got to Ms. Hutchins's room.

I was nervous. But it was a familiar feeling. I'd felt the same way before every prank we'd ever pulled. My hands quivered. My knees melted. My stomach churned like a washing machine, and my heartbeat went as hard and fast as Tabitha Andrezejczak on the snare drum. Everything was sharper, brighter, like the world was a YouTube video that had suddenly adjusted to HD. Alex used to feel the same way.

We both loved that feeling.

I went straight to the windowsill. A tidy line of forty-eight bean plants leaned toward the sunshine.

I darted a glance over my shoulder.

No movement, no sound from the hallway.

I lifted the spray bottle. I hit the first plant labeled *WATER* with a good spray of cleanser. "Pure acetone," Mr. Jackson had said. If it could destroy the intestines of a star pitcher, what would it do to a twiggy bean plant?

One after another, working quickly but carefully, I sprayed every water-fed plant. Then I got a watering can and watered every Coke-fed plant. Done.

I headed to the side board with the cleanser, and not a moment too soon.

"Hey there, Soren!" said Ms. Hutchins.

I jumped. "Where did you come from?"

"Oh, just grabbing—now, where did they go—aha!" She waved a manila folder of quizzes. "Almost forgot them, but what's an evening without a stack of grading? Come on, I'll walk you out. Leave the supplies. I'll get them to Mr. Jackson tomorrow."

Phew. Close call.

"That's your dad picking you up?" she said once we were outside.

"Yep."

Dad rolled down the window. "Evangeline! Hello."

"Good to see you, Jon! Angelica and I have missed you at yoga class lately!"

"Yeah, I've had my hands full with this one." He nodded back to Ivan, snarling in his car seat. "Takes after his big brother."

"Uh-oh," said Ms. Hutchins. "Well, come to yoga anyway. Ditch the kid; get your Bikram on—"

"IVAN NOT KID!"

"Really, sweetie?" said Ms. Hutchins. "What are you?"

"IVAN TIGER!"

"It's a phase," Dad said wearily.

"I understand why your yoga practice is—er, on hiatus."

"Eighteen-year hiatus."

"You know," mused Ms. Hutchins, straightening to stretch her back, "there are definite perks to being a teacher."

"Sending them home?"

"Exactly." She waved. "See you tomorrow, Soren. Don't let your brother bite anyone's leg off!"

She thought that was pretty funny. I think it hit too close to home for Dad and me. He turned on the radio, but it didn't drown out Ivan's growls.

# CHAPTER FIFTEEN

"NEVER, IN MY ten years of teaching," said Ms. Hutchins, "has an experiment gone so poorly."

Nobody was supposed to hear that, I don't think. She muttered it to herself as she walked among us, watching us measure our Coke plants (as green as a rain forest) and our water plants (the gray-yellow that Ruth turns when she reads in the car). "Are you *sure* you've been treating your plants according to the labels?" Ms. Hutchins asked me and Flynn. "The Coke one's getting Coke? The water's getting water?"

"Of course," said Flynn, his face cloudy. He gently shifted a leaf to measure the water plant's full height, but the stem was so brittle it broke. The leaf wafted to the floor. "I don't understand it."

"I don't either," said Ms. Hutchins. "It's almost like someone—but no. Couldn't be."

Flynn shot me a look. I put my face close to the ruler I was using to measure the Coke plant. "Seven inches," I said, "and one, two, three, four, five of these little tick marks, um, so, five-sixteenths—"

I could feel myself blushing. Alex always told me I needed to control my blush better. We used to practice that, too, throwing accusations at each other and seeing how long we could make it before we cracked. I was never very good.

"I guess it's just one of those things," said Ms. Hutchins.

"Guess so," said Flynn, but even with my face buried in the ruler, I could tell he was still looking at me.

I GOT AN email from Alex that night:

> So, I took your advice and just did it. I snuck in during recess. The math room was empty. I covered half the desk in Post-its, and then the teacher walked in.
> Not good.
> I hate this place.
> I really hate this place.

That was the whole thing. I checked, but she wasn't online. I wrote back:

> WHAT?!?! NOOOOO!!!!!!

She wasn't online the next night either, and she hadn't responded to my email. I kept checking all weekend, and she never wrote back and never signed on.

. . .

WHEN I LEFT my last Tuesday detention, Flynn was alone on the playground, juggling a soccer ball. Left knee, right knee, right heel, up and over, bump from the forehead, left knee, roll down the shin to the toe— "Oh, hey," he said, doing a little jump move to catch the ball between his knees.

"Why are *you* here?"

"Same as you. Waiting for your dad."

"Yeah, but why are you *here*?"

"Mr. Brandoon was helping me arrange one of my original songs for choir and band. He's pretty into the idea."

"Cool."

"Yeah." He passed me the ball. We kicked around for a few minutes, ranging over our weedy-dirty field. When my pass went wide, he ran for it and dribbled back, but he didn't pass. "Hey," he said. "Mr. Brandoon and I were in the Fine Arts office."

"So?"

"So," he said, still not passing me the ball, "I was giving him a preview of 'Jim Bob, the Red-Nosed Piglet,' my latest. You want to hear it?"

"Not right now." The way he was holding on to the ball, it was making me nervous. I did a few butt kicks just to have something to do with my body. "Then what happened? Pass."

He passed. "Well." I trapped the ball between my feet. "This lady walked in. Tall and really pale?"

I kicked him the ball. "I think you're talking about Ms. Babbitt. She's the drama teacher."

"Figures. Because she said, 'What a day, Barry, what a day! Children! *Children!* I am exhausted!' Then she collapsed onto the table. Not really collapsed. It was all fake."

"That's Ms. Babbitt for you. She's very dramatic."

Flynn started to juggle again. "She stayed in the office for the rest of our meeting. She ate a whole king-sized chocolate bar and moaned occasionally, but mostly she was on her phone."

"I'm not surprised." I couldn't figure out the point of the story. I saw our Honda at the stoplight down the block, and I said, "Dad's here."

Flynn tucked the ball under his arm. I slung my backpack over one shoulder and we walked to the pickup circle. "Well, *I* was surprised," he said delicately, "because I thought you were staying after school to help Ms. Babbitt build sets."

Oh.

*Oh.*

"I—I was—she told me what to do and then left, probably went straight to the Fine Arts office. . . ."

There I went again, babbling whenever I tried to lie. That was my main tell. Alex always fiddled with her glasses. Hers was more obvious, but mine was harder to stop. All she had to do was sit on her hands.

Dad pulled up. "Don't tell Dad," I said hurriedly. "Please, Flynn."

"What have you been doing, then?"

"I got detention. You know. The milk thing. I didn't want to tell Mom and Dad. I've been cleaning classrooms."

79

"Alone?" said Flynn. "Have you cleaned the science room?"

He was looking straight ahead, his profile tipped to the sky, but I could tell he knew.

"I don't care what you tell your parents," he said. "But the *science,* Soren. How could you?"

"It's funny," I said weakly.

We were right by the car. Flynn stopped. "You have to tell Ms. Hutchins."

"No!"

He wrapped his fingers around the handle to the front door. I guess he was getting shotgun. "Either you tell her," he said, "or I do."

"Flynn! You *can't!*"

"What I can't do is let someone mess with a scientific experiment." He opened the door. "Uncle Jon! Thanks so much for the ride! How are *you* today?"

# CHAPTER SIXTEEN

TUESDAY IS EXPERIMENTAL Food Night at our house. I dawdled over Dad's latest: broccoli slaw with peanuts, tofu, and a spicy peanut-ginger dressing. It wasn't as gross as it sounds, but it involved a lot of chewing. "My voice teacher in New York gave me a bunch of exercises that strengthen the facial muscles," Flynn told me as I massaged my jaw. I was still at the table with half my dinner while everyone else bustled around me, cleaning up the kitchen. "I can pass them along if you'd like."

"Soren's just trying to get out of cleanup," said Ruth, shooting me an evil glare from the sink.

"Am *not!*" I said.

"To ensure domestic tranquility," Mom said smoothly, "we'll leave Soren the drying and putting away."

They were all in the living room by the time I finished eating. It sounded like they were playing charades. It sounded fun. I marched over to the mountain of clean, wet dishes stacked by the sink, and the same questions that had been racing around my head for hours did another lap.

Was Flynn actually bothered that I was messing up the experiment? Or was he a tattletale looking for an excuse?

Would he tell Ms. Hutchins? Or should I call his bluff?

What would Alex do?

And what had happened to Alex, anyway?

I glanced at Dad's laptop. I was risking trouble—I hadn't asked permission *or* finished the dishes—but before I knew it, I'd abandoned the sink and dried my hands on my pants and signed in. (Everyone knows Dad's password is "fr33d0m" plus the year Ivan graduates from high school.)

Finally! She was online. I clicked on her name and she picked up right away. "Where *were* you?" I said. "Oh my gosh, Alex, I have so much to tell you. Are you okay? What happened?"

"I got caught."

"Right, you said, but—"

"My parents took away my screen time. Since grounding wouldn't make much sense for someone who has no friends."

"That's not true! You have friends!"

She ducked closer to the screen. "I hate it here, Soren. I. Hate. It. The math teacher, she got all mad at me for wasting Post-its! Which I bought with my own money!"

"What better use for Post-its *is* there?" I agreed.

"She made me stack them neatly so they could be reused. And then the vice principal called my mom."

"What did the other kids think of the prank? Did they laugh?"

It was probably the Internet being crappy, but her eyes looked all blurry, and there was a tiny chance she was crying, or about to. "She caught me too fast. I had all the Post-its restacked by the time they came in. All they saw was me being sent to the office."

"It's okay," I said. "It's a minor setback. You'll do something better."

"You only get one first prank, one time when no one suspects you, no one's on the lookout—and I wasted it."

That first part was true. After Alex had confessed to the plastic ants, she was always at the top of Principal Leary's suspect list, and some suspicion rubbed off on me because I was her friend. Luckily, my parents were oblivious. Once, my mom had to wash Silly String out of my hair, and she didn't say a thing.

Alex said, "My mom's training new employees right now, but she says that as soon as she trusts them with Ubercut, we can drive up for a visit."

"Really?"

"It'll be short, she said, but I can spend the whole afternoon with you. We should prank together. Since I'll never pull off anything here."

"Yeah, maybe," I said. "Unless I've been caught out too."

"How are the bean plants?"

I took a cautious look around, but all I heard was guessing and laughing and clapping from the charades game in the living room. "Fine. Except. Well. What would you do if . . . if someone found out about your prank?"

"You're getting blackmailed?"

"He said he'll tell Ms. Hutchins unless I tell her first. But I don't even know if he's serious."

"Who?" said Alex. "Soup?"

"No, no—"

"Billiam Flick? He *would* be a blackmailer."

"He would," I agreed, "but no, not him—"

"Well, then, who?"

"It doesn't matter. What should I do?"

"Poison," said Alex. "Just kidding. Pay him? Persuade him not to tell? Blackmail him back? If you'd tell me who it *is*— WHAT, MOM?"

She turned away. I heard footsteps from my end too. Flynn popped into the kitchen. "Just getting a special treat for the charaders!" he trilled. "Wait. Why are you on the computer?"

Alex came back. "It'd be a whole lot easier for me to help if I knew— OKAY, MOM, JUST A SEC—"

"I thought you were drying the dishes," Flynn said.

"I *was*," I told him. "I *am*."

"Great," he said. "I'll keep you company."

"Soren?" said Alex. "My mom's making me get off. Quick, tell me who—"

Flynn came up behind me to peer into the screen. "Who's that?"

"Yeah, who's *that*?" said Alex.

I had no other option: I slammed the computer shut.

"Was that a girl?" said Flynn.

84

I glared at him. "I don't need your company."

He straightened. "Okay. I'll leave."

Every time I'm mean, I feel awful about it two minutes later. It's that two-minute window that's the problem.

"Do leave," I said. "Stay out of my life."

He left. I finished the dishes. Two minutes passed, and I felt awful. I went upstairs and lay on my bed. Our house is small and the walls are thin, and I could hear them playing charades, rounds of clapping and laughing, Ivan yowling in joy. He probably got to act out being a tiger. That's his favorite thing in the world to do, especially when he gets to bite Mom's leg. The five of them, they sounded like a family. I looked at the cracks in the bedroom ceiling. In my old room there was a turtle, but here I didn't know the animals yet. I bet Flynn didn't see the turtle. It took a while to find it. You had to squint. It was the kind of turtle that only came out if it really, really felt at home.

# CHAPTER SEVENTEEN

PRINCIPAL LEARY APPEARED on the projector screen. "Good morning, students and teachers. We've got several announcements this morning. Art Club will meet during lunch in Mr. Rilling's room. . . ."

Soup whispered, "*Stunning* tie."

It looked like a blackboard, and down the front it said *A B C* in wobbly, chalked letters.

"He's worn it before," whispered Tabitha. "Last April, I believe."

Jéro busily tabulated the Video Announcements Necktie Betting Pool results. "Ouch," he said, glancing at Chloe. "She's got a problem."

I peered at his notes.

"She's down like seven bucks," he said. "She should just cut her losses. But no . . ."

He pointed to her name. *Polka dots all month*, it said. *Odds: 80–1.*

"I think she's trying to win back all her money at once," said Jéro.

Chloe was slightly teary as she scrawled a note for him. *Put it on my tab. New bet: Christmas tie tomorrow.*

It was only October.

"Five hundred fifty to one," said Jéro.

Leary was still droning on. "If you'd like to audition for the winter play, *Alice in Wonderland,* you can sign up in Ms. Babbitt's room. The Library Helpers will meet after school today for a fun hour re-alphabetizing the picture books. That's all. Thank you. It's a lovely day for learning."

Ms. Hutchins snapped up the projector screen. "Class," she said.

Her left eyebrow had a slight twitch.

"We need to have a serious discussion," she told us.

I couldn't believe it. Flynn had told her.

"A *serious* discussion."

We all sat up straight and opened our eyes wide and solemn, trying to look innocent. Ms. Hutchins angrily paced under the THINK LIKE A SCIENTIST banner. I wished she'd decided to talk to me alone instead of calling me out in front of the whole class. "I have received information that's *very* disturbing," she said. I craned forward to see the paper in her hand, but it was folded too small to see the writing. "Someone in this class—one of our very own—has made a disastrous decision."

I tried not to squirm. She was really building this up.

"The results of our Coke-versus-water experiment have been severely compromised. *Someone*"—she waved the paper—"has tampered with the bean plants. *Someone* has sabotaged our experiment."

"Who?" asked Billiam.

I could feel the flush starting. I'd gotten in trouble before, of course, but always with Alex. This was different. I was all alone, and soon everyone in the class would turn toward me—

"I don't know," said Ms. Hutchins. "It was an anonymous tip and it named no names. But I've done a quick soil survey, and I have reason to believe it's correct."

"But why?" said Poppy. "Why would someone do that?"

"All I can say, guys, is not everyone cares about scientific integrity," Ms. Hutchins said sadly. "Science speaks the truth, and that's why I love it. It has no agenda, no motives. And scientists have a sworn duty to add their contributions, however tiny, to the mass of human knowledge, to what we have learned to be true about the universe."

The class was enthralled. She sounded like a teacher in a movie. I wondered if she'd written out the speech beforehand.

"But," she said, and took a long pause, "*but,* this can't happen when someone chooses to spoil science for everyone else."

She had the whole class shaking their heads.

"We'll need to abandon our bean-plant experiment. What a waste of time and resources. It's a shame."

She turned to find a whiteboard marker, and I glanced at Flynn. He was gazing forward, so innocent-looking it didn't even seem like he was trying to look innocent. He probably thought I'd be grateful that he hadn't told her it was me.

Well, I wasn't. I wouldn't get in trouble, sure. But my prank was still ruined. My harmless, hilarious prank.

Ms. Hutchins wrote *Scientific Ethics* on the board. "Who can explain why ethics play such an important role in a scientific experiment?"

There was a strip of air between Flynn's seat and Flynn's butt; that's how hard he was raising his hand. "An experiment without ethics means nothing," he said. "If scientists cheat on their results, we can no longer trust science."

"Exactly!" crowed Ms. Hutchins. We all relaxed. She'd come down from that red zone of teacher anger. "And if we cannot trust science, then what, class?"

"We're no longer human," intoned Soup.

Ms. Hutchins gave him a weird look. "I was thinking more along the lines of losing confidence in the medicines we take, the foods we eat . . ."

"Right," Soup said quickly. "That's what I meant."

"Ethics are essential in science," said Ms. Hutchins. "And sadly, unethical procedures are rampant. Many experiments are sponsored by someone who is set to profit. Did you know that nearly every study about the benefits of milk is funded by the dairy industry?"

Ah, the vegan agenda we'd come to know and love. Flynn nodded along.

"I've changed the plans for our next unit," Ms. Hutchins

told us. "We'll be exploring scientific ethics! It's a fresh look at our theme, 'Think Like a Scientist.' We owe a lot to our anonymous informer."

*What about our anonymous culprit?* I wanted to ask. We owed a lot to *him,* too.

CAUTION
CAUTION
CAUTION
ION
CAUTION
CAUTION

# CHAPTER EIGHTEEN

THAT NIGHT WAS Make Your Own Taco Night. I filled three shells with meat and dumped on cheese and sour cream and salsa. Dad had put out some vegetables, but I never bother with those.

I risked the target seat next to Ivan's high chair, since he seemed too busy packing his nose with guacamole to throw anything at me. "Flynn!" Mom called up the stairs. "Dinner!"

Flynn scooted into the kitchen. "Ooh! Is this farm-fresh zucchini?"

"Picked it today," said Dad. Gardening is his stress relief. He hauls out the playpen, plops in Ivan, and weeds for hours. "We had a bumper crop."

"Tragically," said Ruth.

Dad eyed her. "What was that, young lady?"

"*Magically*," Ruth said smoothly. "I've always thought zucchini has a magical taste, you know."

"Really," said Dad.

"Magical like Bertie Bott's Every Flavour Beans," I said, trying to help her out.

"Yeah, the booger-flavored one," Ruth muttered to me.

"Excuse me?" said Dad.

"The *sugar*-flavored one," said Ruth.

"Zucchini *is* a rather sweet vegetable," said Dad. "You've got a very sophisticated palate, young lady."

Ruth basked. Flynn filled his tacos with so much zucchini he'd never get them closed. I'd been avoiding him since science class. I'd played Quidditch instead of soccer at recess, even though running around with a broom between my legs was obviously not going to end well, and I'd dawdled on the walk home from the bus stop so he and Ruth could get ahead.

"Well, Flynn," said Dad, "your mother Skyped me while you were at school today."

I watched Flynn. He didn't even perk up. He just swallowed his bite and said, "Oh?"

"She misses you, but she's doing well. She sold another tapestry."

"Yeah, she texted me," said Flynn.

There were times when I wouldn't have minded being thousands of miles away from my parents, but Flynn always seemed weirdly nonchalant about the whole business. Maybe he was used to it since his dad moved to Berlin when Flynn was a toddler. I guess Ruth was thinking the same thing. She said, "When's the last time you saw your dad?"

"He visits New York every year, just about," said Flynn. "But we're not really that close."

"Are they still officially married?" I said.

I got a scowl from Mom, but Flynn didn't seem to care. "Yep," he said. "I guess why bother getting a divorce if you don't have to."

"Would you guys bother getting a divorce?" Ruth asked our parents.

"That's not in the picture, honey," Dad said at the same time as Mom said, "Yes."

He glared at her.

"Hypothetically," she added. "If we were in the same situation as Flynn's parents. Which we're not, Ruth."

"Hmph," said Dad.

"I see," said Ruth.

Dad turned grumpily to Ivan. "Ivan, we don't put salsa in our ears."

"IVAN LIKE SALSA!"

Grimly, Mom began to excavate Ivan's ears. A strained silence fell. Flynn was the only one who didn't get the message. He hummed as he drizzled hot sauce over his zucchini mountain.

The tune sounded a lot like a Christmas carol.

"So!" I said. "I have a question. A hypothetical question."

"Some of us," Dad said pointedly, "seem to enjoy hypothetical thinking."

"*Honestly*, Jon," huffed Mom.

"Say you see someone breaking a rule," I said. "But it's not hurting anyone. Would you tell?"

"Ooh," said Dad. Nothing cheers him up like a good ethical dilemma. "Is there such thing as a victimless crime?"

"Never," said Mom.

"Well, *that's* simplistic," said Dad.

"Maybe it seems like you're not hurting anyone," she said. "But when you dig a bit deeper, you'll no doubt find that you are."

"But what if you're making people happy, too?" I said. "More people than you're hurting?"

"And what about questioning authority?" said Dad. "Civil disobedience? Principled rebellion? Do we *want* to raise a child who unthinkingly accepts every rule handed to him?"

"I don't think we're in any danger of that," said Mom, just as Ivan cackled.

Stupidly, I looked over.

"Hey—no—don't throw tha—" I said.

He nailed me in the forehead with a loosely packed ball of ground beef and sour cream.

*"Ivan!"*

A rivulet of sour cream trickled down my cheek.

"Straight to the bathtub, boys, both of you," said Dad, his voice tight. "And I am putting *you,* Ivan, straight to bed after that."

"NO! DADDY WON'T!"

"I'd like to see you stop me," said Dad. He stripped off his shirt in preparation for handling Ivan. I took off mine and used it to wipe my face. I was furious. At Ivan, technically, but really at Flynn. As I walked by him on my way out of the kitchen, I gave his chair leg a good hard kick. He jolted forward. Zucchini fell off his fork into his lap.

"Oops!" I said in a totally fake voice. "Sorry! I'm such a klutz!"

Dad was busy getting Ivan into an armlock, but I was sure Mom saw. She didn't say anything. Moist chunklets of meat slid down my neck. I got to the shower as fast as I could.

# CHAPTER NINETEEN

"RUTH, SOREN," said Dad when we got home the next day, "I'd like you clean the chicken coop this afternoon."

"Nooooo," Ruth and I wailed in unison.

"Do not whine," said Dad. "You two took responsibility for the chickens, and part of responsibility is not whining. In fact, I'd like you to do it now. Before snack, before homework."

Flynn slunk around the corner. "I'll help."

"Thanks," said Ruth, "but you don't want to do this job. Help us some other time."

"But I want to help you guys now," said Flynn. He glanced at me. Did he look nervous? Eager? Both? It reminded me of him with the green tea, right before I'd taken a sip and spewed it across the kitchen.

"We don't need you," I said. "We don't want you either."

Do you ever get like that? Where you're mad at someone but also—or mostly—mad at yourself because you're acting so mean? And since you're mad (at yourself), you act worse (to them)?

It makes no sense, and I do it all the time.

"Come on, Soren," said Ruth. "Don't be a butthead."

"Don't *call* me a butthead."

"I won't call you a butthead if you'll stop acting like a butthead." She put her hands on both sides of her head and pressed inward, so it kind of looked like there was a crack going down her face. "Butthead!"

I didn't want to laugh but it made me. When you do that right and you have puffy enough cheeks (heh heh), you *do* look like a butthead. "Fine," I said. "He can come."

We trudged outside. Flynn headed straight for the coop. "So how do we do this?" he said.

"Wait!" said Ruth. "Wait. Wait. Wait."

Flynn froze, his fingers wrapped around the door handle.

"Back away," said Ruth.

Flynn reversed. When he was safe, Ruth shook her head. "That was a close one. *Never* get close to Martha without armor."

The coop is right next to the garage, where we gathered the necessary supplies. Ruth put on her bike helmet while I got my garden gloves. She gave some Rollerblade pads to Flynn.

"Knee pads?" he said. "To deal with a rooster?"

"Any little bit helps," said Ruth.

I turned to her. "You want to take Martha duty or poop duty?"

This was a tough decision. She bit her lip. "I'll take Martha."

"What about me?" asked Flynn.

"You can watch," I said, not looking at him.

"I want to help," said Flynn.

"You can," Ruth assured him. "Right, Soren? But watch the first round so you get the hang of it." She tightened the straps of her bike helmet. "Ready?" she asked me.

"Good luck, soldier," I said.

"Good luck, pooper-scooper," she replied.

We shook hands, squared our shoulders, and marched into the line of duty. The first step was to get the other chickens out of the way. That wasn't hard, since they're literally birdbrains. I had the garage-door remote, and Ruth had a bag of frozen corn. "Open the coop door, Flynn," said Ruth as soon as Dotty waddled near it. "Just an inch or two."

He opened it. I nudged Dotty out the door onto the grass. Ruth rattled the corn kernels and Dotty perked up instantly, following Ruth on the short walk to the garage. We repeated the process for Potty, Hatty, Eugenie, and Betty II. As soon as we had all five hens in the garage, Ruth jogged out and I hit the close-door button. The hens looked around in confusion: *Where is our corn? Why is that large object descending from the sky? Wait—why is it all dark in here?*

They started squawking, but they were no longer our problem.

But Martha, remember, can't handle being penned up. The coop is see-through, so he doesn't mind that, but the garage? He goes nuts. The one time we'd tried to stick him in there, he went on a homicidal rampage. (We ate most of Betty I, and buried the rest of her in the vegetable garden.) So we have to get him out in the yard for long enough to clean the coop.

"Here, Martha!" said Ruth.

He looked at us suspiciously, wondering what we'd done with all his wives.

"Here-here-here!" Ruth clucked like a chicken. Martha seemed interested. Ruth made her arms into wings and flapped them invitingly. "Martha! BAWK-bawk-bawk-bawk!"

Martha jumped at her. Ruth took off across the lawn, Martha in pursuit. I dove into the chicken coop with the shovel and began shoveling out the old bedding. I was going so fast I stirred up a cloud of dirt and cobwebs and feathers and poop. I tried not to breathe in. Chickens are gross.

"BAWK-bawk-bawk-bawk!" I heard Ruth say.

I popped my head out. They were on the other side of the lawn, Martha's beak mere inches from Ruth's backside. "COCK-A-DOO-ARGH-ACK-ECK-EH!" he cried.

I ducked back in. Shovel, shovel, pant, pant, pant. I'd almost emptied it.

"AHHH!" Ruth shouted. "CODE RED!"

I shot out of the coop just as Martha shot in. "So much for advance warning," I said, my heart pounding.

"He's getting smarter," Ruth said defensively. "He faked me out and changed direction."

"Well, be on the lookout. You know what happens when you're alone with Martha in the chicken coop."

"Scars," she said.

She didn't mean emotional scars, either.

At least we had a break: the next step was to hose it down, and Martha can stay in for that. We took turns spraying the walls. Pebbles of hardened poop turned into trickles of poop water. Martha hunkered down in the corner and glared at us.

"Can I have a real job now?" said Flynn.

I swapped out the shovel for an ice scraper and trowel.

"I want to help," he said.

"You don't have to," said Ruth.

"You really don't," I said, relenting. "I wouldn't wish this job on anyone."

"It'll go faster," said Flynn.

Ruth's eyes met mine. "He's right. And given Martha's ever-sharpening wits—"

"True," I said. "Very true." I gave Flynn the scraper. "This round's for all the little crap. You scrape; I'll trowel it into the bucket."

"And be careful," said Ruth. "Get out when you hear—"

"*Code red,*" said Flynn. "I was listening. I know."

We did a ritual group hug in case one of us didn't make it.

Ruth cried beguilingly, "Oh, Martha! I am waiting out here! Waiting just for you!"

Martha stuck his head out of the coop.

"I am a beautiful chicken lady, Martha!"

She flapped and did a sort of shimmy. Martha, intrigued, took a step forward.

"Come here, Roosterlicious!"

He took the bait and started chasing her again. Flynn and I leapt into the coop. "Martha doesn't like being tricked," I panted as I dumped leaves and poop chunks into the bucket, "so each cleaning stint gets shorter and shorter."

"Got it," said Flynn, scraping busily.

We'd done three-fourths of the floor. I heard Ruth clucking. "You know, Flynn," I said, shoving some sweat off my forehead with the inside of my elbow, "this goes a lot faster with you helping."

"CODE RED! *CODE RED!*"

Flynn and I dove for the door. I let him go out first. We made it just in time.

This time Ruth was the one who looked traumatized.

"Guys," she whispered, "I think he really thought I was a chicken."

"Isn't that the point?"

"He had an expression that was all . . . *lovey-dovey,*" she said in horror.

Flynn put a hand on Ruth's shoulder. "I'm so sorry."

"Thanks, Flynn." She took a deep breath. "Okay. Okay. I'll be okay."

"We're so close," I said. "One more time."

"You better clean fast," she said grimly. "I am not having an egg with Martha."

Squawking, she took off across the lawn. As soon as

Martha started chasing her, Flynn and I launched ourselves back into the coop. We worked fast. With a grunt, he scraped the last section. "Go ahead and get out," I told him. "I'll just get this into the bucket—"

"No, it's okay." With his bare hands, he helped me dump the scrapings into the bucket. It was brimming with disgustingness.

"Thanks."

"No problem," he said, tossing in a half-dead worm. "I think we're done."

We were. The plywood floor practically sparkled. "Let's get out of here," I said. "Go ahead—no, after you—"

"AHHH! SORRY! CODE—"

Martha was in the coop.

He stalked toward us.

We were cornered.

"Holy mother of . . . ," Flynn muttered.

I clutched the bucket to my chest. "Nice rooster. Nice Martha."

Martha took two slow, ominous steps toward me. I glimpsed Ruth's terrified face, peering through the wire grate. "Save yourself, Flynn," I whispered out of the side of my mouth. "I'll distract him."

"No," said Flynn, tightening his lips. "We escape together, or not at all."

Martha's beady little eyes were fixed upon me.

"Oh God," said Flynn.

I, too, turned to prayer. *Dear God,* I thought, *save us.*

*Please save us. I'm sorry for all my sins. I'm sorry for being a jerk to Flynn. I'm even sorry for the Urine-Filled Squirt Gun Incident in fourth grade. I will be a better person, I promise.*

*All I ask is that we get out of here unscarred.*

No.

*All I ask is that we get out of here* alive.

Martha minced another step closer.

"*Do* something!" hissed Flynn.

We needed to calm Martha down. "Marthie," I cooed, "don't you want to take a nice little nap?"

He didn't.

"Aren't you sleepy?"

He wasn't.

Panic jolted my stomach. He took another step. We needed to get him to sleep. What puts things to sleep— *think*, Soren, dang it, *think*—aha!

"Martha want a lullaby?" I said encouragingly.

Another step closer.

"Rock-a-bye, Martha, in the treetop . . . ," I sang. I was tuneless, my voice shaking.

His sharp beak trembled in anticipation of the kill.

"When the wind blows, the cradle will pop . . ."

Wait. Were those the right words?

"The cradle will . . . bop?"

That didn't sound right either. *Plop? Drop?* I did remember a certain grisly touch to the song, but—

"Soren," said Flynn. He stretched his left hand far to the that side of the coop. "When I snap, go for it."

I saw the brilliance of his plan.

Martha's tiny head swiveled to follow Flynn's hand. With his arm fully extended, Flynn snapped his fingers.

Martha's whole body jerked. He fluttered his wings and dove to the left corner of the coop.

Flynn and I made a break for it.

Ruth was ready. As soon as we cleared the door, she slammed it shut. Martha hit the grating and hit it again, throwing his body against it, furious that his prey had escaped. "COCK-A-DOO-ARGH-ACK-ECK-EH!" he screamed in rage.

It was a near-perfect escape.

The only hitch, actually, was that I'd tripped over Flynn on the way out. The bucket flew out of my arms. I fell splat on my face, and bits of chicken poop rained down all around us.

# CHAPTER TWENTY

"I SEE WHY Ruth warned me away from this job," said Flynn. She'd gone inside, but we'd stayed out to hose down the coop one last time.

"Thanks for helping," I said. "You saved my life."

"I'm sure the lullaby thing would have worked eventually."

I made a noncommittal "hmm."

"You want a turn with the hose?" he asked.

We fell silent, watching Martha stalk around the coop, dripping wet and highly resentful. We couldn't put in fresh bedding until the floor had dried overnight (the chickens slept in the garage; Martha just had to deal), so our job was done, technically. But I wasn't ready yet to go back to the house. "Hey," I said. Mom says it's better to talk about stuff than to simmer in resentment. She always says that, *simmer in resentment*, which I like because (a) it's a real-life example of metaphor, and once I told it to Mr. Pickett, our Language Arts teacher, and he said I had *an excellent ear for idiom*, which is another metaphor, and (b) it's a *good* metaphor, because that's what it feels like when you're angry but not saying anything: you're a pot and you're bubbling, boiling, low enough that people'll only notice if they come really close, but *you*, pot you, can't relax. You're on constant heat.

So I said, "Hey."

"Hey what?"

All in a rush, since just because it's good to talk about stuff doesn't mean it's easy, I said, "Hey, I wish you hadn't told Ms. Hutchins about the prank because first of all it was going to be really funny and second I worked really hard on it and you ruined it and I know it's probably stupid to work hard on something like a prank but I used to have this friend and that's what we did together and I miss—"

That's the thing with talking in a rush: sometimes stuff comes out that you don't expect.

"What I mean," I said, "is I think pranks are important. I think they're like mini protests. Tiny ways of saying, *We're here!* And I'm careful. I always think about whether they'd hurt people, and if they would, I don't do them. I'm not that kind of prankster."

"I know," said Flynn. "I know you're a good guy, Soren."

I don't know why I cared so much about hearing that from Flynn.

"But I still disagree," he said. "You think pranks are important. Okay. But I think science is important."

"So do I!"

"And messing with an experiment, it's . . ." He wiggled

106

his mouth like he couldn't get the right word out. "It's like Ms. Hutchins said. Science is all about truth. So making science say something untrue—that's just not right. Science *is* truth."

The look on his face, I'd seen it before. I'd seen it on Ms. Hutchins when she talked about animal rights and on Dad when he talked about equal justice under law and on Mr. Pickett when we'd had that metaphor chat.

Maybe that was what I looked like when I talked about pranks.

"Do a different prank," said Flynn. "One that doesn't mess with a science experiment."

"You think so?"

"Sure. You think pranks are important, right? You like doing them? So do a prank."

I thought, I bet that's why I've been walking around all gray and gloomy. Not because I was mad at Flynn, but because I missed the prank. I missed having something to look forward to, something to think about when I was falling asleep or bored in math.

"Will you help?" I said.

"I don't think so," said Flynn. "I just don't like breaking rules. It's not fun for me."

What *was* fun for him, then?

"But maybe there's someone else who'd help."

Did he even *have* fun?

"And I'll cheer you on from the sidelines."

"Let's go in," I said. "I've got some planning to do."

. . .

DAD WAS AT the stove, stirring something that looked sickeningly similar to the contents of Ivan's diaper after he tried cauliflower for the first time. "Dad," I said, "what are the lyrics to that one lullaby? 'Rock-a-bye baby, in the treetop . . .'"

"'When the wind blows, the cradle will rock.'"

"Rock?" I said. "That doesn't even rhyme!"

"'When the bough breaks, the cradle will fall—'"

Ivan looked up from the floor, where he was using silverware to build a prison camp for Gloria (now sporting a leg cast) and his other Barbies. "WON'T!" he shouted.

"'And down will come baby—'"

"IVAN WON'T!" He hurled a fork across the room.

"'Cradle and all.'"

"IVAN *WON'T* GO TO BED!"

"That's a weird lullaby," I said.

"Perfect for weird kids," said Dad, smiling. "You used to love it." He poked me with a wooden spoon. "Dump in those peas for me, would you?"

# CHAPTER TWENTY-ONE

THE NEXT MONDAY, Ms. Hutchins kicked off the new Ethics in Science unit by making us talk about what *ethics* was, which turned out to be a good idea because someone, I'm not going to say who, thought it was a type of cheese.

"What's a synonym for *ethical*?" said Ms. Hutchins.

"Good," said Goldie.

Ms. Hutchins wrote *good vs. bad* on the board. "Give me another pair."

"Right versus wrong," said Flynn.

"Fair versus unfair," said Lila.

They got on the board too. Then she counted us off into groups of four for case studies. I got Tabitha, Olivia, and Flynn. Flynn, of course, grabbed the group worksheet as soon as it floated onto our desks. "We have to read the situation, discuss the ethical issues, and then do a skit for the class," he said. "Want me to read the situation out loud?"

"Yes!" said Olivia. "Please do, Flynn!"

"Sure," said Tabitha, one hundred times less enthusiastically.

I hate being read to, but Flynn and I were getting along, so I wasn't about to protest. "'Case number four,'" he read. "'Sam is working on an electrical-circuit lab in science class. Sam is a good student and knows he's doing everything right.'"

"Arrogant slimeball," whispered Tabitha, catching my eye. I laughed.

"'But when Sam does calculations to see if his data match the formulas in his science book, he discovers that his data must be wrong.'"

"Ha!" said Tabitha. "Serves him right."

"'He suspects the equipment is not working properly, but his teacher, Mr. Volt, is helping a clumsy fellow student.'"

"That can be you in the skit, Soren," said Tabitha.

"Hey!" I said. "No!"

"Typecasting," said Olivia. They giggled.

"One of *you* can be the clumsy student. I'm Sam the Science Star."

Flynn glared at us. "I'm trying to read." We quieted down. "'Instead, Sam does the math to figure out the correct set of data and simply changes his own data to match what he has calculated.'"

"Now what?" said Olivia.

"We have to talk about whether there's anything wrong with what Sam did, what his other options were, and what we'd have done if we were Sam."

"And we have to plan our skit," said Tabitha. "I feel like this story could be way more exciting."

We didn't have much time to practice before it was our turn to present. I actually ended up volunteering to be Clumsy Student because it was the smallest part. It's funny: I don't get nervous talking in front of the class, but if you turn it into a skit and make me pretend to be somebody else, I instantly get butterflies. Flynn was the teacher, and Olivia was Sam.

"It was a bright and sunny day," said Tabitha, the narrator, "when Sam the Science Star and his klutzy friend walked into the science lab."

Olivia pranced onstage, shoving imaginary glasses up her nose. I took one step and tripped over my own feet. Already people were laughing more at our skit than they had at anybody else's. Success.

"I love science," said Olivia. Ms. Hutchins crossed her arms and frowned, probably because this lover of science was talking in a super-nerdy chipmunk voice. "And today's the electrical-circuit lab! Hurray!"

"Get to your lab stations, class!" said Flynn, who made a very believable teacher. "We've got a lot to do today!"

"The class began to work with the circuit," said Tabitha. "But the other student was having trouble."

"May I help you, uh, Bob?" said Flynn.

"Wait, my name is Bob?" I said, forgetting I was supposed to be in character. Everyone laughed. "Uh, yeah. Help! I dropped all the batteries!"

"I love this lab!" chipmunked Olivia. "And it's so simple, too!"

"While Mr. Volt was busy helping Bob," said Tabitha,

"Sam the Science Star was putting together the electrical parts. But then—*ZZZZZZZ!*"

This had not been rehearsed, but Olivia went with it. She flopped to the floor and twitched violently.

"Sam the Science Star was being electrocuted!" Tabitha cried. "He thought he was good at science, but he thought wrong! *ZZZZZ! ZZZZZ!*" Olivia convulsed on the floor. The class was in hysterics.

"I'll rescue you, Sam!" I yelled.

"But little did Bob know," said Tabitha as I did a slow-motion run toward Olivia, "that electricity can be conducted through the human body. When he made contact with Sam"—I touched her—"*ZZZZZZZ!*"

Now both of us were flopping around on the floor. "*ZZZZZ! ZZZZZ!*"

"*Cut!*" yelled Ms. Hutchins, marching to the front. "Cut! Now! That is *not* what's supposed to happen in your skit! What about your ethical issue?"

"We were getting there," said Tabitha.

"We were just livening it up a bit," said Flynn.

Flynn? Defending bad behavior?

Wow.

I twitched one last time, just for fun, and got to my feet. Olivia and I brushed off our pants. "You've wasted your classmates' time," said Ms. Hutchins, "and they don't appreciate that."

"Yes, we do!" said Soup. "That was the best science skit ever!"

"Marsupial, I didn't ask for your input," she said, her lips tight. "Now, the four of you, let's get on with the lesson. Please explain your ethical issue for the class."

"Should we continue the skit?" said Olivia hopefully.

"*No.*"

LILA CAME OVER to our group after the bell rang. "Well played," she told us.

"We got cut off way too soon," said Olivia. "Ms. H has no appreciation for the arts."

"Well, she's a scientist," said Tabitha. "What do you expect?"

"Not true," said Flynn. "Look at me. I'm into banjo, drawing, *and* science."

"That's because you're weird," I said. In a nice way, though. The way you tell your friends they're weird because you like them. I hoped he'd get it. He smiled and flushed and focused far too hard on sliding his science folder into his messenger bag, so I was pretty sure he did.

"Get to Language Arts, kids!" said Ms. Hutchins. "Chop, chop! Mr. Pickett will blame me if you're late!"

Flynn edged behind me in the scrum at the door. "You know how you were looking for new pranking partners?" he whispered. "I don't think you have to look any farther."

# CHAPTER TWENTY-TWO

"YOU'RE GOING TO prank with the triplets?" said Alex when we video-chatted after school. "Well, okay."

"'Well, okay' *what*? You're the one who suggested them."

"True."

"And you should have seen them in science class. They're funny."

"I know they're funny. Remember their mystery video for Language Arts last year?"

It had involved their golden retriever, a trampoline, a fedora, a trench coat, and at least four ketchup bottles' worth of fake blood. Ruth and I still watched it on YouTube every few months. It was a modern classic.

"They're not epic pranksters like us," I said. "Not yet, anyway. But they like to stir things up. Plus they live next door. They're perfect."

"Perfect," echoed Alex, but her voice was flat.

"So what's your problem?"

"I don't have a problem."

"Fine."

We were quiet. She tugged one of her braids. Finally, she said, "Have you asked them yet?"

"No. I wanted to run it by you first."

She perked up a bit. "Oh."

"What's wrong?"

"I don't know," she said. "Nothing. I guess—I don't know. It's weird for me to imagine you pranking with people who aren't me."

"You're the one who suggested it!"

"I know. It's just weird. That's all I'm saying." She shrugged. "But go for it. Ask them. They'd be good."

"And the two of us are going to prank when you visit, right?" I said.

"If you even want to."

"Of course I want to!" She had no idea, I thought, how much I missed her. No idea how much her leaving had screwed up everything about this school year. "You're the best person to prank with. I'd never even consider the triplets if you were around."

She smiled. One of those post-tears smiles, shaky and hopeful. I peered at the screen, but the sucky Internet plus her glasses made it impossible to tell if she'd actually cried.

"How's Ol' Butt-Braid?" I said.

"Her name is Sophia, Soren. *Sophia.*"

She'd always be Ol' Butt-Braid to me.

"She came over after school last Friday."

"What'd you guys do?" I said.

Alex flushed and started fiddling with her glasses. "Um, we watched some stuff online, and then my mom let us make trail mix, and then, um, we just sat around." She wiggled the frame of her glasses so her nose got battered from side to side.

"Why are you messing with your glasses?"

She ripped her hand away from her face. "I'm not."

"You were." I was grinning broadly now. I'd caught her. "Looks like someone's telling a lie."

"I was adjusting them."

"You were straight-up playing with them. That's your tell. Fess up. What'd you *really* do with Bu—Sophia?"

Alex slumped. "Rats. I'm out of practice. Er, we . . ."

I saw her hand sneak up to the side of her face.

"Don't even think about lying."

"Um. Wemadepaperdolls."

Had I heard what I thought I'd heard? "Say that slower."

"We. Made. Paper. Dolls."

I stared at her in both horror and glee. She shook her head. "I know. I know."

"You go from a life of crime to a life of making paper dolls?"

"Sophia really likes them. She's good at them too. She taught me this trick for making the clothes stay on—and you know what, Soren? It was fun. It was actually fun. I'm not even embarrassed. It was *fun*."

. . .

THE TRIPLETS COMPLAIN all the time about how they're allowed online only on weekends. Their parents are the strictest in the class. Dad and Ivan were outside, harvesting (curses) even more zucchini, and Flynn and Ruth were sprawled out on the living room floor with Settlers of Catan. I had an opportunity. I grabbed the landline.

The last time I'd touched it was when Alex and I had recorded the outgoing message to say, "Greetings! You've reached Slinky Sally's, the Best Snake Vet in the Midwest!" Then we posted fake advertisements on a lot of reptile-enthusiast message boards. My parents got so many random voice mails.

I couldn't believe Alex had a new friend.

Now *I* was the one who felt weird. I wanted to be in Minneapolis, cutting out mini blue jeans and ball gowns. Making up characters and voices and plots. And I didn't want Ol' Butt-Braid around either.

I shoved away those thoughts and dialed the phone. It rang four times. "Hello?" said a male voice.

"Um, hi. This is Soren Skaar. May I speak to the triplets, please?"

"Which one?" said the person at the other end, who sounded too young to be their dad.

"Doesn't matter."

The other end laughed. "They *do* have separate personalities, you know."

"Right. Yeah."

"So which one do you want?"

"Uh, all three? Do they do conference calls?"

He snorted. "For a fee, probably. Hold on." I heard a clank and a muffled shout: "HEY, DOOFAE, YOU'VE GOT A PHONE CALL!" With a rustle, he was back.

"They're on their way. Do you go to their school?"

"Yeah."

"Cool. Listen. Do you have any dirt on them?"

"Dirt?"

"You know. Stuff I'd find useful."

"Useful?"

"I'm Ethan. Their big brother. Home for a visit. Look, those girls have been tormenting me for eleven years, three months, and seventeen days."

"You did that math quick."

"They announce their age every morning at breakfast. You know how they are. Imagine what it was like to live in the same house as them. Outnumbered, outsmarted, outmaneuvered."

"I'm so sorry."

"Thanks, man," he said, sounding touched. "So—they're coming—quick—a little blackmail fodder?"

I scrolled through my memory. The triplets were constantly causing trouble, stirring the pot, but they stayed under the radar. The teachers thought they were angels, mostly because they were blond and round-faced and girls. "Just say the words Noodle Incident," I said. "They never got caught for that one. They'll flip."

"You're my hero. Here they are. Shh. Nice chatting."

"What were you *chatting* about?" I heard one of the girls say suspiciously.

"Oh, nothing," Ethan said airily. "Here's Soren."

"Soren? Soren Skaar? He called? On the phone?"

"Quaint, no?"

A pause.

"Hi," said a voice into the receiver. "It's Tabitha. What do you want?"

"I want to collaborate," I said.

# CHAPTER TWENTY-THREE

WHEN FLYNN HAD first arrived, he and Ruth had stuck together on the walk to the bus stop, mostly talking Settlers of Catan strategy. I'd trail behind, partly because I'm never in a hurry to get to school and partly because there's something about know-it-all-ness that turns my stomach in the morning, and Flynn, frankly, is a know-it-all when it comes to Catan.

Walking alone had given me a lot of time to think about how it used to be. There'd been three kids then, too, a pair and a spare, but back then it was Alex and me together with Ruth trailing behind, since we never let her in on our pranks. It had been a depressing walk this year. It was when I missed Alex the most.

But lately, ever since the chicken coop, all three of us walked together. And ever since the triplets and I had started planning a prank together, they'd wait on their porch until we came by. So we were this huge pack, throwing pinecones and rating Halloween decorations and practicing our *cock-a-doo-argh-ack-eck-eh*-ing. It was different. I liked being part of a pack. It was fun.

Even if Flynn was still a know-it-all.

On the day of the class spelling bee, he was crabby. "No reason," he said when I asked why he wasn't laughing at Olivia's spot-on Principal Leary impression.

"Are you mad at me?"

"No."

"Then why are you in a bad mood?"

"It's not all about *you*, Soren."

"Then what's it about?"

"I'm just crabby, okay? It happens. My mom says it runs in the family. Artists are moody, she says. It's the way we are."

I went up ahead with the triplets and Ruth.

At the spelling bee, I nailed *apologize* and had a lucky guess on the number of *c*'s in *recommend*, but then I stuck an *e* in the middle of *orchard*. I wasn't upset. My only goal was not to be the first one out.

Flynn was still in. And he was still in when it was down to three, and still in when Tabitha misspelled *scepter*. (She "accidentally" kicked an empty chair on her way back to her seat, just like me at dinner that one time.) He was still in when Kiyana messed up *pandemonium*, and he spelled it right to win.

"Our champion!" said Mr. Pickett. "Congratulations!"

Everyone clapped the way you're supposed to clap in class, a.k.a. quietly so it doesn't go through the walls and make other classes jealous that you're having fun, but I whooped. "That's a Skaar!" I yelled. "That's my boy!" Soup and Jéro and Freddy laughed.

"Indeed," said Mr. Pickett, frowning at me. He put the alphabet crown on Flynn's head. "Flynn will be our representative to the school bee next month, and we'll all be rooting for him!"

I whooped again. Finally, Flynn cracked a smile.

AT RECESS, I had a job: scoping out whether it was possible to sneak into the gym during recess. The triplets and I were getting ready for P-Day. That's Prank Day, of course, but the *P* also stands for something else, because the only way to talk your way inside from recess is to convince Mrs. Andersen that you have to twirl some chocolate soft-serve onto the big white cone. If you know what I mean.

I staggered over to her. "I need to use the bathroom," I said.

"You can't wait?"

I tried to look strained. "It's an emergency."

Mrs. Andersen tilted her head to the side.

"It's just, egg sandwiches at lunch, and after last night's burrito—"

She winced. "Go. Go."

I lurched into the school. As soon as I was out of view, I started walking normally, but fast, to the gym. There was an all-school assembly next Thursday. It'd be after lunch—they always were—so if the triplets and I could infiltrate the gym during recess . . .

Would it be locked?

I tried the doors.

Nope.

Bingo.

I peeked in, expecting to see nothing but a shiny sweep of floor. But Flynn was sitting on the stage. His legs were hanging off, and his ankles looked all bony and knobbly, poking out from the bottom of his skinny jeans. He wasn't on his phone or reading or doing last-minute homework or anything.

"Hey," I called. The sound echoed in the big empty room.

Flynn looked up. "Hey."

"Why aren't you out at recess?"

"I don't know."

"You won the spelling bee."

"Yep."

"I didn't know you were that good at spelling."

"Guess I am."

"Winning didn't cheer you up?"

"Guess not."

Weird. If I'd won—well, that would never happen. Not in the real world. So yeah, if I'd won, I'd have been *extremely* cheerful, because it would have meant I'd slipped down a wormhole to an alternate universe, which is a major dream of mine.

"You were right about the triplets," I said. "We're planning something good."

"I don't even want to know."

Just as well. If he didn't know, he couldn't tell. "Won't you come outside?" I said. "Jéro's trying to get a soccer game going. We need you."

"Don't feel like it."

"Are you homesick?"

"I just want to be alone."

"Momsick?"

"Bye, Soren."

"Oh." I stood there sort of awkwardly. I watched the laces dangle off his one untied shoe as he swung his feet against the stage. "You have a lot of friends here," I tried. "Everyone likes you. Goldie and Kiyana and those girls, and Jeremiah, and all the teachers—"

"Do you know what *alone* means?"

Fine. If he wanted to sit in the gym, missing the best part of the day, probably about to get in trouble for skipping, well, I'd let him. If he was uncheerupable, I wouldn't try. "Your shoe's untied," I told him, and I left.

# CHAPTER TWENTY-FOUR

IT WAS P-DAY. My secret alarm went off before the sun rose. I stumbled out of bed, pulled on a sweatshirt while Ruth and Ivan snoozed, and tiptoed down to the garage.

The triplets were already there, with their identical squashed noses and wispy hair and bleary, early-morning eyes. "Hey," said Olivia.

"No time for politeness," said Lila, swishing a legal pad through the air. "We're here for a reason."

"Oh, stick it up your ear, Lila," said Tabitha, who is not a morning person.

"I don't know about you," said Lila, glaring at her, "but *I* am trying to make sure this plan goes smoothly."

"Yeah, I'm sure nobody else wants that. . . ."

Lila licked the end of her pencil. "I'm taking the high road," she said. "I can't hear you down there. Let's run through the checklist. Backpacks?"

"Check," we all said.

With a totally unnecessary flourish, she made a check mark. "Duct tape?"

"Check."

"Thirty-seven alarm clocks, each set to 12:37 p.m.?"

We'd had to raise money for this prank: two lemonade stands and a weekend spent raking leaves for old Mrs. Olson. Then we'd gone to Goodwill and Salvation Army and three garage sales and bought up all the alarm clocks that blasted out *BRRRING!* Now they were synced to the second in the corner of the garage.

"*Check.*"

"Load 'em," said Lila with satisfaction.

Our backpacks were chunky and jangling with clocks. We were ready.

IT WAS KIND of embarrassing to claim a number-two-related emergency during recess for the second week in a row. I didn't want Mrs. Andersen to think I had particularly high-maintenance intestines. Actually, I didn't want Mrs. Andersen thinking about my intestines at all. But I sacrificed my dignity, described breakfast (Raisin Bran) and lunch (three-bean chili), and got permission to hobble inside the building.

The triplets were waiting for me at our lockers. "How did you all get in at once?" I said as I retrieved my clock-filled backpack. "Did you *all* say you had to—"

"Ew!" squealed Olivia. "No!"

"They let us move as a unit," said Tabitha, shrugging. "It's a triplet thing."

We headed to the gym. "Walk with purpose," I told

them. "Like a teacher sent you on an errand." That was another thing Alex and I used to practice. We'd stride down the second-floor hallway in her house. . . .

I felt a pang. She should have been here.

The gym was empty. Folding chairs were already set up for the assembly. "Go, go, go," muttered Lila. We scattered across the floor. With a strip of duct tape, I attached the first alarm clock to the underside of a chair. When I stood, it was invisible. I laughed aloud. Somebody'd be in for a big surprise when their butt started ringing at 12:37 p.m.

We stashed twenty clocks in the audience and tucked ten on the windowsills. Two we put in the ball closet; two we camouflaged near the scoreboard timer; two we tangled in the soccer nets. Olivia, holding the final clock, hesitated. "I know we planned to put it in the lectern," she whispered urgently, "but what if Principal Leary sees it before 12:37?"

"Stop thinking!" hissed Lila. "Start acting!"

"Won't he be suspicious?"

"Just *put* it somewhere!"

Olivia shoved it under a chair in our sixth-grade section. I lunged in with a strip of duct tape.

Our work was done.

BECAUSE OF THE all-school assembly after recess, we hadn't had video announcements that morning during homeroom. The gambling crowd all groaned when Principal Leary took the stage: his necktie had normal, boring gray-and-blue stripes. "The house won today," said Jéro as

127

he did the calculations. "Nobody expects normal. Not from Principal Leary."

Supposedly, the reason for the assembly was to celebrate our first-quarter achievements. Leary started by giving straight-A certificates to every single kindergartner. It went on from there, with smaller and smaller percentages from every grade. They said that was because school got harder, but had anyone asked, What if actually we were getting dumber? What if school was backfiring?

Maybe there was an experiment you could do to figure it out.

Oh no. Was I *Thinking Like a Scientist*? I hate it when teachers get into my head.

I'd gotten a B in Language Arts because I'd started my book report at ten p.m. the night before it was due and a C+ in math because fractions, so I clapped while Flynn, Jéro, all three triplets, Goldie, Kiyana, and a few other people accepted certificates of merit. "And now," said Principal Leary, "I have several reminders about how to conduct yourselves within these hallowed halls."

That was the real reason we had these assemblies: so Principal Leary could lecture us about rules. He likes a captive audience. That's probably why he's a principal.

It was 12:23. Fourteen minutes to go. "In fact," Leary said happily, "I made a slide show."

The first slide said THE A TO Z OF RULES, REGULATIONS, AND REMINDERS. I got comfortable. Thirteen minutes left.

I'd missed *A*, whoops. "*B* is for *Bathrooms*," said Leary.

"No horseplay or gossip in the bathrooms. Bathrooms are to be used for one thing only."

"We shouldn't wash our hands afterward?" called out Sam Goldberg, a third grader.

"You know what I mean, Sam," said Leary. "*C* is for *Cafeteria Conduct. . . .*"

I swiveled around to find the triplets. Olivia was gazing in Flynn's direction. Lila was admiring her certificate, and Tabitha was folding hers into a paper airplane.

"*F,*" said Leary. "*Fights,* whether of *Fists* or *Food,* are strictly *Forbidden.*"

Seven minutes.

"*H* is for *Hallways,* where students should be seen and not heard," said Principal Leary.

Two minutes.

"*L* is for *Lockers.* No food is allowed in lockers, as well as no drinks, no electronics, and no biohazardous waste."

One minute.

"*M,*" Leary began, but he didn't get to say what *M* was for, because—

*BRRRRRINNNNGGGGGGG!!!*

Everyone leapt out of their seats. Principal Leary bobbled the wireless microphone, which hit the floor in an explosion of static. Mr. Pickett let loose the highest, shrillest shriek I've ever heard.

I basked.

It was chaos. It was like a fire alarm but better. The noise came from the windows, the chairs, the closet, the timer, the nets. Everyone's reactions only made it more chaotic. The younger kids, on mats at the front of the gym, were rolling around, or yelling, or both. The third and fourth graders practiced their murder-victim screams. Lila and Olivia were on the aisle, and they jumped up to knock the big red exercise balls off their racks. The balls bounded across the gym, bouncing off the heads of anyone who'd stayed sitting down.

Flynn gave me a pointed look. I widened my eyes and opened my mouth in shock: *Me? Why on earth would you look at* me?

He cracked the tiniest of smiles, and I cracked one back. We'd done it.

# CHAPTER TWENTY-FIVE

"IT WORKED?" said Alex.

"Yes!"

Those new purple glasses plus the lurchy Internet made it hard to read her expression, but I could tell that she was nowhere near as excited as I wanted her to be. "It was *chaos*," I said again. "The clocks wouldn't have been that noisy by themselves, but once everyone started screaming—you know how little kids are, one screams and the rest have to scream too—"

"Yep."

"It was like flicking over a domino. Just starting something and watching what goes down. Remember what that feels like?"

"I remember."

"You know what *I'd* forgotten about pranks?" I was grinning like a goofball and going on way too long, but I was feeling so great. Even tarping the chicken coop before this afternoon's rainstorm hadn't brought me down. "I'd forgotten the adrenaline. It's like a roller coaster. But way better, because you're the one who designed it."

Alex nodded.

"And Leary actually called me into his office to 'discuss a few matters'—you know, how he always did with you. . . ."

Ever since those blasted plastic ants.

"But I said I was innocent and he believed me. He said that without your influence, he doubted I'd try anything. So it's actually—"

"A good thing that I'm gone?" Alex said flatly.

"No! That's not what I was going to say!"

I was going to say it was *kind* of a good thing.

A very, very small good thing. That obviously I would trade in a flash to get her back.

"We're driving up on Saturday," she said. "If you even want to prank with me anymore."

"Of course I do!"

"You don't like the triplets better?"

"No. *No.* We should prank all together. All five of us. It'd be epic."

"I'm only there for an afternoon. We don't have time for anything epic."

"It'd be fun anyway."

"I don't know."

Ruth knocked on the dining-room door. "Sorry, Soren," she said, "but Dad says I have to do my online math stuff now."

"Dad says?" I said suspiciously.

"He does!" yelled Dad from the kitchen.

"Okay. I gotta go, Alex. Bye."

"Bye!"

I x-ed out.

"Why didn't you argue?" Ruth asked me.

"Did you want me to?"

"Well, it would give me more time not doing math."

I shrugged and stood up. I didn't even push the power button, which is an annoying but satisfying thing that Ruth and I traditionally do to each other when we get kicked off the computer. "All yours."

I wandered to the living room. I looked out the same window where we'd waited for Flynn to arrive. It was still raining. If the prank was a roller coaster, now I was at the end, where you have to pry yourself out of your seat, when your head's rattled and the ground's not as solid as it used to be. I watched the rainwater wash brown leaves into a clump at the bottom of the driveway. The reason I hadn't argued, I could have told Ruth, was that I hadn't wanted to talk to Alex anymore. She was acting like a drip, and I was a bit sick of her. I'd never felt that way before. She was my best friend.

AROUND NOON ON Saturday, Alex's mom texted Dad to say they were half an hour away. Mom had taken Flynn and Ivan to the farmers' market, and the quiet house made me feel even jumpier. I went out to kick on the woodpile until their car pulled up and Alex got out.

"Alex!" cried Dad, jogging out of the house. "Alex Harris! What a sight for sore eyes! Welcome back!"

"Hey, Mr. Skaar."

He went over to the driver's window. Alex and I nodded at each other. It wasn't like we were going to shake hands or hug. I bobbled the ball between my feet. "Yep," I said.

"Yep."

"What's up?"

"Not much. You?"

"Not much."

It was a tad awkward, you might say.

Meanwhile, Dad was shouting into Mrs. Harris's window, "Welcome back to Camelot! Your home away from home! Smell that clear country air! Soak in these prairie vistas!"

Dad claims he doesn't act different after his Saturday-morning run. Ha. He basically transforms into a human exclamation point. A sweaty one, too.

"Your dad's sure in a good mood," said Alex. She quirked an eyebrow. "Might I guess—runner's high is involved?"

I grinned. There she was. The person who got me. I didn't have to explain the backstory because she'd been around for the backstory. "It's Saturday morning," I said. "Nothing's changed."

"Well, well, well!" Dad was saying. "So Ubercut is a success! I can't say I'm surprised. My follicles miss your scissors, Marilyn!"

I rolled my eyes at Alex.

"See you around six!" said Dad. "And you"—he did a little spin move and pointed at Alex—"you must be hungry! Come on in, dudette!"

Usually parents make things more awkward, but sometimes they're just so over the top and weird that they have the opposite effect and destroy everyone else's awkwardness, like when a comet gets absorbed into the sun. Well, that's what happened. Dad grilled ham-and-cheese sandwiches and then he grilled Alex about her new life. Ol' Butt-Braid, apparently, took a class in "scissor art" and was trying to get Alex to sign up too. "How nice!" said Dad. "How civilized! I wish Soren had a hobby that was so . . . so *quiet*."

"Soccer is quiet," I said.

Ruth slunk around the corner. "The whole house shakes every time you miss the woodpile. Oh. You're here. Hi, Alex."

"Hi, Ruth."

They've never gotten along. Well, that's not true. Really, Alex has never accepted that Ruth is a person. Alex doesn't have little siblings, so she sees them as tiny and annoying beasts who are always underfoot and/or trying to butt in. And sure, they're annoying, but what your friends don't see are all the times your siblings *are* your friends. They're always around. They're better company than real friends, sometimes. I feel like in books and movies the person with siblings despises them, and the only child wants to play with the other family's babies, but in my experience, anyway, it's the opposite.

"Want to go outside?" I asked Alex.

"The great outdoors!" said Dad. "The freedom of child-hood!"

"Can I come?" asked Ruth.

Alex grimaced and shook her head at me as if we were behind Ruth's back, which we weren't. Ruth saw the whole thing.

Darn.

But what could I do? Alex was only here for the afternoon. "Sorry, Ruth," I said. "We've got something we're working on."

"Let them have their time!" trilled Dad. "Ruth, come with me. Ivan's about ready for big-boy underwear, and I think I remember where we packed away Soren's. You can help me organize it."

"Dad!" I said. "Stop talking about my underwear!"

"Though we might have to buy some new pairs, to be honest. Soren was so big by the time he finally got toilet-trained that Ivan might not fit—"

"*Da-ad!*"

"Not to mention the stains— What, Soren? Something wrong?"

I groaned. "Forget it. Come on, Alex. Let's go outside."

# CHAPTER TWENTY-SIX

FROM THE TREE platform, we could see the triplets in their backyard, rummaging around in a longish patch of grass.

"What are they doing?" said Alex.

"Let's ask them," I said.

"I don't know—"

"ANDREZEJCZAKS!" I hollered. They jumped and looked up, but they couldn't find us. The tree platform has a lot of camouflage, mostly because it's half-finished. That's why we don't call it a tree house. Dad and I were building it together, but then Ivan got born.

Alex said, "Do we have to—"

"YOO-HOO! UP HERE!"

Tabitha pointed, and Lila's and Olivia's gazes followed. They jogged toward the tree platform. "Trust me," I told Alex quietly. "They're fun."

I unfurled the rope ladder, and Olivia grabbed it first. "Don't mess with my ankles while I'm going up," she told her sisters.

"Of course not!" cried Lila.

"We would never!" said Tabitha, wounded.

Olivia rolled her eyes and flew up the ladder like she didn't believe them at all. "Oh my gosh!" she said when she saw Alex, who'd sat with her back against the trunk of the tree. "It's you!"

"Hey."

"Wow. Alex Harris. I always knew you were good at pranks, but Soren's been telling us *how* good." Olivia reached out her hand. "It's an honor to be in your presence."

The corner of Alex's mouth twitched into a smile, and I could have kissed Olivia. (In a totally non-gross way, like on the back of the hand or something. And only if nobody was watching.) "What's he been telling you?" said Alex.

"Well, a lot is still classified, he says," said Olivia, and Alex gave me an approving nod, "but he told us a few details. Like that you were the one who got the kickball trophies out of Leary's office."

Alex would put that on her college application if she could.

"And how you stockpiled duct tape for months before Tapegate."

Alex grinned. She couldn't help it. Nobody in their right mind would call any Andrezejczak triplet "the nice one," but Olivia is as close as it gets. "I heard about the Alarm Clock Incident," said Alex. "Very impressive."

"Thanks!" said Olivia. "Though we really should be thanking *you*."

Alex's expression soured. "Because if I hadn't left, you wouldn't have gotten to work with Soren?"

"No! No! Because you trained him so well."

"Soren's taught me a lot too," said Alex.

"Aww," said Olivia.

"Aww," mimicked Tabitha.

Quick as a snake, Olivia reached out and pinched her neck.

So much for the nice one.

"You'll regret that, Olivia," said Tabitha.

"You'll regret mocking me, Tabitha."

"You'll regret making me regret it, Olivia."

"You'll—"

Lila clapped her hands. "People! People! It's time to get to work."

"True," said Tabitha, instantly switching gears. "Look at the collective prank power in this tree house."

"Tree platform," I corrected her.

"We'd be stupid not to take advantage of this opportunity."

"That's what we were thinking too," said Alex.

Yes. *Yes.* I knew she'd come around.

"How much time do we have?" said Lila.

"Just this afternoon," said Alex.

Just an afternoon. It was a crumb, and I used to have a cake.

Lila whipped out a legal pad. I don't know where from. It's one of her special talents, whipping out legal pads from nowhere. "I'll take notes while we brainstorm," she said. "Ideas, please!"

WE WERE LONG past brainstorming, deep into details, when Ruth and Flynn wandered over. "What are you guys doing?" said Ruth.

"Quick!" said Alex. "Pull up the ladder!"

"Who's that?" I heard Flynn ask Ruth.

"Alex, Soren's friend," Ruth said. "Hey! Guys! What's going on up there? Can we come up?"

"You mean, *may* we come up," said Flynn.

Alex was rolling up the rope ladder, so the answer to both questions, obviously, was no. "Not this time," I said, feeling a punch of guilt.

"Oh, come on," said Olivia. "Can't they?"

Olivia likes Flynn. Plus she has a soft spot for younger sisters because she's the runt.

"You guys will make the platform collapse," said Alex. "Five is as many as this thing can hold."

That was honestly true. I could hear ominous creaks every time anyone shifted position. "Let's play Catan tonight," I called down. "The three of us."

Ruth lifted a shoulder. Flynn didn't say a word. They beat their retreat back to the house.

"I feel kind of bad," said Tabitha.

"Me too," said Olivia.

"I play with them all the time," I said. "Seriously. All the time. And Flynn doesn't even like pranking. He told me."

"The thing about pranking," said Alex, "is that if you let everyone in on it, there's no point. There's no *prank*."

Lila fluttered the pages. "Back to the plan."

I'd be extra nice to Ruth and Flynn tonight, I thought. I'd make it better.

But not now.

# CHAPTER TWENTY-SEVEN

HERE ARE THE instructions for our small, domestic prank:

1. Sneak into the kitchen and find a box of uncooked macaroni. You also need Scotch tape. And one sandwich bag for each toilet you want to target.

2. Put a little handful of dry macaroni in each bag. Maybe ten pieces. Not much.

3. Go to the bathroom. Close the door like you're actually, you know, going to the bathroom.

4. Tape the bag to the underside of the seat. Make sure the macaroni's spread out enough that the seat looks flat when you close the lid.

5. Wait.

With five experts, it didn't take long to hit every bathroom in both houses. Mom popped in just as we'd all met up in our living room for step 5. "Alex!" said Mom. "We've missed you so much!"

"Speak for yourself," I said.

Alex looped back her leg and nailed me behind the knee. I crumpled to the floor. "Gotcha," she said.

"Nice one," said Mom, high-fiving her.

"Thanks for supporting your child," I told her.

"You deserved it," she said. "How *are* you, Alex?"

I waited for their chatting to die down. "Where are Ruth and Flynn?" I asked Mom as soon as it did.

"They're walking to Coneheads," said Mom. That's the ice cream shop in town. "They took Jim Bob in the stroller."

"Flynn agreed to get near Jim Bob?"

Mom gave me a look. "Don't be mean, Soren."

"I'm not. I was just wondering. So they'll be gone for another hour?"

"At least," said Mom.

Good, because I had a feeling they would not take it well if they were the ones who fell for the prank.

"Let's play Pictionary Telephone," said Tabitha. Before long, we were howling over how demented our drawings got. It was so fun I wished Ruth and Flynn were there too.

We almost missed Dad lumbering down the hall, the newspaper folded under his arm.

"There he goes!" I hissed. "P-Day! P-Day! The moment has come!"

"*Shh!*" said all four girls together, so hard that the breeze from their mouths practically knocked me over.

"Keep playing," said Tabitha. "It'll look suspicious if we don't."

Luckily, we were at a naturally quiet part in the game,

everyone sketching the phrase that the person next to them had written. Nobody was paying much attention to drawing, though. We heard the bathroom door close. The fan whirred on as Dad turned on the light, and then there was silence.

And then—

"AHHHH!"

We were wide-eyed, trying not to laugh.

"LUCINDA!"

Dad rushed down the hall, holding up his pants with his hands.

"Yes?" said Mom. "Is there a problem?"

"I—I'm—"

"What's going on, Jon?"

"Nothing like this has ever happened before—"

"Nothing like *what*?"

We tiptoed into the kitchen and peeked around the doorframe. Mom was peering up at Dad, her work laptop open in front of her.

"Jon?" she said. "Are you all right? And why aren't your pants zipped?"

"Well—"

"One of those scalawags clog the toilet? Well, the plunger's where it always is. Unless Ivan had it up in his crib again—"

"It cracked," Dad whispered urgently.

"The plunger? That clogged, huh—"

"The seat."

"The *what*?"

"I cracked the seat."

"You *what*?"

"Lucinda," said Dad in despair, "I must have sat down too hard—I was in a bit of a hurry—or maybe it was on its last legs—but I sat, and the seat, well . . . It broke."

"You broke the toilet seat?"

I made the mistake of looking at Tabitha, who was bright red and quietly shaking. I had to stuff the collar of my shirt into my mouth.

"Yes," whispered Dad. "I don't know what to say, Lucinda. I heard it crack."

THE DOWNSIDE TO this prank: it's clearly a prank. Mom marched right in to check out the damage, and it was pretty obvious that a bag of macaroni hadn't casually strolled over to the toilet and taped itself under the lid.

But the upside: nobody can be that mad. We were doubled up laughing, flopped on the floor, when Mom and Dad came storming into the living room with the macaroni. "It just crunched, right?" I managed.

"I sat down," Dad said darkly, "and that crack—it was dead-on the sound of a toilet seat breaking." The ends of his belt were still flapping around his thighs. "You should have seen me. I was up like a shot."

That was enough to send us into another gale of laughter. Mom and Dad started laughing too.

"Why didn't I think of this one myself?" said Mom.

"Did you booby-trap any other toilets?" said Dad. "No. You know what? Don't answer that question."

"Maybe we'll go over to the Andrezejczaks' for a while," I said innocently. "See what's going on over there."

Mom lifted her eyebrows at Dad. He shook his head, but not like *no*. More like *why even bother?*

"Be back before dinner," said Mom.

"Have fun," said Dad.

"I don't think you have to tell them that, Jon."

ALEX SAID THERE was a hope that when her mom came back at six, we could persuade her to stay for dinner, and we'd eat really slowly, and it'd end up too late to drive to Effie, where they were going to stay with Alex's aunt, and they'd have to spend the night with us.

No such luck.

Mrs. Harris whipped into the driveway at six o'clock sharp. She came up to the door to get Alex and thank my parents, but you could tell she wanted to hit the road. She was bouncing on her heels and she kept glancing at her phone. "I trusted my new stylist," she told my mom. "I left my whole business in her hands. And now I've got a text that she snipped a man's ear!"

"Snipped it, or snipped it off?" I said.

"Given my luck, snipped it off," said Mrs. Harris. "Why did I leave for a day? Who up and leaves the thing they care most about? *Abandons* it?"

"But what about the ear? Can they reattach it?"

"Probably not," she said gloomily.

I *knew* it. Those haircutters always get way too close with the scissors, and Mom never believes me when I tell her I'm in danger. "I am never getting my hair cut again," I said.

"I'm positive it was just a nick," Mom said to both me and Mrs. Harris. "Everything will be fine, Marilyn. Give him a coupon for a free haircut and he'll settle down."

"He'd better," said Mrs. Harris. "Go take one last bathroom run, Alex, because we're going all the way to Minneapolis and we're not stopping."

Mom ran her hand through the back of my hair. "You're getting pretty scruffy, Soren. Thanks for reminding me. I'll make an appointment for next week."

Ugh.

"Bye," I told Alex when she got back. "See you—see you next time."

"Bye," said Alex. "Yeah. See you. Bye, Soren."

This was the second time I had to watch Alex drive away, not knowing how long it'd be till I'd see her again. It didn't get any easier.

# CHAPTER TWENTY-EIGHT

THAT NIGHT IT rained, and it kept raining straight through to Monday morning. That didn't stop Dad from making us walk to the bus stop. "You know the rule," he said. "Skaars walk unless . . ."

"It's below zero with gale-force winds," Ruth and I recited glumly. Dad has a lot of call-and-response sayings like that. "Trash goes in . . . ," he'll say, and we'll chant, "The proper receptacle!" Or, "Skaars are too nice to . . ." "Act exclusive!" He's trying to mold us in his image.

Flynn and Ruth and I set out together, but they started speed-walking right away. They were sharing Flynn's Metropolitan Museum of Art umbrella. I didn't have an umbrella, just a hood, and Dad had made me wear these janky, too-big rain boots I couldn't go fast in. "Hey," I yelled. "Wait up."

Flynn's head bent toward Ruth's, and I heard her giggle. They started walking even faster. "Guys!" I called.

No response. I kicked a wet bundle of leaves. All that did

was throw a bunch of water down the boot, so now my sock was soggy too.

The triplets weren't on their porch. I thought about waiting for them, but I was worried I'd miss the bus and Dad would be mad and I'd be late and Ms. Hutchins would be like, "Your *cousin* was on time." So I sloshed on, getting farther and farther behind.

When I got to the bus stop, the triplets and Ruth and Flynn were all clustered under the gigantic umbrella. "I can't wait to change into my tennis shoes," I announced. Nobody looked up. I elbowed my way in. "How'd you get here so fast?" I asked Lila.

"Mom drove us," she said. "Look."

They were huddled around the worm in Ruth's palm. "I saved him," said Ruth. "He was stranded on the sidewalk."

"Ruth," I said, "there were hundreds of stranded worms."

"Yeah, but only one was Mr. Wiggly."

He was definitely wiggly. That much I'd give her. "*You* like worms?" I asked Flynn quietly.

"Nope. That's why my hands are in my pockets." He shook his hair off his forehead. "Yours are too."

I looked down. Yep. I gave Flynn an embarrassed grin. "Guess so." I couldn't be squeamish—I had a reputation to maintain—but honestly, I don't like worms much either. It was those pink, pointy ends they had. No thanks.

"I think Mr. Wiggly knows you're the one who saved him," Olivia told Ruth. "Look, he dances a bit whenever you get your face near."

The bus pulled up, clanking and splashing. Flynn wrestled with his umbrella and the rest of us lined up to get on. "If Mr. Wiggly's so smart," I told Ruth, "we should use him in a prank."

"No! He's my friend!"

"What better fate for a friend than to be used in a prank?" said Tabitha.

"You guys have one-track minds," sighed Flynn.

"Don't even think about touching Mr. Wiggly," said Ruth.

The bus was damp and steamy, and my socks were so wet I could feel my toes pruning, and all the seats were gone so I had to sit with Billiam Flick. But I found myself in a good mood. It was fun to get along with people. It was a lot better than fighting. We rattled to school. What if Mr. Wiggly ended up in Principal Leary's pocket? Or in a teacher's microwave lunch? Not that any of these pranks would happen, but there was no harm in imagining.

FLYNN WENT TO Goldie's after school to work on their science presentations, so Ruth and I went home alone. "How's Mr. Wiggly?" I asked her.

"He died in math."

"Me too," I said. We'd had a polygon quiz.

"Mr. Snyder let us bury him in the hamster cage. We had indoor recess so we did a whole funeral. Wallaby sang 'Tears in Heaven.'"

"Wow. Sounds sad."

"Nah, it was fun. Hopefully I can find Ms. Wiggly on the way to school tomorrow."

That reminded me. "Do you think Dad would let me have the triplets over?"

"No. No way. It's a school night and you haven't done your homework."

"How do *you* know I haven't done my homework?"

"Have you?"

"Well, no."

"Ha. Told you. Why can't you meet them on the tree platform?"

"Because it's pouring rain."

"I could help you sneak them in," said Ruth, perking up. "Call them up. I've got just the plan."

TABITHA PICKED UP after one ring. "Hello?"

"Oh, hey," I said, relieved it wasn't some weird relative. "I want to do another prank."

"Me too."

"But we've got to be inside—"

"Tell him we can't have friends over on school days," said Lila in the background.

"I *know* that, Lila," Tabitha said snippily. "We want to plan too, Soren—"

"Tell him I've got a new legal pad," I heard Lila say.

"I can talk to him myself—no—quit it—"

There was a bump and a lot of staticky feedback.

"Hello, Soren," said Lila smoothly into the receiver. "*Ouch!* Tabitha!"

"Can you guys get out of the house?" I asked.

"Sure, we're allowed outside. But it's raining, in case

you didn't notice. And maybe we could get an exception and invite you over if we'd done our homework already, but we haven't even started Ms. Hutchins's giant presentation, and that's due the day after tomorrow."

"I don't even know my topic." I paused, distracted. But I had to shake it off. I'd worry about the presentation later. "No, but listen. What I've been trying to tell you: Ruth can sneak you in."

"Really?"

"She's got a plan."

Another bump. More static. "Tell Ruth she's amazing!" Olivia shouted into the phone. "Ouch, Lila! Stop that—*ow*—"

Lila was back. "Hi again. We'll be over straightaway."

"Give us thirty minutes," I said. "And come to the front door."

"But you guys never use the front door."

"Exactly."

TWENTY-TWO MINUTES LATER, Ruth rambled into the kitchen. Dad was cleaning out the cabinet beneath the sink, and Ivan was whizzing around in his baby walker. He uses it even though he can walk now, I'm sure because he can get up some serious speed.

"Can I make scrambled eggs?" Ruth asked Dad.

"Sure."

Ruth whisked a few eggs, turned the stove up to the max, and gave me the thumbs-up. I sidled out of the kitchen and went to the front door.

"WHEEEEE!" I heard Ivan shout.

"Ivan!" said Dad. "Ruth, could you corral him on that side of the kitchen? I've got a lot of dangerous household chemicals out over here."

I couldn't see, but based on the furious screaming and revving of wheels, Ruth was holding Ivan by his collar. I peeked in. When I saw a wisp of smoke from the stove, I ducked back to the front hall.

"SET IVAN FREE!" Ivan yelled.

"Just a sec, Ruth," said Dad. "Let me get the bleach onto a high shelf—"

"He's really pulling," panted Ruth.

"One second—"

And there it was, the smell of burning eggs. If you've never smelled it, don't. It's kind of like the yolk of a hard-boiled egg plus a fart, but it's all warm and smoky too.

"Your eggs!" shouted Dad.

*BEEEEEP! BEEEEEP!* That was the smoke detector.

"Oh no!" cried Ruth, sounding only the tiniest bit fake. "I totally forgot!"

"Get that pan off the stove!"

*BEEEEEP! BEEEEEP!*

"Should I let go of—"

There were pounding footsteps, clattering wheels, and a clang.

"WHEEEEEE!" yelled Ivan.

I opened the door. The triplets darted in.

"Up the stairs," I muttered. "And step on it."

*BEEEEEP! BEEEEEP!*

They started to run upstairs, me on their heels, but our plan had one major flaw:

Dad sprinted to the front door to fan out the smoke.

We were caught red-handed.

"Do not move," he said.

The triplets and I froze midstep.

Dad fanned the door back and forth. Cold air rushed in, and a raft of raindrops. With one last, drawn-out, resentful beep, the smoke detector fell silent.

Ruth peeked into the hallway. "Oh," she said sadly. "Caught."

Dad surveyed me and the triplets, stock-still on the stairs. Ivan, smirking, wheeled out to the hall. After automatically checking Ivan's tray for the bleach bottle, Dad looked back to me. "I guess I knew that someday you might try to sneak a girl up to your room. But I always thought it'd be one, not three."

"School project," I said weakly.

"You know what?" Dad said. "I'm done. I'm just done. I throw up my hands."

Ruth and I shot each other alarmed looks. Ever since Ivan was born, we'd worried that Dad might crack. "Daddy . . . ," said Ruth.

"I'm fine," he sighed. "Ivan and I will have a nice bracing glass of pomegranate juice. You go work on your"—he paused—"school project."

# CHAPTER TWENTY-NINE

"ALL THE WAY UP," I told the triplets on the stairs. "We'll use Flynn's room." The room Ruth and Ivan and I share was filled with dirty laundry and Duplo, and if you step on Duplo barefoot you basically die, it hurts so much.

"Where *is* Flynn?" said Olivia.

"He's at Goldie's. They're working on their science presentations."

Tabitha clapped her hands over her ears. "LA LA LA SCIENCE PRESENTATIONS ARE NOT A THING LA LA LA—"

"It only counts as procrastination if you feel anxious and terrible," Lila explained. "So we have this new strategy where we convince ourselves that major projects don't exist."

Olivia, tearfully twisting a lock of hair, said, "Yeah! It's great!"

"We'll get it done," Lila assured her. "We always do."

"Get what done?" said Tabitha.

"Nothing!" said Lila. "Nothing at all! No deadlines! No projects! We're free!"

Personally, I preferred feeling anxious and terrible. I opened Flynn's bedroom door. "Whoa," I said.

The room was totally different from when it'd been mine. He'd covered one of the slanted attic walls with a sheet of butcher paper, and it looked like he was in the middle of coloring and drawing and doodling all over it. It was like the cave paintings we'd learned about in social studies, except Flynn is way better at art than cavemen.

"This is super cool," said Lila.

"Flynn is amazing," moaned Olivia.

"Hey, look, Soren," said Tabitha. "There's you."

I looked. It was a cartoon of Ivan tricking me into sitting on play dough. There was me, yeah, and there was a clod of brown stuff on the butt of my pants. "Great," I said flatly.

Now that I was looking closely, I saw one familiar scene after another. There was Flynn steeping me that poisonous green tea. There was Flynn at the block party, holding his phone and surrounded by girls. There he was, grinning at his desk, as Ms. Hutchins read aloud the anonymous tip that'd ruined my prank. There he was walking to the bus stop with Ruth, and, yeah, if you followed the road like ten inches back, there was me, walking alone.

"I don't get how he's good at science *and* soccer *and* banjo *and* art," said Tabitha.

"*And* drawing every time I've ever looked stupid!" I said in a chipper voice.

"He's so amazing," said Olivia.

I sat on the floor so I'd have to crane way up to see the mural or whatever you wanted to call it. Those dumb pictures had made me crabby. "Moving on," I said. "Let's plan."

"What are we planning?" said Ruth, lingering by the door.

"We?" said Lila.

"I can stay, right, Soren?" said Ruth.

I shrugged. "If they're okay with it."

"Of course we are," said Olivia. "We wouldn't even be in here without Ruth."

"But can she keep a secret?" said Lila.

"I can!" said Ruth. Her back was ruler straight and her eyes were wide. "I'm good at secrets!"

"Prove it," said Tabitha. "Tell us something you've never told anyone else."

"Trick question," said Ruth. "I won't."

Lila and Tabitha nodded. "She can stay."

"I'll ask Dad if we can borrow his laptop," Ruth said, and shot down the stairs.

"Why?" wondered Tabitha.

I shrugged. When she came back, I said, "Ruth? Why the laptop?"

"To video-chat Alex," she said, like *duh*. "You weren't thinking we'd plan without her, were you?"

Well, yes. I was. Based on the nonplussed looks on the triplets' faces, they were too. Alex had called us the Dream Team after the Crackaroni Incident, but—well, we'd forgotten all about her.

Ruth hadn't forgotten, and Alex wasn't even nice to Ruth.

"We weren't sure she'd be online," I told Ruth.

But she was. I panned the screen so she could see the whole room. "The Dream Team is back!" she said. "Oh, and you, Ruth. Is this your old room, Soren? What happened to the wall up there? Are those drawings?"

"Never mind that," I said quickly, tilting the screen to center on my face. "We've got our next all-school assembly in a couple of weeks. Want to help us plan something?"

Alex frowned. Her glasses slipped down her nose. "My mom says we can't visit again until she's a hundred percent certain nobody's going to cut off an ear the second she leaves town."

"Oh."

"She said definitely not November. Maybe December."

"Oh. Shoot. Okay."

"So . . ."

"So what?"

"So let's plan a prank for then."

"Sure, we will," said Lila, neatly sliding in front of me, "but what about now?"

Alex bit her bottom lip. "Just, I think you should wait till December."

I grabbed the screen so I was the one in it again. "Alex. We can't wait till December."

"Why not?"

"Because it's only October! What are we going to do in between?"

"Plan the December prank."

"And pass up any other opportunity?"

"We're the Dream Team," said Alex. "Well, minus Ruth."

"Yeah, but—"

"And the Dream Team shouldn't prank when only four people are there."

"Five," said Ruth under her breath.

"You shouldn't leave me out," said Alex.

"You could do something down there."

Alex snorted. "Yeah, right. The way they secure this school? And Sophia hates pranking. She's always like, 'Why is that even fun?'"

I shook my head. If someone doesn't immediately grasp the joy of pranking, they're beyond hope.

"Listen," said Lila, taking advantage of my momentary lapse to regain control of the laptop, "we're pranking now. That's decided. So either you're cool with it and help us, or—"

"I just think you're being a little mean," said Alex. "You *could* wait for me."

*But you moved away!* I wanted to say. *I never wanted you to move, Alex, but you did, and what else am I supposed to do?*

Lila swiveled so Alex couldn't see her face. She mouthed at us, *What should I say?*

"I got this," said Tabitha. She scooched forward. "Alex?"

"Imagine how epic December could be—"

"We're having trouble hearing you." Tabitha frowned at the screen. She grabbed the top of the screen and shook it back and forth. "Alex?" she said in a faraway voice. "We're losing you—bad connection—are you—"

She slammed the laptop shut.

"Done," she said.

We all stared at the laptop there on the rug. A second ago it had been talking, it had been Alex's moving face, scowling, glasses shifting around—and now it was just a hunk of plastic. Technology was weird.

"That's what we do when our mom's out of town and trying to give us chores," said Tabitha.

"It's not very nice," said Ruth.

"Nope," agreed Tabitha. "We're Slytherins."

"Big picture, it *is* nice," said Lila. "She doesn't need to know we're pranking without her. She can think we're waiting, and we'll forget to mention whatever we do."

"I'd rather know the truth if I were her," said Ruth.

"But you're *not* her, are you?" I snapped.

What? Where did that come from?

"No," said Ruth, "but—"

"Go away," I said. "You're just proving you're too little to be here."

I guess I thought, At least I can do *one* thing Alex would approve of.

"Go away, Ruth," I said again.

"You said I could stay!"

"*They* said you could stay. But you're my little sister, so I get to decide." Right then it felt like everything had been better in the old days, and that's the most helpless, hopeless feeling. "And I decide no."

Ruth stomped her foot.

"Very mature," I told her.

She drew herself up as tall as she could. Her eyes got big as she tried not to let tears come out. There was no way she'd cry in front of older girls. Ruth has a lot of pride. "I am *extremely* insulted," she said. "If it hadn't been for me, you wouldn't have even gotten them in the house." On her way out, she whirled around to toss one more thing over her shoulder. "Don't think I'm going to wash that egg pan for you."

IF YOU'VE EVER been over to your friend's when they fight with their sibling, you know it's the second-most awkward situation in the world, number one being them fighting with their parents. I'd seen it plenty (Soup can't even ride in the same car as his sister Wallaby without name-calling), but I'd never been the one who caused it. Not because I'm noble. Just because Ruth and I are, usually, cool.

The triplets were tactfully silent. After a while, though, we started reliving the Alarm Clock Incident. That cleared the air. Olivia did an imitation of Leary when the clocks went off—"*M,* children, is for—AHHHHH! HELP!"— and we were all rolling around like the kindergartners on their mats.

"We've got to do another prank," said Tabitha. "That was the most fun I've had since we forced Ethan to go ice fishing for his boxers."

Lila's legal pad was scrawled with ideas by the time the door opened.

"Oh," said Flynn. "Hey, everyone."

"Oh my gosh," said Olivia, sounding like she'd been sucking on a helium balloon. "It's *Flynn.*"

"Hi, Olivia."

She turned bright red and scooted back so she was half-hidden by the desk. "Hi!"

"I'm back from Goldie's," Flynn told me.

"We can see that," I said. "Um, is it okay that we're in here?"

"I guess." He didn't sound totally sure, but he perched on the windowsill and played the piano on the seams of his pants. "What's up? Are you working on your science presentations too?"

"What science presentations?" said Lila. "What in the world are you talking about?"

"Nobody here's started," I said.

"They're due in two days!" said Flynn.

"LA LA LA—" the triplets began.

"What are Dad and Ivan doing?" I asked Flynn. "Are they okay?"

"Your dad is lying flat on the kitchen floor. Ivan is driving trucks over his face."

"Back to normal, then," I said, relieved. "Er, did you happen to see Ruth?"

"She's reading *From the Mixed-Up Files of Mrs. Basil E. Frankweiler* on the couch." Uh-oh. Isn't that book about a girl who runs away from home because her brothers are so annoying? "She looks mad," Flynn added.

"I bet she does," said Tabitha.

"Poor Ruth," said Olivia.

"You don't know anything about it," I told them. "So don't pretend to."

There was an awkward silence.

"So," said Flynn.

"So," said Lila.

The awkwardness continued. Three other people thought about saying, *So*.

Finally, I glanced at the mural on the wall. "We *would* ask you to hang out with us," I said, "but you wouldn't like what we're doing."

"Oh."

I wanted him to leave. I wanted him to get the hint.

"So," I said at last, "you're kind of interrupting."

"Well," said Flynn, "you're kind of in my room."

As a unit, the triplets stood. "We're sorry!" said Olivia. "We'll go!"

"Let's go downstairs, Soren," said Lila.

"Don't boss me around in my own house," I told her. I turned to Flynn. "And you should remember that your room is actually *my* room."

"Whoa," Tabitha said. "Chill."

Didn't she know that the worst, the absolute number-one worst thing to be told is "chill"? I went from annoyed to mad to furious in about half a second, and I grabbed a corner of butcher-paper mural and tore it. I tore it twelve inches, a jagged diagonal rip that went right through a careful, colorful cartoon of Flynn playing the banjo while a bald dude and a ponytailed lady, obviously my parents, bowed in worship. "You can *have* this room," I said. "At least I'm living in my own house."

Flynn turned a deep red. I spun to leave, but not before I saw the way his eyes had gotten all watery. It was the second time that day I'd made someone cry. I knew I was supposed to feel sorry, but it didn't hit me right away. It didn't hit me for a while. For a while it felt like when you've won a soccer game, not just won but really pounded them, and you're walking off the field and you give your counterpart on the other team that little look, chin up, square in the eyes: *I'm better than you.* It was like the surge you get when you win a random arm-wrestling match at lunch and everyone shouts, "OHHH!" Until the sorriness hit me, I felt like a champion. Then it hit me, and I wanted to cry myself.

# CHAPTER THIRTY

FLYNN HAD A stomachache and didn't come down for dinner. Mom went to check on him, and after we ate she took up a plate of food and stayed up there for an hour at least.

I figured I'd be in for a Big Talk, so I spent the hour preparing arguments in my head. He didn't like pranking, he'd *said* that, so I wasn't acting exclusive, and about the room, the thing is, as Mom knew, in a big family, or even a medium family in a small house, it's not a huge deal to use someone else's room. Sometimes there's just no other place to go. We hadn't snooped or messed anything up, well, except the mural that had gotten torn, but that was practically an accident—

But Mom didn't say anything about it.

Also, I would have asked whether she'd noticed that the most embarrassing moments in her son's life were depicted in graphic detail on her nephew's walls, and what did she think about *that*.

Nope. Nothing. She did make me wash the egg pan, though.

The next day, Flynn went over to Goldie's again. Her dad dropped him off right before dinner. He slid into his seat and said, "Wow, Uncle Jon! Homemade pizza!"

"Homemade *cabbage* pizza," Ruth corrected him. It was Experimental Food Night again. "Don't get excited."

"Cabbage is my favorite!"

"There's acorn squash and caper pizza as well," said Dad. "Have a slice of each."

"What did you and Goldie get up to?" said Mom.

"First we had snack," said Flynn. "Mrs. Grandin made Snickers salad. It was amazing. I'm really coming around to Midwestern cuisine."

I was having a tough time choking down the cabbage pizza, and I think what happened was that I took a way too big bite and actually clogged my ear canals for a few seconds. Everything's connected in there. By the time I managed a swallow, both Mom and Dad were glaring at me.

"Soren," said Dad, "Flynn says he and Goldie spent most of the afternoon working on their Ethics in Science presentations for Ms. Hutchins."

"Well, actually, we've been working for weeks," Flynn said. "Today was for the finishing touches."

"And they're due *tomorrow*?" said Mom, still glaring.

"I'll be fine!" I said.

"Flynn is done. Have you even started?"

"In a way," I hedged.

"What way?"

"Well . . ." I considered saying I'd made half the Power-Point already, but that was an easy one to check. "I know what my topic is."

That was *almost* true. I couldn't have named it, but I did know where I had it written down.

As long as I hadn't thrown away that piece of paper.

It had to be in the pocket of my Adidas soccer pants.

Unless they'd gotten washed.

"I thought you'd vowed to stop procrastinating," said Dad.

"No, I said *soon* I'd vow to stop procrastinating," I said.

Nobody even cracked a smile. That was how I knew I was in trouble.

I WAS LOCKED in the dining room with Dad's laptop and a cowbell. The laptop was for working; the cowbell was for ringing if I had to go to the bathroom. Then Mom or Dad would come grant permission and stand there scowling until I got back.

At nine or so, Ruth popped her head in. "Flynn's making Snickers salad," she said. "He found the recipe online."

"Cool," I said, not raising my eyes from my PowerPoint. I was still choosing a visual theme, but that was probably the most important step.

"Dad gave him Snickers from the Halloween stash, and he's microwaving them and mashing them up with marsh-mallows and peanut butter and Rice Chex."

Those were four of my all-time favorite foods. "That sounds disgusting," I said.

"Too bad," said Ruth, "because I was going to ask if you wanted me to bring you a bowl."

"Wait, really? Will you really—"

With her sweetest smile, she said, "Nope. Just kidding."

She skipped off.

My mouth was watering.

"I guess Flynn's eating processed sugar these days," I called, and after a minute, "Who's acting exclusive *now*?" Nobody answered. But I could hear the beeps of the microwave and Ivan chanting "GLOOP! GLOOP! GLOOP!," so I bet they could hear me.

They could definitely hear me.

I couldn't believe they were taking *his* side.

# CHAPTER THIRTY-ONE

IT WAS TWO a.m. by the time I finished *Fudging Data: A Very Big Problem in Scientific Research*, the worst PowerPoint I'd ever made. I relied heavily on animations, twirling letters, and GIFs to cover up the fact that I'd done hardly any research. To be honest, I had to fudge some data myself. I would have considered the irony, but I was too busy collapsing into bed.

Approximately ten minutes later, Mom yelled, "Flynn! Soren! Ruth!"

I flinched.

"Flynn! Soren! Ruth!"

I rolled over.

"Rise and shine!"

I squinted my eyes open. The sun seemed extra bright.

"Blerg," I said to Ruth, forgetting that she was mad at me.

"Blerg yourself," she said, obviously forgetting too. She hopped out of bed. "It snowed! First of the season!"

That was why it was so bright. The sun was glaring off it, like the world was carpeted with fluorescent lights.

"You think we'll get a snow day?"

"No. It's not much. I can still see grass blades." October snow is usually pretty wimpy. Besides, we're so good at plowing up here in northern Minnesota that it takes a major blizzard to get a snow day.

"CHILDREN!"

"I'm up, Mom!" called Ruth.

"Me too, Aunt Lucinda!" yelled Flynn.

I closed my eyes. I'd rest for one more minute, let Ruth take her turn in the bathroom—

"SOREN EBENEZER SKAAR! YOU'LL MAKE US ALL LATE!"

I jolted awake.

"IF YOU DON'T GET YOURSELF OUT OF BED WITHIN THREE SECONDS, I'M COMING TO GET YOU OUT OF BED MYSELF!"

That made me jump. You do not want Mom to get you out of bed. Once she literally picked up the footboard and dumped me out, like she was having one of those superhuman-strength moments that normal moms get when they're saving their child from a flipped car or something.

I got on the bus like, *Phew.* Sometimes you want to go from the frying pan to the fire just for the change of scenery.

MS. HUTCHINS IS always peppy on presentation days, mostly because she gets to use the bingo machine she bought at an antiques store in Duluth. It's basically a bird-cage full of numbered Ping-Pong balls, and you pull a lever and they all hop around like water bugs and then one ball falls down the chute. Ms. Hutchins loves it. She danced over and set them popping and sang out, "Our first victim is . . ."

The Ping-Pong ball glided down the chute. We held our breaths.

"Number . . ."

She drags this out, I swear.

"Nine!"

We're numbered alphabetically. Twenty-three kids breathed a sigh of relief. Goldie stood.

"Hi!" she said. Goldie loves presentations. She was wearing a blazer, total overkill but probably doing great things for her grade. "My PowerPoint is called *Why We Shouldn't Experiment on Animals.*"

I half closed my eyes. I meant to mentally rehearse my presentation, but I must have dozed off. I was jerked awake by the applause as Goldie bowed left, right, and center.

"Thank you!" said Ms. Hutchins, glowing. "What a *wonderful* start! I hope you all will take Goldie's professional, well-mannered presentation style as a model."

She pulled the lever on the lottery machine. "Number . . ."

I crossed my fingers and prayed for salvation.

"Seventeen!"

Me.

Rats.

Reluctantly, I pulled up my PowerPoint on Ms. Hutchins's computer. "Er," I said, "hello. My topic is . . ."

I blanked.

"Um . . ." I turned around to look at my slide. "Oh, right. Fudging data."

It went downhill from there.

I've blocked out most of it, so, sorry, you don't get all the grisly details. I do recall reading authoritatively from one of my slides, "Amazingly, 37.2 percent of scientific data is entirely made up."

"Really," said Ms. Hutchins dryly.

"Yup," I said, sensing imminent disaster and clicking onward fast. The next slide was the second to last. Thank goodness. "So if you ever become a scientist," I said, "you should never make up data."

"*That's* your takeaway for the class?" said Ms. Hutchins.

"Um," I said, "I think there's one more slide."

I'd made the last slide in a delirious haze at two a.m. I had no recollection of what it was.

"In conclusion," I said, hoping it was some sort of conclusion.

I clicked.

Oh no.

Well. I didn't have a choice. I had to go for it.

"Always remember," I read with gusto, "when you fudge data . . ."

I clicked, and the rest of the motto twirled onto the screen.

". . . you say 'fudge you' to the scientific community!"

The class exploded into laughter.

"Soren!" said Ms. Hutchins. "Utterly inappropriate! What were you thinking?"

"I guess I thought it was catchy."

"You should know better."

"Sorry, Ms. Hutchins."

Oops.

# CHAPTER THIRTY-TWO

YOU ONLY GO into Mom and Dad's bedroom if (a) you're deathly ill or (b) you're in the biggest trouble of your life. Or, once, when I decided that having the flu was a great chance to stockpile vomit ice cubes, both (a) and (b).

"Sit on the couch, young man," said Dad.

"We've seen the online grade book," said Mom.

They loomed over me. I'll spare you the lecture—I'm sure you can imagine it—but basically, I was grounded until my science grade improved. "But it's not about the grade," said Dad, trying to make himself feel better about his parenting. "It's about attitude. It's about work ethic. We want you to do your best, Soren, and your best is not a presentation that gets a . . ."

He peered at the laptop.

"A seven."

"Ouch," I said involuntarily. It sounded really bad when you said it out loud.

"How is a seven even *possible*?" said Dad.

"Ms. Hutchins is a really hard grader," I said.

"Then how did Flynn get a ninety-eight?"

"Well, Flynn should have gotten a hundred, so—"

"You should have gotten a nine?"

IT'S HARD TO plan a prank when you can't leave the house. On Friday, when I should have been planning with the triplets, or playing on Jéro's dock with him and Soup and Freddy, or kicking it with Alex, my real best friend—on Friday, when Flynn went rollerblading with Goldie and Kiyana, when Ruth went to Wallaby's sleepover birthday party, when even Ivan, *Ivan the Terrible,* had a playdate— well, on Friday, I took the bus straight home, alone.

"It's just you and me, Soren!" Dad crowed. "And I've got exciting plans for us!"

"Really?"

"Father-son bonding!"

I hoped he wanted to play catch. We used to throw around all the time, but then Ivan was born. "I'll get the mitts," I said.

"It's time for the Great Chicken Migration!"

"Wait, what?"

"I've taken a deep dive into the chicken-farming blogosphere, and we're going to move them to the mudroom for the winter. It'll be good for both their egg production and their mental health."

"But the mudroom's full of our stuff!"

"That's where you and I come in."

"Must be nice to have a kid," I muttered. "Forced labor."

"You're referring to your life, or mine?" said Dad.

We started clearing out the mudroom. It was like an archaeological dig, a layer of boots and coats drifting over the summer rubble of deflated water wings, unpaired flip-flops, and the badminton net. Finally we got to the distant past: crumpled vocabulary quizzes and dried-out stink-bug corpses. "Whew." Dad surveyed the lawn, where we'd dumped all the stuff. "This is a bigger job than I'd imagined."

"Maybe we should take a break," I suggested. "Finish up tomorrow when everyone's home."

He eyed me. "What do we say? Chores build . . ."

"Character," I finished grumpily.

It took a few hours, but by the time we sorted all that crap and dumped in pine shavings for the chickens' bedding, I was actually feeling good. I'd never admit this to Dad, but there's something weirdly fun about working hard enough to sweat and get hungry, especially if you're working outside. "We'll keep their feeder out in the yard," said Dad, "so they'll get exercise and fresh air."

"Hopefully they'll do their pooping out there too," I said.

"We can always dream."

"*You* can. I have better things to dream about than pooping."

He laughed, and I felt a warm *pop!*, like I was a can of Coke that someone had just opened, like I was all fizzy and alive. "Look at this nifty heat lamp I ordered," said Dad.

"Why? Won't it be warm in the mudroom?"

"Not warm enough, and it's for light, too. We'll set it to turn on at four a.m. If the chickens don't get a fourteen-hour day, they'll go into a molt and stop laying eggs."

"Would that be so bad?"

"You know your mother," he said. "She won't buy feed if they aren't producing."

Mom grew up on a farm in North Dakota. She doesn't believe in pets.

"You lure them in while I set up the lamp," said Dad. "Then I think we'll be done."

I scattered a trail of feed from coop to mudroom. "Bawk-bawk-bawk!" I called. Pecking and chattering, Dotty, Potty, Eugenie, Hatty, and Betty II waddled along the trail. They hopped in, nipped around, and settled down. Chickens aren't easy to stress out.

But Martha was still lingering in the coop.

"Come on, Martha!" I said, keeping my distance. "Here, boy!"

"COCK-A-DOO-ARGH-ACK-ECK-EH!" Martha screamed. He didn't move.

"Martha! Martha! Don't you want to be nice and warm for the winter?" I said.

He swiveled his head, but only because Mr. Nelson's car had pulled into the driveway. Flynn hopped out. "Ooh!" he said. "Are we winterizing the chickens? I've read about this!"

I skulked back. When I'd seen him whispering with the

Goldie gang at recess, I'd gotten that being-talked-about feeling, which was confirmed when they spent all social studies shooting me evil looks. But he hadn't said a word to me. I'd also seen him taking the Scotch tape up to his room, probably to fix the mural, and probably, while he was at it, to draw another picture of me looking bad. He had several new options.

Dad was giving him a tour of the mudroom. "But we're having trouble getting Martha to recognize his new home," Dad said.

"Relocation is hard," said Flynn. "What about a treat? Something to soothe him?"

"COCK-A-DOO-ARGH-ACK-ECK-EH!"

"Excellent idea!" said Dad.

"I'll get some yogurt," said Flynn. "Martha loves it."

How would *he* know?

But sure enough, when he came back with a dish of plain yogurt, Martha hopped happily into the mudroom. "Wow," said Dad. "Flynn, what would we do without you?"

"Yogurt's good for his digestive health, too!" said Flynn.

Dad slung an arm around his shoulders and pulled him close. "*Thank* you."

I trudged after them into the house. You could really tell they were related from the back. Their hair lay the same way, and their shoulders, too. "We'll do an easy dinner," said Dad. "How do veggie burgers sound, Flynn?"

"With hummus?" he said. "And pickled red onion?"

"Wonderful!"

FLYNN AND RUTH were refusing to walk with me again. They'd speed-walk if I walked normally and they'd dawdle back if I tried to catch up. Flynn I could handle, I guess, but it really annoyed me that he'd gotten Ruth on his side. She wouldn't have even remembered she was mad at me without his constant reminders.

Luckily, the triplets stuck with me. "Let's make this spelling-bee prank happen," I said, eyeing Ruth and Flynn twenty feet ahead. We hadn't had any good ideas yet, but it wasn't till tomorrow.

"Whatever we do, let's be careful," said Olivia.

"Naturally," said Lila, rolling her eyes. She doesn't like her authority being questioned, especially by the runt. "Nobody wants to get caught."

"No, I mean . . . let's make sure we don't ruin the spelling bee."

"Why?" said Tabitha. "Because darling Flynnie's in the bee?"

"No!" said Olivia, blushing. Obviously, she meant, *Yes!*

Lila shrugged. "We'll do the prank at the end of the assembly. After the bee's over."

"But what's our prank?" I said.

Tabitha's eyes glinted. "I have the perfect idea."

She told us. Olivia shook her head. "Ruth would never let us borrow him," Olivia said. "He's like a pet to her. No. He's like a *son.*"

"Who says we'll ask her?" I said.

"He'll be fine," said Tabitha. "He'll like it."

"And Ruth will think it's funny," I said. "Eventually."

"I don't know," said Lila. "She's already mad at us for leaving her out. And then if we use—"

"It's a great idea," I said. I looked ahead at Ruth and Flynn, trudging along with their heads bent close, his messenger bag bumping her giant green backpack. "Let's do it. Once she sees how funny it is, Ruth won't mind at all."

# CHAPTER THIRTY-THREE

"SHUSH!" MS. HUTCHINS kept saying as we found our seats in the gym. "Silence, sixth graders!" It had no effect. The spelling bee hadn't started yet, though the fourteen kids who'd advanced from the classroom competitions were already seated onstage. There were about ten teachers up there too, trying to figure out how to turn on the mike.

"Anyone want to bet on the winner?" said Jéro.

"I'll bet a nickel on Flynn," said Olivia.

"Ten cents on Justice," said Soup. "He won last year."

"The winning word," cried Chloe, wildly waving a dollar bill in Jéro's face, "will be *reindeer!*"

"Soren?" said Jéro. "Want to bet on your cousin?"

I nudged my backpack, which was unzipped at the top, a bit farther under my seat. "I'm good."

Mr. Pickett must have bumped the right switch, because his words suddenly filled the gym. "This mike design is bullpoop"—he didn't say *bullpoop,* though—"that's what it is, absolute bu— Wait, is this working?" He turned bright red and thrust the mike at Principal Leary.

Leary shook his head at Mr. Pickett, who slunk back. It was nice to know that teachers could get on principals' bad sides. It made them seem almost human. "Welcome to the spelling bee," said Principal Leary. He explained the rules while I peered over Jéro's shoulder to see whether anyone had won big by predicting Leary's solar-system tie. Pluto was featured right down by the tip. I guess it was an old one.

Macintosh Avery had drawn the first seat. "Your word, Macintosh," said Principal Leary, "is *nonchalant.*" Macintosh is a third grader who comes up to about my knee, but he nonchalantly whipped it off.

Next up was Gordon Spinner, a second grader. "*Scenic,*" said Principal Leary. Gordon missed the first *c* and burst into tears, but he got a solid round of applause for being the first loser.

Nevaeh Diggs got *chandelier.*

Rob Diedrich Jr. got *patrician.*

John Lovinsky missed *imbecile,* which is kind of funny if you think about it.

Flynn, wearing a tuxedo T-shirt and pants that stopped in the middle of his calf, was next. He got *artisanal.* I zoned out. Spelling's boring even when it's you who's doing it. The spellers finally burned down to three: tiny Macintosh, reigning champ Justice, and Flynn.

I'd been zoning out on Tabitha's ponytail, which I didn't know until she turned around and I realized I'd gone kind of cross-eyed. "Is something wrong?" she said.

"No, I'm fine."

She raised her eyebrows. *But are you* ready? she mouthed.

I was. Three spellers left. It'd be soon now. The plan was to set off the prank the second the winning word was spelled, before anyone had time to leave.

Justice went down on *dromedary*. His eyes welled up. I quickly looked away.

Macintosh got *pachyderm,* and rattled it off like it was *cat.*

Flynn got *trattoria.* His voice was shaking, but he nailed it. Then Macintosh screwed up *fracas* pretty hard. There was a *q* involved. Flynn had to spell it right to win. He stepped up to the microphone.

"*Fracas,*" he said. "*F—*"

I lifted my backpack to my lap. Lila and Olivia were on either side of me, and they leaned forward to give me cover.

"*R—*"

I opened the backpack. Jim Bob, curled cozily inside, blinked as he woke up from his morning nap. He looked groggy. My greatest fear was that he'd go right back to sleep. The prank would fail, and fail hard.

"*A—*"

I set the backpack on the floor and nudged at the bottom with my foot. I figured it'd take him a minute to discover his escape hatch and make a move, but he nosed out right away. He took off down the row of seats. "Grab him!" I hissed at Lila, and she swiped at him, but it was too late. There was a flutter of squeals and laughter as he poked his way down the row.

"C—"

"Stop him!" I whispered, waving frantically, but nobody heard me. Jim Bob reached the center aisle. Like a midfielder who breaks out of a clump of defenders and hits his stride in the open grass, he took off across the shiny wooden floor.

"A—" said Flynn, and then he saw Jim Bob. "CATCH IT!" he shrieked into the mike.

Now the whole gym looked to where he was pointing. Some kids laughed. Some kids screamed. Amid the uproar, Jim Bob made a beeline for the stage.

Flynn was totally safe up there. No piglet can jump four feet, not even at a dead sprint. But he freaked out. He shrieked again and leapt off the stage, knocking over the mike as he went. It hit the stage floor with an earsplitting burst of feedback. Jim Bob was startled. He turned tail and charged the fifth grade. A few of them were so scared they scrabbled up the gym walls to get away, like he was a rat. Principal Leary rummaged for the mike on the floor. "Catch it!" he cried into the mike. "Teachers! Students! Someone! Someone catch it!"

Jim Bob darted back and forth, oinking. He'd panicked along with everyone else. Chairs were flying as kids dove for safety.

"CALM DOWN, EVERYONE!" yelled Principal Leary into the mike. At the noise, all four of Jim Bob's short legs left the floor. When he landed, he took off even faster in the other direction.

"CATCH THAT PIGLET!" Principal Leary shouted at the top of his lungs. "FACULTY, I AM TALKING TO YOU!"

But the teachers were standing against the walls of the gym with faces that were like, *Not* my *problem.* Principal Leary tossed the mike aside and left the stage with a flying leap that was actually pretty impressive for a dad-aged guy. He took off after Jim Bob, his face purple with rage, the solar-system necktie flapping behind.

Kids sprang out of his way. Jim Bob maintained the narrow distance between them for a while, but as they approached the fourth-grade section, Leary was gaining. He dove. He missed.

"HEY!" yelled a high, furious voice. "THAT'S MY PIGLET!"

Kicking and flailing, Ruth emerged from the mass of fourth graders. She took off in a trot toward Jim Bob. "Here, Jimmy!" she called. "Here, Jimmy-Jimmy Bobkins! Here!"

Jim Bob didn't hear her. He started sprinting back toward the front, eyeing Flynn.

Leary, grasping a side stitch, stopped altogether, but Ruth picked up the pace. So did Jim Bob. I bet he heard her footsteps and thought it was still Leary. He was heading straight for Flynn. Flynn tried to shove Macintosh in front of him, but since Macintosh was about as big as Flynn's left leg, he didn't offer much protection.

Ruth sprinted, but Jim Bob sprinted faster. Ten feet away from Flynn, Jim Bob hit another gear, bounding down the aisle. Flynn's face was pure terror. Jim Bob leapt into

Flynn's arms. For a moment, Flynn clutched him, and then Ruth caught up and snatched him away.

"My darling!" I heard her cry in horror, before the whole gym was overtaken with excited shouts and banging applause.

Ruth ripped her gaze from Jim Bob and turned toward the sixth-grade section. She stared at me. Even from fifty feet away, the stare burned.

"Oh dear," Olivia whispered. "She's not very happy, is she?"

I slowly shook my head.

# CHAPTER THIRTY-FOUR

WE GOT DISMISSED to the playground for emergency recess. I tried to catch up with Ruth, but she (and Jim Bob) got whisked away to Leary's office. Then I went over to the triplets by the fence, but Tabitha said, "Go play soccer. It looks way too suspicious to have you here right now."

I got drafted onto Kiyana's team. Jeremiah passed to Goldie, who tapped it to Billiam, who took it on a quick run down the wing. I charged, but Billiam blew past me and shot on goal. Kiyana did this feetfirst dive thing and just managed to knock it out of bounds.

Jeremiah lined up for the corner. A scrum formed around the goal, all eight of us jockeying for position, and I marked Jack. Jeremiah's kick soared. The scrum exploded like a firecracker. Jack leapt left and scorched a perfect header into the goal.

Ouch. My fault. I wasn't playing my best. I was all twitchy and high-energy, and that's not right for soccer.

You have to concentrate. It was like my mind was still in the gym, like it had become a spooked piglet itself, bouncing from one wall to the next, in one direction and another.

My team jogged back up to midfield. We were only down one, and then we were tied when Kiyana scored on a beautiful floater from twenty yards out.

Goldie was about to take their kickoff when Flynn appeared. "You want to play?" she said.

He didn't say anything, but he nodded. "We get him," said Billiam. "We're down a man."

"A person," said Kiyana.

"Whatever," said Billiam. "As long as we get Flynn."

There wasn't really any arguing, not when it was five versus four, so Flynn jogged over to their right wing. Of course Goldie passed it to him. "Mark your man!" yelled Kiyana to our team.

"Person!" yelled Billiam.

She ignored him. "Spread out!" Flynn passed so much that we'd learned how to face him: let him do what he wanted and cover the rest of his team. Let them make the mistakes, basically.

I was left to mark Flynn. I ran up to him, expecting him to pass as soon as I got there, but instead he took off down the wing. And I mean took off. I'm pretty fast, and before that day I'd thought I could beat him in a race, but I'd never seen him go all out. He was flying.

A bunch of his teammates were open, open enough to

pass to, anyway, but he didn't even consider it. He hosed me—I was five feet behind, then ten—and swept the ball into the top left corner of the net.

"GOOOOAALLLLLLL!" Billiam screamed. He ran over to chest-bump Flynn, but Flynn wasn't having it. Flynn didn't even smile. He jogged back up to the line, barely winded, and he said, "Take the kickoff."

That was how it went for the rest of the emergency recess. If we'd ever wondered what Flynn was really capable of, now we knew. He scored on midfield shots, on dribbles, on headers. He scored with his right foot and his left. He didn't break a sweat and he didn't crack a smile. It was 8–1, maybe 9–1, when Mrs. Andersen knuckle-whistled us in. "VICTORY!" yelled Billiam, raising his arms in ninety-degree angles and doing this robot dance thing, but Flynn just slumped down, like he was a puppet and the game was his string, the only thing holding him up. He started back toward the school immediately.

"What's with him?" said Jéro.

I shrugged.

"He could go pro," said Soup. "He could get free cleats."

"Yeah, he's really good," I said. I wished I could be a good sport, the kind of loser Dad always says we should be, but I felt like the bad kind of loser, the kind who shouts about unfairness and kicks the dirt and never wants to play again. I said, "Too bad he's scared of piglets."

Jéro and Soup and Freddy laughed. I thought it'd make me feel better, but it didn't really work.

I'D TRIED TO keep a low profile after school, but I had to come down when I was called for dinner. I was nervous. Ruth knew it was me, and Flynn probably did too. What if they'd told Mom and Dad? Or worse, Leary?

"Set the table, Soren," Mom told me.

"For six?"

"I called your sister in, but Flynn has another stomachache. Five."

Ruth came to the kitchen door holding Jim Bob.

"You know the rule," said Mom. "No animals inside."

Usually when Mom says that, Ruth and I mouth *except Ivan* at each other. But she didn't look at me. "Fine," she told Mom. "I'll eat slops. I'm not leaving him alone until he feels better."

"Honey, he's just a piglet—"

"Lucinda," said Dad, "let her be." He gave Ruth a PB&J for her and some unsalted peanuts for Jim Bob, and the two of them went back outside.

"Four," Mom told me.

The door between the kitchen and the mudroom is glass, so if you had the right seat, you could watch the chickens from the table. They were boring—mostly they pecked at nothing and readjusted their feathers—but that evening, dinner was even more boring. Ivan's always quiet on spaghetti nights because he's busy painting his entire body orange. Mom talked about a work thing and Dad gave her advice that she viciously tore to shreds, which is a thing they both enjoy. I was just grateful they didn't ask me any tough questions about how, exactly, Jim Bob had found himself at the spelling bee.

Like I said: they were clueless.

I loaded the dishwasher without being asked. (Obvious sign of a guilty conscience, but I couldn't help it.) Afterward, I went to shoot on the woodpile. It was dark, but there's a light on the garage that helps a bit.

*Pow!*

*Pow!*

*Pow!*

Ruth heaved herself up the hill from the pigpen. "Hi," I said.

"Hi."

I shuffled the ball between my feet, mostly to have something else to look at. "Is he, um, okay?" I said.

"He's not back to normal. But he lost that wild look in his eyes after he got the peanuts."

"Oh, good."

"Here," said Ruth. "Pass."

I passed. She shot. "So," she said as it rebounded. "That was you, right?"

I cringed.

"Well?"

I wished I could lie. But I couldn't, and to be totally honest, it wasn't because lying's wrong; it was because I didn't think Ruth would buy it. "Me and the triplets."

"Wow," she said. Her voice was quivering. "Jim Bob is my favorite person in the world, and you *kidnapped* him? You kept him in your *backpack*?"

"I didn't zip it all the way!"

"He could have died!"

"I put a banana in there! Which he ate! He couldn't have been too unhappy!"

She kicked the ball at me, hard. I barely managed to snag it before it went into the street. "Are you mad at the triplets too?" I asked.

She considered. "Not as much. You're the one who stole him."

"That's unfair."

"Besides," she said, "that was really mean of you, what you did to Flynn."

I passed back. "It's his fault he's scared of a harmless piglet."

"No. With the bee. He was about to win. Now they have to replay the last word tomorrow."

"He'll probably win anyway."

"Maybe," said Ruth.

"Pass."

She set a firm foot atop the ball. "He knows it was you," she said. "And I bet he thinks you did it on purpose."

"Well, we didn't bring Jim Bob to the spelling bee by *accident*—"

"No. I mean. That you targeted him."

"Of course we didn't!"

"Well, he was about to win and you stopped the bee. And you knew he was scared of Jim Bob."

Obviously we hadn't targeted Flynn. How were we supposed to know he'd be the last speller? The real problem, anyway, was that Jim Bob had escaped one letter too soon. "What happened with you and Principal Leary?" I asked Ruth.

"He said that as soon as he found out who brought the piglet, they'd get expelled."

"Expelled?"

"He was really mad. He wrenched his knee on one of those diving leaps."

"Did you—did you tell him you thought it was me?"

She gave me a withering look. "Of course not."

"Oh. Good. Phew. Thanks."

"I told him it definitely wasn't you. I told him I saw inside your backpack on the bus and it was full of books."

"Ruth . . ." I was a bit overcome.

"And I told Mom and Dad someone must have snuck over here and stolen Jim Bob. I said maybe Billiam Flick. You know Mom's thing with him."

Billiam wrote his name in the wet concrete when we got our driveway repoured. Mom's held a grudge ever since. The poor kid was six.

"Well. Thanks, Ruth."

"You don't deserve a sister like me."

I really didn't. "I'll give you my dessert tonight."

"Just because I'm not getting you into trouble," she said,

"doesn't mean I'm not still extremely mad. And so is Flynn."
Abruptly, she turned and headed inside.

"Wait—Ruth—"

She didn't stop. She hadn't even kicked me the ball. It began to roll down the slight slope of the driveway. I started to jog after it, but then I stopped too. I didn't feel like kicking anymore.

# CHAPTER THIRTY-FIVE

"GOOD MORNING," Principal Leary said on the screen.

"A new tie!" whispered Soup.

Jéro scribbled hurriedly. New ties always gave him a lot of calculations. This one featured a globe surrounded by the words *World's Coolest Elementary School Administrator*.

How much competition was there, anyway?

"We have several announcements," said Principal Leary. "The Lego League will meet after school in Mr. Rashid's classroom."

Beside us, Chloe had gone all pale and sweaty.

"Are you okay?" said Tabitha.

Chloe braced both hands on her desk to keep herself upright. She looked like she might faint. Or barf. I scooched my own desk a few inches away.

Principal Leary continued. "The Future Engineers of America will meet with Ms. Vicari after school at the circuit board."

"Chloe?" said Tabitha. "Did you lose another bet?"

"I thought he'd go with stripes," said Chloe weakly. "And I bet it all."

"Class!" said Ms. Hutchins. "Stop talking!"

"I bet it *all*," Chloe said again.

"Attention up here, please!"

"My iPod—my guinea pig—"

"Eyes open, mouths closed!"

"The shirt off my back—"

"Who won the shirt?" said Soup.

"*Shush!*" barked Ms. Hutchins.

"One final announcement," Leary said. His grim tone plus Ms. Hutchins's orange-zone anger made everyone shut up, though Chloe was still rocking from side to side. "Yesterday, our school community was disrupted. We lost several minutes of valuable instructional time and had to reschedule the final word of the spelling bee. Furthermore, on a personal note, your fearless leader injured his knee." He turned the webcam to a brace strapped over his pants. "If you were the one behind this inappropriate and disrespectful act," he said, righting the camera, "don't think you'll get away with it. And the rest of you, as upstanding members of the Camelot Elementary community—if you saw something, say something. It is your duty."

I went rigid. Most likely, someone *had* seen something.

And that wasn't even mentioning Flynn.

"If you have information," said Leary, "please speak with a trusted adult. The safety and peace of our school depend on each one of you."

He stared out at us for a length of time somewhere between "awkwardly long" and "Is the webcam frozen?"

"Thank you," he said at last. "It's a lovely day for learning."

DAD CAME BACK from his Saturday-morning run with his usual runner's high plus a box of doughnuts from Mamie's Donuttery. Mamie's doughnuts are basically clouds dipped in frosting. I had a cinnamon cruller while Ruth had a cream-filled. Ivan got pink sprinkles, and Flynn, who was reading a book in his lap, had a toffee crisp.

Our parents paged through the *Camelot Roundtable*. "Mateo Luna is running for town council again, I see," said Dad.

"And Gerald Flick's heirloom butternut squash won second place at the county fair," said Mom. "We should pop over for a look."

"Can we have the comics?" I asked.

A few minutes later, Mom said, "Well, well. Jim Bob made the paper."

We craned to see the headline: SOME PIG! HOG "SPELLS" DISRUPTION AT SCHOOL BEE.

"Let me see that," I said, my heart pounding. Had Leary sicced a reporter on the case?

"Looks like total chaos," said Dad.

Mom, skimming the article, said, "Flynn! You didn't breathe a word! How modest you are!"

# Some Pig! Hog "Spells" Disruption at School Bee

BY HENRY DUCK, STAFF REPORTER

The annual spelling bee at Camelot Elementary School was given a "streak" of excitement when a piglet interrupted the proceedings.

Kiyana Nelson, 11, said, "Usually the spelling bee is really boring, but this year I loved it!"

As Flynn Skaar, 12, was at the microphone, spelling what could have been his winning word, the piglet was let loose. He or she (bystanders were unsure) streaked through the assembly with students and faculty alike in hot pursuit.

Louis Leary, 49, the school's principal, was not pleased. "We at Camelot Elementary take spelling very seriously," he said. "Whoever did this showed a lot of disrespect to the students in the competition, not to mention those of us who risked life and limb to chase the beast."

The piglet was eventually apprehended, but the perpetrator remains at large. The next day, a replay of the last word was given to the two finalists. When Skaar stumbled over *viscera,* Macintosh Avery, 9, took the crown. Beaming, he said, "I owe it all to my parents, my teachers, and my personal hero, Noah Webster."

This reporter would guess that none of the students will forget how to spell *pig* anytime soon!

"Well, I should hope not," said Ruth.

"I see no culprit is mentioned," said Mom. "Should I call Principal Leary? Tell him that it may well have been Billiam Flick?"

I gave a nervous twitch.

"*I* think we're focusing on the wrong thing here!" said Dad. He pulled Flynn into a side-armed hug. Flynn squirmed away, probably because Dad was still sweaty. "We are in the presence of greatness! Flynn Skaar, second place in the spelling bee!"

"Thanks, Uncle Jon."

"Spelling must not be genetic," Dad mused. "Why, I could barely spell my own name when I was your age. Always put an *h* in there. What an accomplishment, Flynn! Are you thrilled?"

"I should have won," he said. "All I had left on *fracas* was the *s*, but I was rattled during the replay. Macintosh kept jangling his lucky charm bracelet, the one with the tooth of Noah Webster—"

"Excuse me?" said Mom.

"He bought it on eBay. Certified authentic." Flynn shook his head. "It threw me off. I confused *viscera* with *vicissitude*."

"Still amazing," said Dad. "We should celebrate! We'll bake a Silver Medal Speller cake!"

Ivan perked up at the word *cake*. "IVAN LICK BOWL!"

"We don't eat raw eggs, remember, not after Daddy read the latest from the CDC—"

"IVAN LIKE RAW EGGS!"

"Raw eggs make us sick, Ivy, remember? Sick at both ends?"

"IVAN LIKE SICK!"

"I'm in no mood to celebrate," said Flynn. Without warning, he stood and left. His footsteps took the two flights to the attic.

"Oh dear," said Dad.

"He's taken it hard," said Mom.

"Soren and Ruth," said Dad, "I hope you know that your mother and I are proud of you whether you get first place, or second place, or dead last place."

"Honey," said Mom, "are you sure that's the message you want to send?"

# CHAPTER THIRTY-SIX

THREE MINUTES AFTER I sat down at the computer, Ruth claimed she needed to do research for her social studies project. "This is what happened the *last* time I needed to use the computer!" I said.

"And it'll happen the next time too," she said sweetly. "And the next, and the next, and the—"

I stomped out. Not before pushing the power button, though. And a few hours later, while Dad was distracted with building Duplo towers for Ivan to demolish, I grabbed his laptop and took it up to our closet. I wasn't supposed to, but I didn't know what else to do. I had to talk to someone. Someone who got me.

"Alex?" Her face jumped onto the screen. "I have some things to tell you."

"I thought you might."

"Okay. So." I took a deep breath. "Let's start with the last time we video-chatted. . . ."

I told her everything. I told her we'd hung up on her on

purpose. I told her we'd pranked without her, and I told her all about the prank.

"Now Ruth's mad and Flynn's mad and you're probably mad too," I said, "and it's all my fault."

"What about the triplets?" she said. "Don't they deserve some blame?"

"They asked if Ruth would care about us using Jim Bob, and I said no. They didn't know Flynn's scared of him. And you—you're *my* best friend. I'm the one who's supposed to be watching out for you."

I squirmed, which was a mistake since I was sitting on a pile of toys. I got stabbed in the butt by a dump truck. "And here's the worst part," I said. "I *wanted* to make everyone mad. It wasn't an accident."

That's what I'd realized lying in bed last night. I'd looked at the dark contours of the furniture and listened to the slow sleeping breaths of my sister and brother and I'd finally stopped fooling myself. "I wanted to blow everything up," I said.

"But why?" said Alex. "That's not why we prank."

"I don't know. I guess it was easier to make things worse than to make them better."

"I'm not that mad at you."

"Even though we hung up on you?"

"Well, that was annoying. Tell Tabitha she's way too obvious. She needs to shake the screen more."

"And distort the audio. Mess with the volume button, maybe?"

We both paused, lost in thought, and I could tell that'd be added to our list of Things to Practice.

"But anyway," said Alex, "I was talking to Sophia about the prank thing, and she said that if *she* moved and told me I could only do paper dolls when she visited, I'd think that was stupid."

"Oh."

I couldn't decide whether to be grateful to Ol' Butt-Braid for making my case for me, or annoyed that she'd managed to convince Alex that paper dolls were as cool as pranks.

"Plus, now you owe me," said Alex.

"Yeah."

"I got my mom to promise me we'll visit in December. She picked a random Thursday, since apparently that's the day Ubercut gets the fewest clients. December thirteenth. I get to skip school and come to school with you. We've got a chance to do something amazing."

"Wait. One more thing, Alex . . ."

I hadn't gotten to my last point, the last thing I'd realized when I couldn't sleep. Which was this:

I'd retired from pranking.

Not fake retired, melodramatically mentally retired, like I'd kept saying at the beginning of the school year. No. This time, I was done.

I couldn't trust myself. I'd hurt too many people.

"Whoopee cushions?" said Alex. "Stink bombs? Water balloons?"

"None of them," I said. "I can't. Because— OW!"

The closet door had been ripped open, and I'd jumped, and I'd landed right on the dump truck.

"Soren, Soren, Soren," said Dad, sighing. "Where do we even start with you these days?"

"Oh. Hi."

"Computer, please."

I handed it over.

"Huh?" said Alex's tinny voice. "Because what, Soren? Why can't you?"

Dad righted the laptop. "Hello, Alex."

"Oh! Hi, Mr. Skaar."

"We sure miss you here in Camelot. But *this* guy"—he clumsily angled the laptop toward me—"has not been authorized to use technology in his bedroom closet. As he well knows. I'm not sure when you'll talk to him next, so you'd better say goodbye."

"Bye," I whispered.

Alex stared at me. "Because *why*?"

The laptop closed.

ON MONDAY, Ms. Hutchins said, "Now that you've wrapped up your Ethics in Science presentations—some of you more successfully than others—it's time to return to our study of experimental design."

"More bean plants?" said Goldie.

"More Coke?" said Freddy.

"If you want!" Ms. Hutchins gave a *wait till you see what's in store for you* smile. It's always a bad sign when you get one of those from a teacher. "Class, you'll really get to think like a scientist. Because it's time for . . ."

She paused expectantly, but nobody drum-rolled.

"Science fair!"

She explained each step. We'd have to ask a question, and do background research, and formulate a hypothesis, and design an experiment, and execute the experiment, and analyze the data, and make a trifold presentation board, and present to outside judges during a special evening event on December 13—

December 13!

Science fair was the day of Alex's visit. This was the best prank opportunity I'd ever have. Alex, the triplets, and me—and a hundred kids and parents packed into the gym, a gym cluttered with scientific apparatus and experimental animals and trifold boards—

"This is a huge project," said Kiyana.

But I couldn't prank. I'd retired for a reason.

"It is huge," agreed Ms. Hutchins.

Flynn loved science. Science fair would probably be the highlight of his year. If we pranked it, he'd never forgive me.

Nope. No prank. I'd gone too far before, and I couldn't go back now.

Retirement, I'd started to realize, meant saying *nope, no prank* for the rest of my life.

"You'll write an individual research report," said Ms. Hutchins, "but you'll share the rest of the work with a partner."

"Soren!" hissed Jéro. "You want to—"

"An assigned partner," she said.

"Maybe she'll put us together," I whispered.

"No way," he said.

He was right. Sometimes teachers put girls who are friends together, because they have this idea that they're nice and docile. Boys, though, never get put with their friends. Especially boys who maybe don't behave perfectly every second of every day. But I bet we'd behave better if we did work together. Ever think of *that*, teachers?

"Jéro and Lila," Ms. Hutchins read from her list.

They both groaned.

"Goldie and Kiyana."

They squealed in delight.

"Marsupial and Evelyn. Jeremiah and Emily. Olivia and Tori."

I looked around the class. There weren't a lot of people left. Billiam was unpartnered, which was bad, but so was Tabitha, and *her* I wouldn't mind—

"Soren," said Ms. Hutchins, "and Flynn."

I froze. I'd never expected this. Nobody else was with their original lab partner. And nobody else was with their cousin.

Flynn had been avoiding me hard lately. At school he was always with a group, always moving, and at home he was always in his room, adding scenes to the *Soren Stinks* mural, I guess.

"Your initial idea is due next Monday," Ms. Hutchins said. "Go forth and think like scientists together!"

# CHAPTER THIRTY-SEVEN

I DIDN'T SEE how I was going to think with Flynn if he wouldn't even talk with me. Sometimes Ruth and I will try the silent treatment on each other, but it never works. What happens is we keep thinking of good insults and breaking the silence to say them, and at some point both of us accidentally forget we're mad. The funny thing is, that's how Mom and Dad fight too.

So to me the silent treatment had been kind of a mythical beast, the unicorn of getting mad. I'd read about it, but I was pretty sure it didn't exist in real life.

It does.

Flynn pulled it off for eight solid days. Eight! He refused to make eye contact and shunned me at school and ignored me at the dinner table. I couldn't even tell him I'd retired from pranking, because he refused to acknowledge me. Every time I thought I'd pinned him down, he'd get this distant, confused look and cup his hand around his ear and say, "What's that noise? It must be the wind."

Ruth was still mad at me too, but her madness was like our Internet connection. It went in and out.

"Do you have after-school plans?" Dad asked me on Friday morning.

"Nope." Though hopefully the question meant I wasn't grounded anymore. I'd been doing all my science homework plus participating with Flynn-like frequency, and although my grade wasn't going to get a certificate of merit, at least it was in the double digits.

"Then why don't you come with me to Ivan's new class at the rec center?"

I shrugged. "Okay."

"We can talk."

Uh-oh. The word *talk* was ominous these days. "Okay."

Flynn went home with Kiyana. Ruth got off at our bus stop, but when the triplets turned down their driveway, she followed.

"Wait," I said. "You're going *there*?"

"I'm teaching them how to play Catan," said Ruth.

"Ethan loves it," said Tabitha. "So the plan is, we're going to become secret experts and then pound him next time he comes home."

"He'll be so mad," Olivia said dreamily.

"That sounds fun," I said, kind of hoping I'd get invited. I paused. Nobody said anything. "Too bad Dad wants me to hang out with him," I said to save face.

"Too bad," said Olivia. "Otherwise you could have come too."

Darn. I should have paused longer.

"Have a good afternoon!" called Lila.

Ruth didn't even smirk at me. Maybe she felt a little bad for stealing my friends and leaving me out. Or maybe she was so happy she forgot all about me. Either way, I deserved it, but that didn't make it easier.

IVAN CHARGED ME when I got home. Well, I assumed it was Ivan, since it was three feet tall, had limbs, and was attacking me, but I couldn't be positive since a helmet with a mesh mask covered the whole head-face-neck region. "IVAN FIGHT!" the figure cried, smacking my thigh with a wooden spoon.

It was definitely Ivan.

Dad dove in and grabbed the spoon. "Say *en garde* before you strike!" he told Ivan. "Remember how we practiced?"

"EN GARDE!" Ivan chopped at my leg with his hand.

"Sorry, Soren," said Dad, scooping him up. "His new class is Fencing for Toddlers. We thought it might provide an outlet for his natural aggression."

"IVAN KNIGHT IN SHINING ARMOR!"

"You've had a lot of questionable ideas," I told Dad, "but this is the worst."

We sat with the other parents in the bleachers at the rec center. The instructor made the toddlers all line up and lunge across the gym (several fell over in the attempt), and then he gave them cardboard wrapping-paper tubes. "I'm glad they aren't getting real swords on the first day," Dad said.

"They're getting real swords?" I yelped. "When?"

"Once they've mastered the basics."

One small girl lay flat on the floor while two others battered her. Ivan, with a determined expression, was hitting himself in the head. "So, never," I said.

"Let's hope not," said Dad. He squeezed the back of my neck. "You know, you were exactly the same at that age."

"I was not."

"Luckily, you've grown up. You're completely different now."

Was he being sarcastic? He stared with a straight face at the instructor, who was wringing his hands and yelling, "Fencers! Fencers! You should be practicing your first-position stance!"

"Really?" I said.

"You should *not* be whacking each other!" said the instructor. "Or yourselves!"

"Sure," said Dad. "You don't cause any trouble at all."

"Sarcasm is the lowest form of humor," I said, which he says to us all the time.

"True. I guess I should just come out and say it. It was you with Jim Bob, right?"

I jumped. That was *not* what I'd expected. I'd thought the talk today was going to be about No Technology in the Bedroom Closet.

"Well?" said Dad. "Let's skip the part where you play innocent, okay?"

"Ruth told you, didn't she?"

Dad snorted. "Soren. Someone brings the Skaar piglet to school, releases it in the middle of an assembly, and causes total chaos. I don't need Ruth to tell me who did it."

He had a point. "When you put it that way . . ."

"I know you know this," said Dad, "but taking Ruth's piglet, that wasn't the nicest move."

"Yeah."

"You're going to need to make it up to her."

"I know. And Flynn. He would have won."

"Second place is wonderful."

"Not to Flynn."

The instructor had succeeded in getting all the kids to sit on the floor, nice and far away from each other. He wiped his brow. "Let's try that again," he called, "*without* the swords."

"Poor guy," Dad and I said at the same time. We laughed. I glanced over. Dad didn't seem that mad. In fact, he didn't seem mad at all.

"Are you going to tell Mom?" I asked.

"Eventually," he said. "In 2030, maybe. Or 2040. Not that I'm keeping secrets from my wife, but does she need to know *now*?"

"Definitely not."

"This guy I knew," said Dad, "his junior year of high school, as soon as he got his driver's license, he borrowed his brother's pickup truck. He drove it out to his best friend's family's farm, and they loaded it up with two pigs. On them, they painted '#1' and '#3.'"

"Then what?"

"They brought them to school. Released them. The admins rounded them up pretty fast, but everyone had to stay outside for three more hours while they looked for #2."

I laughed. "That's amazing."

"I guess what I'm saying," said Dad, "is that I should be blaming myself."

"Wait."

"Yep. That guy? That was me."

I stood up in the bleachers, I was so discombobulated. "YOU?"

"And my best friend?" continued Dad. "That was your mother."

"MOM?"

"It was her idea." He sighed. "We should have known better than to combine this sort of genetic material."

"But you guys are *anti*-prank!"

And then I thought about it.

How they drove me around to buy alarm clocks and never asked why.

How they looked to the side whenever I came home covered with Jell-O, and never interrogated me about how I'd gotten a whole can of Silly String in my hair.

How they gave me a twelve-pack of whoopee cushions for my sixth birthday.

How, when I rubber-banded the handle of the sink sprayer so it'd shoot water when you turned on the faucet, and Mom got it right in the face, *after* she'd put on her work makeup, she'd laughed.

"Whoa," I said.

My world was shaking.

"Even so," said Dad, "here's something I didn't learn till I was, oh, twenty-nine. There's a time and a place for pranking, and it's not always, and it's not everywhere."

"I know. I'm retiring."

"No! Soren! A prankster of your talent!"

"I've done too much damage."

Dad reached around my back and pulled me in. "You and Ruth and Flynn are going to be okay."

"Do you really think so?"

"I really think so." He squeezed me in to him, and I fit my shoulder in the warm nook under his arm. After bath but before bed, when we were little, Ruth and I got to settle into those nooks so Dad could read Narnia to us. He does voices but isn't annoying about it. I remembered the bristle of his cheek at the end of the day, and the waffley feel of the blanket. When I was little, I thought nothing would change. I thought I was a kid and that was the way it was. But everything that's now eventually turns into something long ago.

"I believe in you," said Dad. "You're learning. You're growing up. That's a good thing, Soren."

"What happened when you were twenty-nine?"

"My two-year-old filled my favorite shoes with ketchup," he said grimly.

"Oh," I said. "That would have been me. Oops. Sorry."

We watched the toddlers sprint around the gym, banging each other with wrapping-paper tubes. "Ivan's having the time of his life," said Dad.

"It does look fun," I said.

# CHAPTER THIRTY-EIGHT

MOM NOTICED FLYNN'S silent treatment. "Give him time," she told me. "Keep trying, but give him time."

The problem was, we didn't have time. Our science-fair idea was due on Monday. Finally, on Sunday afternoon, I cracked and told her about our assignment. "Oh," she said. "Hmm. Well, what if we try neutral ground? Do you think you could work together at Mugshot?" That's the coffee shop in town. "I could drop you off now."

"I can't even ask him if he wants to," I said, near tears, "because he'll say I'm the *wind*!"

The silent treatment, man. It gets to you.

"I'll talk to him," said Mom. I don't know what she said, but Flynn followed her down to the kitchen a few minutes later. I gave him shotgun even though he didn't call it.

Mugshot was packed, as always. We went up to the counter. "One coffee, medium roast," said Flynn to Jo Ann, who's worked there since it was the Kwikky Stoppe & Diner, since before some California tech guy got a cabin up here for the ice fishing and decided what Camelot really needed was an espresso bar. He wasn't wrong.

"Sure, hon," said Jo Ann. "Cream and sugar?"

"No thanks. I take it black."

I stepped up to order. "Cream and sugar, please," I said.

"Coffee?"

"No thanks. I take it white."

"Every man needs a signature drink," said Jo Ann, twinkling as she handed me the cup.

We sat at the creaky table by the window. Flynn got out his notebook. He still hadn't spoken to me. I was starting to wonder whether we'd plan the whole experiment like charades.

"So," I said, twiddling the sleeve on my cup, "um . . ."

He opened his notebook and labeled the page *Science Fair* without looking up. Maybe this was a good time to tell him I'd retired from pranking. He'd be all happy, we'd be pals again, the project might even be fun—

"Just out of curiosity," he said, "are you planning to pull your weight, or should I expect to do the whole project myself?"

"I'm going to help!" I was highly insulted. "You've never worked with me. I'm good at science."

"Riiight," he said. I bet he'd snuck a look at my presentation grade. That rat. "You have any ideas, then?"

He said it like he wasn't expecting anything. "Actually," I said, "I was talking to Jéro's big brother. He said the experiments with people, like psychology, he said they don't do well. It's too hard to figure out what's going on."

"As in, it's too hard to isolate the variables," he said, all condescending.

"Sure."

"I'd concur."

Fine. If he was going to act that way, I'd concur too. Whatever *that* meant. "I was thinking we could do an experiment with bugs," I said. I liked bugs. I also liked that Flynn didn't like them. "And let's split up the work as much as possible. Let's make it like two individual projects, and we'll pretend we did it together when Ms. Hutchins asks."

"Perfect." He drew a line down the middle of the notebook page. "That's just what I want."

It was weird how Mugshot, which was so warm the windows steamed up, could feel so cold. I wanted to leave. Being around Flynn made me feel guilty and sad and mad all at once, and I guess being around me didn't make him feel too great either, because he didn't even bother raising a stink about the bug thing. We went with the first idea we had. We'd get two specimens—pill bugs, maybe—and raise them differently, and see if one did better. Done.

"How are we going to raise them differently?" I said.

"Different diets, maybe. Something like that. We can get full points for the initial idea even if we don't have all the details hammered out." Flynn was the kind of guy who knew where his points came from, so I wasn't about to argue. "Where are we going to get the experimental subjects?" he said.

"You mean the bugs?"

Jo Ann was sweeping around our chairs. "You need bugs? We've got bugs."

"Really?" I said. "What kind?"

"Silverfish, millipedes, stinkbugs. All in the kitchen, free for the taking. And Don caught a couple cockroaches this morning. They're still under a glass. He hasn't gotten around to squishing them."

"Can we have them?" I asked.

"I don't see why not, hon."

"You really want to experiment on *cockroaches*?" Flynn whispered urgently.

"Cockroaches are amazing creatures," I told him. "They're the only animals on earth who'd survive a nuclear holocaust."

"But they're . . . *cockroaches*."

"You do the data and graphs and writing. You do the board. And I'll take care of the experimental subjects."

"Actually," Flynn said, "that could work."

THE WHOLE RIDE home, I watched the cockroaches crawl around their jar, up and down and over each other. I already felt fond of them. They *were* amazing creatures. They were trapped in a jar with only a few holes for fresh air, but they didn't get depressed or bored. They kept on exploring. "Since they're experimental subjects, we should probably go with simple names," I told Flynn and Mom.

"What about A and B?" said Flynn.

"I'm thinking Cah and Croach."

"Don't expect me to remember their names."

"Cah's the one with the longer antennae."

"I don't believe in naming cockroaches."

"If you were a cockroach, I bet you'd want a name."

"What a great idea to make you two partners," said Mom. "I'm going to email that Ms. Hutchins and tell her so."

"Don't," Flynn and I said at the same time.

Mom just laughed.

# CHAPTER THIRTY-NINE

THE NEXT FRIDAY, Mr. Pickett and Ms. Hutchins combined their class time so the whole sixth grade could watch *Hoot*. I love team-teaching days. Ms. Hutchins gives all these super-specific instructions about SILENTLY collecting a mat and SILENTLY crossing the hall and SILENTLY, CLASS, AND I MEAN SILENTLY finding our place in Mr. Pickett's room so we can start the movie WITH NOT A SECOND WASTED, CLASS, WE DON'T HAVE A SECOND TO WASTE; but sorry, Ms. Hutchins, if you cram fifty sixth graders and two non-scary teachers into one classroom—on a Friday!—it's going to get messy.

I reclined on my mat. Hubbub hummed around me. Ms. Hutchins and Mr. Pickett were in a frustrated huddle, trying to figure out which cable to plug in where. We had assigned places in alphabetical order, so I was next to Flynn.

"Let's talk about the experiment," he said, brandishing his science notebook, "since we're stuck together."

Ouch.

"We need to be very careful to choose just one independent variable," he said. We'd been learning about that. It's the thing you change, so, like, what kind of liquid in the Coke-versus-water experiment. You try to keep everything else the same so that you know why the results are the way they are. "How about having two different habitats? At first I was thinking two diets, but we might not see any difference, since cockroaches can survive on practically anything, right?"

"They can go without food for a month," I said. I knew a lot about bugs, mostly because I've always kind of wanted to *be* a bug.

"What if we split a fish tank into two parts, and fill one side with fertilized soil and the other with gravel?"

"Okay."

"*I'd* hypothesize that the roach in the dirt will do better, but I'm happy to incorporate your thoughts, if you have any."

"Nope."

Irritated, he snatched away his notebook and started scribbling on a page labeled *Materials*.

"Can Cah be the one in the rich soil?" I asked.

"I think it should be double-blind."

"I'm obviously going to be able to tell the difference between them."

"Or at least randomly assigned."

"Well, randomly assign Cah to the soil, okay?"

Croach was cool, but Cah was my *man*. The way he

wiggled his antennae when I gave him a chunk of old pizza—it was like he was thanking me.

"Maybe we should try to teach cockroaches sign language," I said.

"That's not a science-fair-style experiment," said Flynn.

"What if I'm thinking bigger than science fair?"

He ignored me. Ms. Hutchins and Mr. Pickett were red and flustered, wielding cables and barking out the occasional "Quiet, please!" I bet lots of people in the room could have figured it out, but teachers never admit their oldness and ask for help.

Flynn was lost in his notebook. We weren't supposed to leave our spots, but I decided I'd risk going over to the soccer guys. They'd borrowed a desk from one of Mr. Pickett's students so they could play paper-clip badminton, a game Jéro invented a few years ago. I'd never played much—Alex and I had mostly hung out alone—but I'd always thought it was fun.

"I've got winner," Freddy told me, "but you're next."

"Match point," said Jéro. Soup served the little bouncy ball onto the desk. Jéro, his regulation 28-mm untwisted paper clip held between thumb and index finger, returned it. They rallied back and forth a few times. Tension grew. Then Soup hit a zinger that rebounded off the corner of the desk. It seemed destined for the floor—but Jéro flung himself to the side and nabbed the ball with his clip.

"Ha!" he grunted.

But he hadn't gotten much wire behind it, and his soft

lob floated over to Soup's side. Soup slammed it back. Jéro was still recovering from his violent dive, so Soup got the point, and the match.

Freddy and Soup spun clips to see who'd serve first. "What's Flynn doing with that notebook?" Jéro asked, wincing as he massaged his ribs.

"Science fair. I hate this project."

"Dude, tell me about it," he said. "I got put with Lila Andrezejczak."

"I'm the one who should be complaining," said Lila. The triplets, as they often did, had popped up out of nowhere. "All you do is veto my ideas."

"Your ideas are stupid!"

"Just because you don't want to do psychology—"

"Yeah, I don't want to test what kind of music makes people subconsciously want to obey your orders, and I think it's creepy you *do*, actually—"

"It's not creepy!" said Lila.

"It's a little creepy," said Olivia.

"But very useful," said Tabitha.

"Got him!" crowed Soup, waving his victorious paper clip in the air.

"Soup-de-dupe! Nice!" I high-fived him.

Freddy sprawled dramatically onto the floor. "I'm over life."

"I'm going to take you *down*, Soup," I said.

Suddenly, there was a burst of music from the speakers. "It works!" cried Mr. Pickett.

"We did it!" said Ms. Hutchins.

They high-fived with both hands.

"Sixth grade! Quiet, please! The movie's about to start! Soren Skaar, why are you out of your assigned spot, and *why* are you holding an untwisted paper clip?"

"You could take someone's eye out!" whispered Tabitha in an uncanny imitation of Ms. Hutchins.

Trying not to laugh, I skittered back to my seat.

# CHAPTER FORTY

FLYNN AND I each had to write our own research report. The rest of the project we divided right down the middle, just as we'd agreed. He drew a diagram of the fish tank while I built a wall between the two habitats. I found Miracle-Gro in Dad's garden supplies and Flynn read the instructions on how to properly fertilize Cah's soil.

"Done," he said as I dumped the gravel into Crouch's side of the fish tank. "Put them in."

"These habitats are kind of bare."

"What do you want to add? Paintings? A coffee table?"

"I don't know. Something." I petted Cah's head with the tip of my pinkie finger. He scampered away.

"Armchairs? Houseplants?"

I knew he was making fun of me. "I just think they might appreciate a sun rock. A few shrubs."

"As long as it's the same between the two," Flynn said wearily. "It has to be controlled."

It was thanks to me that they got varied diets, too. If

Flynn had his way, they'd have been eating bread and water every day, like in a dungeon.

"You may be experimental subjects," I told them, "but I still respect you. I'll treat you right."

Flynn eyed everything I did. "Did you weigh that?" he asked when he saw me feeding them melon for dessert.

"Yes."

"Did you log it?"

"Yes."

"What'd you give them for dinner?"

"One Frosted Mini-Wheat each and three cubes of cat kibble."

"Did you weigh—"

"*Yes.*"

He checked, though. He flipped through the marbled composition book we kept by the fish tank.

I still hadn't told him I'd retired, and I felt like I had to try.

"Just to tell you," I said, "I'm not trying to sabotage this experiment."

He *hmm*ed.

"In fact, I've retired from pranking."

"Have you ever heard the phrase 'too little, too late'?" said Flynn. "Do you know what that means?"

"I'm not dumb."

"Maybe you should have retired before you embarrassed me in front of the whole school."

"Nobody cares that you lost the spelling bee!"

"I panicked when Jim Bob ran at me," he said levelly. He shook his bangs off his face to look me straight in the eyes. "I *shrieked.*"

"Everyone shrieked! Nobody remembers your shriek in particular!"

He shrugged. "I remember. I'm just saying, Soren, claiming you've retired isn't going to fix everything."

I VIDEO-CHATTED ALEX as soon as I was allowed on the computer again. She picked up. "Because *why*?" she said, as if we'd lost Internet connection for two seconds, not two weeks. "Why can't you prank with me in December? Do you know how hard it was for me to get my mom to promise we'd come? It's *science-fair* day, Soren. I looked at the school calendar. Think about the possibilities—our best one yet—"

"I'm retiring from pranking."

She opened her mouth like a goldfish looking for food.

"I'm taking a solid break, anyway. Pranks are not good for me right now."

"Oh," she said. "You decide to retire right before I visit. I see."

"It has nothing to do with that!"

"You prank with the triplets, but I'm visiting and suddenly you're done? How convenient."

I wasn't used to Alex dumping her sarcasm acid on me. "Alex—no—"

"I *knew* you didn't want to prank with me. Even last

227

time, you had to pull in the triplets. Are we even best friends anymore?"

"I'm retiring from pranking, not from being your best friend."

"Those are the same thing!"

"No, they're not!"

"But pranking's all we did together!"

That wasn't true. What about our secret code? What about all the hours we'd spent kicking on the wood-pile, or digging tiger traps in the woods? What about our don't-blush, don't-babble practice sessions? And okay, so maybe a lot of that stuff related to pranks, but that was almost a coincidence. Pranking was just the language we spoke together. We could have had anything in common— soccer, or science, or, I guess, yeah, paper dolls—and we'd still have been friends.

I liked Alex because she was Alex. Not because she pranked.

But why did she like me?

"You don't even want me to be your best friend," I said. "You've got Ol' Butt-Braid."

"*Sophia.*"

"I'll call her whatever I want."

Alex crossed her arms. "Fine. Sophia's my new best friend. So what? Do you even care?"

"No," I said. "I don't."

I moved to x out of the chat window, but she beat me to it. Her face swooshed away.

Retirement wasn't going to fix everything. It might not fix anything, I thought. It might make things worse.

THE WEDNESDAY OF Thanksgiving week, Ms. Hutchins gave up with half the period left and told us that she was going to her in-laws for the weekend and if she wasted one single iota of patience on us she wasn't going to be able to handle them and to please, for the love of God, give her thirty short minutes to forget that she had voluntarily chosen to spend her professional life with eleven-year-olds. Then she collapsed into the beanbag chair at the back of the room. Goldie and Kiyana brought her a cold washcloth for her forehead. "Do what you want, class," she called. "Just keep it to a dull roar."

Jéro and Soup and Freddy were already shoving desks into competition formation. Paper-clip badminton hadn't been big since third grade, but the games we'd played before watching *Hoot* had sparked a revival. I went over. "Can I play?"

"Yes!" said Freddy. He sounded so enthusiastic it was kind of exciting. What with Flynn loathing me, and Alex hanging up on me, and Ruth making my life harder whenever she remembered, I hadn't heard a lot of "Yes!" lately.

Soup beat Jéro while I narrowly edged out Freddy. "You know what?" I said as we swapped seats. "We have almost half an hour till Language Arts. We should organize a class tournament."

"*Great* idea!" said Freddy. He whipped out a sheet of paper. "Round robin or single elimination?"

"Probably elimination, to save time," said Soup.

"But then all the people who haven't played before are going to get out really fast," said Jéro.

"Isn't that the point?" said Soup. "One of the four of us will win."

"Let's have two brackets," I said. "Amateur and advanced."

"Genius," said Jéro. We bent over the paper to seed the brackets. "It's fun having you around, Soren," he added. "You have good ideas."

My neck got all hot. "I've always been around."

"It's different this year," said Jéro.

Freddy squinted at his list of the kids in our class. "Who's missing?" he said.

Alex, I thought, quick as a reflex. I glanced around. I don't know how it happened, but suddenly I got a zoomed-out look at the classroom, like I was God or a TV camera or something. I saw the triplets reading a big book about mythology on the floor behind the begonia. I saw Ms. Hutchins conked out on the beanbag, and I saw the piece of tissue stuck to her upper lip flutter every time she exhaled. I saw Flynn doing Language Arts extra credit with Kiyana and Tori, like any of them needed it. And I saw myself, too. I saw where I was and who I was with, and I saw the things I'd messed up and the things I'd gotten right.

Jéro wasn't wrong. This year *was* different.

"I should obviously be top seed," said Soup.

"Ha!" scoffed Freddy. "I just destroyed you! Nine to one!"

"Only because my paper clip was messed up!"

"Soren should be top seed," said Jéro. "He's got that evil slam move."

It was weird, missing Alex and also being glad she was gone. Those were two feelings that seemed like Harry and Voldemort: *one cannot live while the other survives.* But there they were, lodged in my rib cage.

"Let's flip a coin," I said. "All four of us are good."

# CHAPTER FORTY-ONE

WHEN WE GOT home from school, Thanksgiving preparations were in full swing. Mom had taken the afternoon off to do a last-minute grocery run over the border. It's a Skaar Thanksgiving tradition to, once we're totally stuffed with turkey and pie, top it off with these delicious Canadian chocolates called Coffee Crisps, and we have to go to Fort Frances to get them.

"While Mom's gone," Dad announced, "we're all going to work on a holiday centerpiece for the table!"

"Maybe I'll go to the grocery with her," I said.

"Are you sure?" Dad extended a bowl of oranges and a tin of cloves. "I could sure use someone to clove these oranges!"

I inched away. My thumb still had a dent from the last time Dad tricked me into cloving oranges.

"Or," he said, "you could help Ivan finger-paint autumnal foliage on our Thanksgiving banner!"

A lot of people think Dad's a pretty smart guy, but sometimes all the evidence points otherwise.

"Yeah, I'm definitely going to the grocery."

"Grab your passport and let's hit the road," said Mom. "It's going to snow."

The border's only a few minutes away, and Mom does Zumba with the guard, so we got into Canada fast. We found a parking spot and trundled through flurries into the store. It was packed, even though Canada had their Thanksgiving back in October. Mom had me push the cart—"If I bump into someone they'll get mad, but if you do they'll see you're just a kid"—and she darted around and tossed in food. "Thanks for coming," she said once we were finally in line to pay.

"Frankly," I said, "it was the lesser of two evils."

She laughed. "Maybe so. But I appreciate your company. You're fun to be around, Soren."

What the heck? Twice in one day, Jéro and Mom, saying nice things out of the blue. I scuffed my toe on the wheel of the cart. "Oh."

"It's nice to have you spending more time around the family."

"I am?"

"You've been hanging around the kitchen a lot."

"Because half the time I'm grounded."

"Well, true." We moved forward a foot in line. "Even so."

"And because I'm taking care of Cah and Croach." Their fish tank was in the corner of the kitchen, as far from the food as Dad could get it.

"How's *that* going?"

"Fine."

"You're working okay with Flynn?"

"Yeah."

"Hmm." She shoved the cart forward and almost clipped the heels of the old lady just ahead, who turned and glared at her. "Sorry, sorry, ma'am!"

"That's all right," said the old lady in a long-suffering tone.

Mom grimaced at me. *Oops,* she mouthed, and then said in her normal voice, "I've noticed you and Flynn still aren't talking."

"We're talking about science fair."

"Hmm," Mom said again.

"The thing is," I said, toying with the bars of Coffee Crisp in the basket, "he's really mad at me. I can't explain why. It's too complicated." I hoped she'd buy that. "And I'm really mad at him, too." For the mural, sort of, but mostly I was mad at him for being mad at me. I doubted he'd even thought about what a sacrifice it was for me to retire from pranking.

"Hmm."

"You're going to tell me things would be better if we talked them out, I know, and I'm not supposed to simmer, I know, but he won't even let me try! He won't even talk to me unless it's about stupid *graphs!*"

I was glad Mom hit the front of the line just then because my eyes had filled with tears. Angrily, I swatted them away. I hate crying. You look dumb plus your nose gets all stuffy.

Mom was loading the belt, and I put my head down and helped.

It wasn't until we were in the car, bags loaded, windshield wipers shoving away the snow, that she said anything that wasn't about being careful with the eggs, darn it, Soren, I mean *careful*, do *you* want to stand in that line again, etc. "I know what happened at the spelling bee," she said.

"Dad told you?" The man had no loyalty.

"He didn't have to tell me." She rolled her eyes. "Why you two imagined I wouldn't figure out that one on my own . . . Anyway. You're not going to feel good about yourself until you make things right with Flynn."

"I tried!"

"Did you?"

"I told him I'm retiring from pranking. Which I am. I'm done."

Till I saw the look on Mom's face right then, I'd had trouble visualizing her as a prankster. But her forehead crumpled, and her mouth gaped, and she looked the same as Dad had when I'd made my retirement announcement to him.

Surprised. And sad.

Suddenly I could imagine teenage Mom loading two numbered pigs into a pickup truck.

Come to think of it, she'd come home from work once with a story about how someone had Saran-wrapped her boss's entire office. . . .

And that time she'd given us mashed potatoes and gravy in ice cream dishes with cherries on top—maybe that *hadn't* been an accident, like she'd claimed. . . .

And once I'd found five bucks in Ivan's diaper and she'd said that sometimes babies pooped cash—it was a phenomenon as yet unexplained by science—and for months afterward I'd volunteered to change his diaper in the hopes of finding more money. . . .

*Mom!*

"Soren," she said, unaware that I was rewriting the story of my life, "retirement aside, you *do* need to make it up to Flynn."

"But—"

"I know, I know. You can't apologize, because he'd just cup his hand around his ear and say, 'Is that the wind?'"

"*Right!*"

"So apologies won't work. The thing is, you can't control what he does. You can only control what you do."

"What *do* I do?"

"Act like the person you want to be. Be kind. Think about how it's hard for him."

"It's hard for me, too."

"It is. I know, Soren. It is." She leaned forward, concentrating on the slushy road. "It's hard for everyone. That's kind of the thing about life."

It was dark already. The snowflakes zoomed toward us and then caught the wind up and over the car, like mini skateboarders. I must have fallen asleep, because next thing I knew we were at the border, and then Mom was poking at me and Ruth was saying, "Just because he went with you doesn't mean he doesn't have to help carry in the groceries."

We were home.

# CHAPTER FORTY-TWO

I WOKE UP the next morning to the smell of roasting turkey. Dad was happily pirouetting from sink to oven to countertop. He wore a floral apron, and his forehead was smeared with a large dab of something pinkish brown. "Happy Thanksgiving!" he said. "I am thankful for *you*, firstborn!"

"Yeah, same to you," I said, which was all the holiday spirit I could muster. Three minutes ago I'd been unconscious. I went to the pantry for some cereal.

"Ah ah ah," said Dad, waggling his finger. "We're fasting till the grand meal."

"Dad! I'm starving."

"Hunger," he pronounced, "is the best spice."

"What time are we eating?"

"Six."

"There's no way—"

"Chef makes the rules!" Dad seemed loopy. Probably from low blood sugar.

"You've got something on your face," I told him.

"Ooh," he said, scraping it off and examining it. "Giblets."

BY THREE, I was about to pass out. My stomach felt like it was eating itself.

The turkey was still in the oven. The other preparations were done. Dad's sister and her husband had arrived from Ely, and once Aunt Karen, Uncle Foster, Mom, Dad, and Flynn were deep in a game of Scrabble, I snatched a bag of pretzels and made a break for it.

Ruth was already by the pigpen. Her cheeks were as full as a squirrel's in October. "Sneaking food?" I said.

"Of course not." She swallowed. "I was visiting Jim Bob."

"Sure. Uh-huh. I got pretzels. What'd you get?"

"Hummus." She pulled it from behind her back. "I was desperate. I grabbed the first thing I saw. Thank goodness you got something we can dip. I was licking it off a twig."

We brushed the snow from the downed tree and sat. "I haven't been so hungry since the last time we got sent to bed without dinner," Ruth said. "Remember? The tinsel and the blowtorch?"

"Yes, yes," I said quickly. "No need to get into details." I stuffed food into my mouth. "Wow," I said, muffled. "This is *amazing.*"

"Hunger is the best spice," said Ruth.

We munched. When we were finished, Ruth tried to pick up snow all subtly, but come on, I'm a native. You're not going to fool me. Before she even started to pack it,

I'd sprinted behind the pigpen to scoop my first snowball. It was a free-for-all. We were both panting, moving fast, snatching snow and packing it and flinging it at each other. A small figure darted across my vision. I had just packed a giant snowball, and all my instincts told me to hurl it. I nailed the person in the head.

"Hey!"

It was an Andrezejczak. A very bundled Andrezejczak. I couldn't tell which one.

"Pause!" I yelled to Ruth. "Armistice!"

The Andrezejczak took down her hood. It was Olivia. "It's clear now!" she called back. Lila and Tabitha came out from behind the garage.

"Wait," said Ruth. "They stayed on safe ground while you went out?"

"That's me," said Olivia.

"You're like the one poor penguin that the others shove into the water to test for seals," said Ruth.

Olivia dumped a load of snow from the hood of her coat. "That's me."

Lila and Tabitha marched up. "Hello, Ruth. Hello, Soren," said Lila. "Have you guys eaten yet?"

"Nope," said Ruth. "Nothing."

"So why are you outside?"

"The adults and Flynn are playing Scrabble."

"Same at *our* house!" said Tabitha.

"It's awful," said Olivia.

"We aren't allowed to make any noise," said Lila.

"Us neither!" said Ruth.

"Ethan keeps bluffing," said Olivia, "but Great-Aunt Ermintrude would have to be the one to challenge, since her turn's after his, and she never does—"

"She keeps being like, 'I declare, this young man's vocabulary is *enormous!*' after he's played a word like *KINJROG*, which he claims is an Icelandic knitting needle—" said Lila.

"Our parents are furious—he's beating them by like six hundred points—" said Olivia.

"We had to escape," said Tabitha.

"How'd that thing go?" said Ruth.

"What thing?" I said.

"Just a thing they were planning," said Ruth airily. "A secret thing."

"It went perfectly," said Lila.

"He was so mad," said Tabitha, biting her bottom lip in a devilish smile.

"Come on," I said. "Tell me."

Olivia took pity on me. "Let's just say mayonnaise went in a place mayonnaise should never go."

"That doesn't narrow it down much."

"We put it in Ethan's shampoo bottle."

"Oh. Wow." I really hoped Ruth wouldn't take any little-sister inspiration. "That's bad."

"You should try it on your mom."

"About that . . ." I glanced at Ruth. "I'm retiring from pranking."

I have to admit, I was hoping the announcement would

go like it had with Mom and Dad. Shock, sadness, people telling me I was the talent of a generation, etc. But the triplets just got *aha* expressions. "So that's why Alex emailed us," said Olivia.

"She emailed you?"

"Complaining about *you*," said Tabitha.

"And also—" said Olivia, but Lila kicked her and she shut up.

"And also what?" I said.

"And also, Soren," said Tabitha, "on the way over here, I found something you might be interested in."

"Really?"

"Yeah. Come here."

"What is it?" I took a couple of steps toward Tabitha—

And she stuffed a massive snowball into my face.

I forgot about everything else. It was *on*.

Ruth took my side, Skaars versus Andrezejczaks. We ranged over the whole yard, our fort behind the pigpen, theirs in the vegetable garden. We're better at throwing but they're more vicious, so it was an even match.

We'd just called time-out to catch our breaths and stockpile ammo when we heard footsteps. It was Flynn, looking wan and pinched.

"Soren?" he said. "It's time to feed Cah and Croach."

"I'm in the middle of something."

"They need to be fed at four p.m. exactly. That's how the experiment works."

"*We* haven't been fed yet today."

"That's irrelevant. Do you know *anything* about science?"

And everything Mom told me about Being Kind and Acting Like the Person I Want to Be, all that stuff disappeared the way snow disappears in hard rain. It didn't even have a chance. Here I was, making the ultimate sacrifice, retiring from pranking, infuriating my best friend—and there he was, acting like a jerk.

I was holding a giant snowball I'd been working on, hard-packed with crunches of ice, and I threw it at him.

Not that hard.

Not that soft, either.

It hit him in the face. He wasn't wearing a coat. It exploded all over him. His hair was covered with drifts of snow. His mouth was a small, perfect O.

Everyone gaped, shocked. A few seconds passed. I guess they were seconds. It felt like a month.

In a very small voice, Olivia said, "You shouldn't have done that."

"I *know.*" I kicked the snowball pyramid I'd built, and then I kicked its ruins. They were staring like I was an exhibit at the zoo. "Stop looking at me," I said.

"You're destroying all our ammo," said Ruth.

"I don't care. I'm done with this stupid game. I'm going to go feed my *real* friends."

I stomped toward the house. When I was almost in, I heard Tabitha say, "His real friends are cockroaches?"

"They have names," said Flynn. "And personalities."

They all laughed. I slammed the door.

# CHAPTER FORTY-THREE

ON MONDAY, Ms. Hutchins's skin had the delicately crumpled look of an undershirt that's been in the corner of your room for a week. I guess I wasn't the only one who'd had a rough Thanksgiving. "Today," she said, "you'll be writing a reflection on how your science-fair experiment is going. And yes, it will be graded."

Jéro scooched his desk toward Lila's, but Ms. Hutchins lifted her hand. "Nope. This is an individual assignment."

"But what if our reflections don't match?" said Jéro, eyeing Lila.

"What if one of us has a much better reflection than the other?" said Lila, eyeing Jéro.

"What if one of us makes unfair accusations about the other's quality of work?"

"What if—"

"Class, you have the rest of the period to write," said Ms. Hutchins. "If you have a question, save it for tomorrow. If you have an urgent question, consider whether it's actually urgent."

She returned to her desk.

"If you need me, and you shouldn't, I'll be over here. Just me, my coffee, and my frayed sense of self, trying to forget that my in-laws . . ."

We couldn't hear her anymore, but her mouth was still moving. Nobody in their right mind would have asked her a question. Nobody would have even asked to go to the bathroom. Sometimes it's better to hold it.

I read the first prompt from the board.

**1. What have you learned so far from your research?**

For his individual report, Flynn was researching the chemistry of nitrogen fertilizers. I was writing a paper called *Indestructible: The Life and Times of the Modern American Cockroach*.

> I have learned many fun facts about cockroaches. For example, did you know a cockroach can live for a week without its head? Plus, they can run three miles an hour. And if you're thinking, "Hey, I'm faster," well, your legs are also a hundred times longer.
>
> I have also learned that cockroaches cannot twerk.

I read the next question.

**2. What have you learned about working with a partner?**

I untwirled the spiral of my notebook.

I didn't want to answer that.

Everyone else was working. Soup wore the constipated look he always gets when he has to think. Freddy kept digging around in his ear with his pencil, so it kind of looked like he was writing with a quill dipped in earwax. Jéro and Lila were each hunched over, scribbling fast and furious, trying to outdo—a.k.a. out-tattle—each other.

Flynn was rotating his pencil inside the Statue of Liberty–shaped sharpener he kept in an Altoids tin. A curl of shaving dropped onto his desk. He glanced at me. I jerked my eyes away, but I knew he'd seen me looking.

"Ten minutes, class," said Ms. Hutchins. "When you're finished, stack your notebooks on my desk."

> I have learned many things about working with a partner.

I always start by repeating the question. It makes your answer look longer.

> Sometimes you have to compromise

I tried to erase, since we hadn't done much compromising. But my pencil had the worst eraser ever. All it did was smear pencil guck around my paper.

I scratched out *compromise* and wrote *split up the work*.

> Evenly dividing the work is important. That way, you can do your thing and your

partner can do theirs and you don't have
to talk.

"Five minutes." People had started to file past me to
turn in their notebooks.

Though it'd probably be way more fun if we
actually worked together, so it's kind of sad
the way it's ended up

Where did *that* come from? I tried to erase. But no, not
with this cruddy pencil.
"Two minutes."

and that's why you should let us choose our
own partners next time.

I looked hurriedly up at the board.

**3. If you could start over, what would you do**
**differently?**

I scrawled:

What I would do differently would be

"One minute."
Rats. I scribbled as fast as I could.

to not get in fights with everyone. I actually
hate fighting. And if Flynn and my sister

hadn't already been mad at me, it wouldn't have been such a big deal when Jim Bob

I scratched out that last part so hard I made a hole in the paper.

when something unfortunate happened, but now Flynn will never forgive me. (Ruth has mostly forgotten.)

My handwriting had gotten really messy, and my hand hurt.

I also feel guilty because I get to do all the fun parts of the project, like taking the experimental subjects for walks around the garden, and Flynn is doing the hard parts, like graphs.

The bell rang. "Notebooks on my desk. Soren? Everyone else has finished—"

"Okay! One sec! Almost done!"

Also, I should have made sure I was alone before I tried to teach my cockroaches to twerk. Ruth saw it, and she will never let me live it down.

.   .   .

ONE WEIRD THING happened that evening.

"Have you finished your homework, Soren?" said Dad.

"I'm reading our Language Arts book."

"Reading? Or reading ahead?"

Darn. Dad knew me too well. I hated the way teachers made you read one chapter at a time—just when you were getting into it, the homework assignment ended—so I always read the books in one go. "I'm way ahead," I admitted.

"Do you have other homework?"

"Some math problems in the online textbook."

"Flynn's on the desktop, but I think Ruth has my laptop in the dining room. Tell her I said it's your turn."

Reluctantly, I put down *When You Reach Me*. I dragged my toes all the way to the dining room, leaving two jerky trails in the carpet. "Dad says you have to—"

*Shwop!* Ruth had slammed the laptop shut.

"What were you *doing*?"

"Nothing," she said, way too fast.

Usually she either messages her friends or plays this game where you build fortresses out of cat heads. Or both. But I was pretty sure I'd seen a video-chat window, and a familiar face. A face with purple glasses.

"Go away," she said, clutching the laptop to her chest. "I'll give it to you. Just let me close what I was doing."

I was too surprised to argue.

As I signed in to the textbook, I thought, Should I be suspicious?

# CHAPTER FORTY-FOUR

FLYNN AND I didn't speak for the entire last week of our experiment. I fed the cockroaches and took them out for exercise and noted their measurements, and he worked on the board in his room.

The day before it was due, he stopped by my seat on the bus home. "Hey."

"Hey."

"After you feed them, update the log one final time and bring it up to my room."

I grunted. He headed back to the seat Goldie was saving for him.

"Awkward," said Jéro.

"That's the first time he's spoken to me in a week."

"I *wish* Lila would stop speaking to me. I wouldn't even need a week. I'd take an hour."

"Guess who's visiting tomorrow?" I said.

"Who?"

"Alex."

"Wow," said Jéro. "I remember her. Are you guys going to do something?"

"Like hang out? Of course."

I thought of how Alex had hung up on me. How she had a new best friend, and how she'd emailed the triplets to complain about me.

Probably we'd hang out.

Maybe.

"No. Like an epic prank."

"Oh. No. Not this time."

"What you should do," said Jéro, "is prank science fair. Destroy all the boards so Ms. Hutchins can't grade them. Dump Kool-Aid all over them or something. And I'm not saying you'd *try* to dump Kool-Aid on Lila, but if she ended up in the wrong place at the wrong time . . ."

I laughed. "Yeah, no, not happening. That kind of thing takes weeks of prep."

"You guys are experts. You could do it."

Squirt guns. Or, no, buckets. A few dozen packets of red Kool-Aid powder. And the basketball backboards would be pulled up against the ceiling, so if we could get buckets of Kool-Aid strung up on them ahead of time, all we'd have to do mid-fair would be push the button to lower the hoops. . . . "That'd ruin a lot of people's hard work."

"Isn't that the point?"

"Well, anyway." I wished the conversation were over. "Nothing's happening at science fair."

Jéro elbowed me. "If our board's getting destroyed,

I don't want to bother finishing it. So if you change your mind, give me a heads-up, okay?"

WE GOT HOME. Flynn went upstairs, and Ruth went out to build a snow castle for Prince Jim Bob, Duke of Pork. Dad said, "Soren, will you watch Ivan for twenty minutes while I rest my eyes on the couch?"

"Sure."

"Thanks. He wrecked me today."

"What'd he do?"

Dad shot a grim look at a pile of dirty laundry. "It began with the creamed spinach. . . ."

"IVAN LIKE FEE SEES!" yelled Ivan from the floor.

"Got it," I said. "Go lie down. Ivan, want to help me feed Cah and Croach?"

Ivan lifted a trusting, chubby hand to mine. I walked him over to the windowsill with the fish tank. "There's Cah, in the soil habitat," I told Ivan.

Ivan peered in. Cah (such a ham!) started doing push-ups on his sun rock.

"And this is Croach. He's shy, but really funny once you get to know him. Wave, Croach!"

He sized us up with his glossy black eyes and then scuttled behind his cactus plant.

"IVAN LIKE!" Ivan put his hands flat on the fish tank's glass. Cah twitched, glared at Ivan, and ran away.

"You're smearing their habitat windows," I explained. "How would *you* feel if someone messed up *your* room?"

"IVAN NOT LIKE!" he said, frowning at me.

Oops. Definitely the wrong question to ask, as I messed up Ivan's room all the time. His crib rails made an extremely convenient rack for draping dirty underwear and wet towels. "Let's feed them," I said. I went over to the fridge while Ivan stared at the fish tank. He'd gotten as glazed over as he gets with cartoons. "Leftover spaghetti? No, too hard to measure. What do you think we should give them?"

"CREAMED SPINACH!" said Ivan.

"Uh, no. I heard what that did to you."

"IVAN GO BOOM!"

I winced. "How about saltines with peanut butter?" I chose two saltines with identical salt patterns and used the lab scale to measure eight grams of peanut butter onto each one. "A classic snack."

Ivan watched as I opened the feeding hatch and set down the crackers. Neither Cah nor Croach ever finished their meals, but Flynn said it'd be an experimental no-no to remove the leftovers. This meant the food areas were gross. They liked it, though. They'd hunker there for hours, licking a splotch of yogurt here, a crumb of croissant there. Once I'd seen Cah squatting to take a poop right on top of all the food. I'd looked away as fast as possible. Scientific curiosity is all well and good, but there are some things you can't unsee.

Ivan thrust his hand down the hatch. "No!" I said. I snapped it shut so fast that I caught his hand, and he started to cry. "Sorry, Ivan! Ack, I'm sorry! But don't wake up Dad! Come on, Ivan, shh—"

He sucked his hand and scowled at me.

"Let's go play Barbies," I told him. "Where's Gloria? Is she still in physical therapy for her leg? Will you let me visit her?"

At last, he gave a sulky nod.

# CHAPTER FORTY-FIVE

FLYNN DIDN'T COME down for dinner. Dad sent Ruth to find him while we waited, chicken potpie glistening on our plates. "He says he'll eat later," Ruth reported. "He's got too much work."

"Hmph," said Dad, who likes his cooking to be appreciated. We ate, and Ruth and I did the dishes while Mom cleaned around us. Ivan was playing with his tea set in the corner.

"What's Flynn working on?" asked Mom as she swept the floor.

"The science-fair project, I'm guessing."

"*Your* science-fair project?"

"Well, also his."

"The project you two are doing as partners?"

"Um, yes, that would be the one."

Mom stood there with the broom like a Roman soldier with a javelin. "Then why," she said, her voice steely, "are you down here, not up there?"

"Well, this was his part—we split up the work—"

"*Jon!*" Mom blared.

"Yeah?" said Dad.

"We need to talk to our son. Soren, go to our bedroom immediately." She turned to Ruth. "Do your half of the dishes, and then stop. Not a single fork more. Your brother will finish his half himself."

I THOUGHT I might get some mercy. "He still won't talk to me," I said, but Mom said, "And that means you don't have to do your own science project?"

"I already did my half!"

"Remember our talk at the rec center?" said Dad. "I'm worried you walked away thinking that we condone bad behavior. And that's not at all the case."

"And remember *our* talk in the car?" said Mom. "I know he's not treating you particularly well, but imagine, Soren. What if you had to go live in Brooklyn with Flynn and Aunt Linnea? For a whole year? Go to a new school, make all new friends, come home after school and it's not your *real* home—"

"He's made a ton of friends."

Mom sighed. "You're missing the point."

"What's the point?"

"Right now," said Mom, "the point is that you can't let him do that project by himself."

"Reheat his potpie and take it upstairs," said Dad.

"And don't even think about coming down until the

project's done," said Mom. I opened my mouth. "If you run out of ways to contribute," she added, knowing what I was about to say, "well, keep him company."

"I swear," I tried, "he *wants* to do it alone—"

That got me nowhere.

Mom and Dad stayed in their bedroom, doing this thing they do every few months where they pretend they're so disappointed in their children they can't resume normal life. Ruth had finished the dishes. "You didn't have to do that," I called into the living room, where she was reading *Ella Enchanted*.

"I wanted to," she called back. "I'm pretending I'm an oppressed stepsibling who doesn't yet know she's going to be a queen."

"Oh. Thanks." I actually was grateful, even though that meant I was an ugly stepsister. "Thanks a lot, Ruth."

"By the way," she said, "do you have any water balloons?"

"Yeah, in my sock drawer. Why?"

"Can I borrow them?"

"You can have them."

"Really?"

"Sure." I slammed the microwave door on Flynn's pot-pie. "I owe you."

"Cool. Awesome. Thanks."

"It's kind of cold outside for water balloons."

She shrugged and turned a page. Flynn's potpie spun in the microwave. I strolled over to the window— "AHHH! Ivan!"

He waved. He was still in the corner, playing with his teacups.

"I didn't know you were in here!"

"IVAN QUIET!"

"I know. It was weird."

*Beep! Beep!* That was the microwave.

"SOREN PLAY!"

"I can't right now." I felt a rush of big-brotherly warmth. "But I wish I could."

"IVAN WANT SOREN PLAY!" he yelled, his chin quivering.

"Sorry, Ivan. I really can't." He clearly didn't understand why not. "Someday you'll get it," I told him. "Someday you'll be in this much trouble yourself."

"I hope that potpie is on its way up the stairs!" Mom yelled from the bedroom.

"Gotta go," I told Ivan. "We'll play later."

"I DON'T NEED ANY HELP," said Flynn.

"Well, my parents are making me stay in here until you're done."

"I'd prefer to be alone."

"Well, my parents are making—"

"Fine."

I lay on the bed and watched him enter measurements into Dad's laptop. After a few minutes, I rolled over. Now I was facing the mural. Nope. Not about to look at *that*. I rolled over again. I started mouth-breathing. Supposedly you can hypnotize yourself if you focus only on your breath, eight counts in, eight out—*ahhhhh—ahhhhh—*

"Gah!" Flynn exploded. "Could you *be* any more annoying?" He tossed a sheaf of papers onto the bed. A box of colored pencils followed. "As long as you're trapped here, you might as well color these graphs."

"Whoa," I said, despite myself.

"You won't?"

"No, I just mean, these graphs are really professional-looking."

Flynn ducked his chin. "They're okay."

"They're *awesome.*"

I felt kind of bad my name would be on them. That's how good they were.

"How did you know how to do all this stuff?" I said.

"I googled it."

I colored one bar of the first graph a soft periwinkle. Usually I'm way too impatient to color within the lines, but these were too nice to mess up. I took my time. I shaded the way Mom shaded when she'd take pity on me or Ruth doing geography homework and sit with us and help color in the nations of South America. She taught us how to hold the pencil loosely, how to overlap the strokes so the shade came out even. Coloring. It took me back, back before geography homework, back to dinosaur coloring books, to our old kitchen with yellow walls, where I sat on a pillow for a booster and someone cut me silhouettes of Santas and stars so I could make ornaments for the Christmas tree. I'd had *memories* before, obviously, and I'd have been able to tell you that the past had passed and you couldn't dip back, but I guess I hadn't totally believed it until right then, when I wished I were a little kid and knew I never would be again.

The graphs took a while. Flynn paged through them. "Not bad."

"Thanks."

"No," he said stiffly, "thank *you*. Thanks for doing all the hard parts of the project."

"Okay," I said, "no need for sarcasm."

"No, that's what I wrote about for Ms. Hutchins's reflection thing," he said. "That I flaked and gave you all the tough parts."

"That's what *I* wrote about!"

"You've been tending *roaches*!"

"You've been making *graphs*!"

We stared at each other.

"I thought I was getting off easy," he said.

"So did I."

"ONE LAST STEP," said Flynn at midnight. The board looked amazing. Mostly because of him, but it was true I'd done a lot of coloring. "We're going to display Subject A and Subject B—"

"You mean Cah and Croach—"

"But we also need photographs of them in their habitats." He grabbed his phone. "I should have done this earlier, but, um, I didn't want to get that close."

"They're very friendly," I assured him.

We tiptoed through the sleeping house. Mom and Dad's door was shut. Ruth and Ivan's was ajar, but their room was dark and silent. Flynn flicked on the kitchen light. I went to the fish tank.

"Good evening, Cah and Croach!" I whispered. "Ready for your photo shoot? Wait—what—no—"

I sank to my knees.

The feeding hatch was open. Both habitats were empty.

Cah and Croach had escaped.

# CHAPTER FORTY-SIX

"GONE," I WHISPERED.

"Gone?" said Flynn.

"They must be hiding," I said frantically. "Playing a trick. Cah! Croach! Come out, come out, wherever you are!"

Flynn rattled the fish tank.

"Careful!" I squealed.

But I knew they weren't in there. We'd designed the habitats to be observed. There weren't places to hide.

"How could they have escaped?" said Flynn.

I thought for a minute.

*Oh.*

"Ivan was playing here—by himself—and he watched me open the feeding hatch earlier today—"

"You think he set them free?"

"I know it. He was in here alone after dinner. They're smart, Cah and Croach, but they couldn't have opened the hatch themselves."

"Our project is going to be so messed up if we can't find them," said Flynn.

"*That's* what you're worried about?"

"It's due tomorrow! What else would I be worried about?"

"Their safety!" I said. "Cah and Croach are house pets! They're domesticated! Now they're alone in the wild!"

"I don't know how we'll present our project without them," said Flynn.

"They're going to get lost—"

"We don't even have photographs!"

"Or get eaten—"

"This is terrible," said Flynn.

"It *is*."

"Do you think we can catch some backups and fake it?"

"That'd be like Dad expecting nobody to notice if he swapped Ivan with some other two-year-old from fencing class."

Flynn and I made sudden eye contact, and I knew what we were both thinking:

*I wish.*

"Let's split up the kitchen and search," said Flynn. "You take under the fridge, I'll—"

"No. No. We'll never find them that way." I'd done a lot of research. "Did you know a cockroach can flatten itself out as thin as a dime? They might not be in the kitchen. They could have slid under the door."

"Great," Flynn groaned.

"You don't find a cockroach," I said. "A cockroach finds you."

"And how are we going to make *that* happen?"

"Flynn, you're an expert when it comes to designing an experiment. You can do data and graphs."

"So?"

"You can think like a scientist," I said. "But I can think like a cockroach."

LUCKILY, I'D BEEN observing Cah and Croach so closely that I knew just what food they liked best. "Cah loves beans and sugar and fruit," I said. Flynn found a jar of raspberry jam while I unlidded the Tupperware of last week's lentil stew, which was definitely fermenting.

"Good thing your dad never cleans out the fridge," said Flynn.

"Only when something stinks and it's definitely not Ivan," I agreed. "As for Croach, remember that day we got sushi from Misohungri? That new place on Main Street?"

"I loved that sushi," said Flynn.

"So did Croach. He rolled around in it like Jim Bob in slops."

Flynn arranged a rank California roll on a plate.

"Don't use a plate," I said. "Put it right on the floor. Easier access, and the scent'll travel faster."

"You *do* think like a cockroach."

"Thanks," I said, flattered. Flynn dumped lentil stew on top, and I added the jam.

"Are we all set?" said Flynn.

I surveyed the food. All their favorites. It made me miss them. My mild-mannered Croach, who shimmied his thorax whenever I filled the water trough. My wacky Cah, who'd do anything for a joke.

My throat grew tight. "What if they can't find their way back?" I said. "They've been out for hours, Flynn. . . ."

"They're just getting a taste of the outside world. They'll be back."

I flipped off the lights. The moonlight made the kitchen silver and gray. Flynn and I took up positions on opposite countertops, poised to pounce at the first sign of scuttling.

"I just want my boys to come home," I said.

"Shh," said Flynn. "They'll be here any minute."

THE WATER HEATER popped and bubbled. Snow made a *shirr-shirr* sound as it shifted on the roof. A board creaked, and a train hooted a dreamy, distant whistle. Flynn, crouched on the other counter, was a statue. I could hear the beats of my own heart. We had waited for a very long time.

I stared at the dark mound of food on the floor.

There was nothing.

But then—

There was something.

A twitch in the side of my vision.

I thought it might be eyestrain, or wishful thinking.

But the twitch became a shape. A small, dark shape under the baseboard of the dishwasher.

Flynn saw it too. He bent his head, and I nodded.

Suddenly, the shape made a break for it. A cockroach scurried across the floor. He leapt onto the food.

I eased myself off the counter. As soon as my feet touched the floor, the cockroach felt the vibrations. He tensed. His antennae wiggled wildly. I froze, and he returned to the food.

I couldn't risk another step. I'd have to catch him with one move. I tensed my thighs, ready to leap.

On three, I thought.

One—

Two—

"WAHHHH!" Ivan cried from upstairs.

The cockroach startled and darted left. I dove. He scampered toward the baseboard, but I launched myself at him—my foot slipped on something—I crashed down—but my hands were cupped over the floor.

"Got him," I gasped.

Flynn turned on the light. We both blinked. I peeked into my cupped hands. "I think it's Croach," I said. I put him into the gravel side of the fish tank, and made sure the feeding hatch was closed before I squatted to squint through the glass.

"Yeah, it's Croach." He ran a lap around his habitat and sighed in relief (I'm guessing) as he lay on the sun rock and closed his eyes. "Get some sleep," I told him.

"WAHHHH!" Ivan wailed.

"He's going to wake up your parents." Flynn looked nervously at the mess of cockroach bait. I'd stepped in it, and it was ground thoroughly into the floorboards. "What if they wake up and find us here?"

"That'd be bad."

Flynn turned for the stairs. "I'm fetching him."

"The last person we want here is Ivan!"

"WAHHHH!"

"No," said Flynn, "the last person we want is your mom. And that's what's going to happen in about four seconds. We'll get Ivan, we'll restrain him, and we'll calm him down."

He was right. Keep your friends close, your enemies closer, and your baby brothers closest of all.

A FEW MINUTES later, Flynn tiptoed down the stairs. Ivan, snuggled in his arms, was wearing his gorilla pajamas and holding Gloria. "Ivan understands," said Flynn, obviously for Ivan's benefit, "that we have to be *very quiet*."

"Yep," I said.

"Ivan, can you show Soren what *very quiet* means?"

Ivan put a finger to his lips. He said nothing.

"Wow," I said.

"No sounds from your parents' room," Flynn said. "They must be pretty conked."

"They usually are," I said. "They find their lives exhausting."

"Now what?" Flynn shifted Ivan to his other hip and looked at the trampled food on the floor. "More waiting?"

All three of us gazed at the crab-lentil-jam mush.

"Gross," whispered Ivan.

Flynn set him down. He toddled to the fish tank. I tensed, but all he did was wave at Croach, who waggled a lazy antenna back.

"Free," said Ivan.

"They don't want to be free," I told him. "Life is good in their habitats."

It hurt to think of Cah out there. Scared. Alone.

"Where would he have gone?" Flynn said.

"Out," whispered Ivan. He didn't sound like himself when he whispered. He sounded less like a monster and more like a kid. "Out."

"What?" I said.

Ivan pointed at the door to the dark mudroom, where the chickens slept on their roosts. *"Out."*

# CHAPTER FORTY-SEVEN

THE THREE OF us peered through the glass door. Flynn reached back to turn off the lights so we could see more than our reflections. Slowly, our eyes adjusted.

The hens were bundles of feathers: five plump, sleeping lumps. And there was Martha, a spikier bundle on a roost near the window. The heat lamp was dark, but I knew it'd turn on soon.

"What time is it?" I said.

"Three forty-eight," said Flynn.

"We've got twelve minutes before they all wake up."

"Can't we just turn off the timer?"

I shook my head. "It wouldn't help. They've woken up at four a.m. for weeks now, so they'll wake up at four a.m. today."

"Out," said Ivan.

The mudroom floor was six inches deep in pine shavings and straw, all gray and tangled in the moonlight.

"We don't even know he's out there," said Flynn.

"I bet he is." Ivan was right. If I knew Cah—and I knew Cah—he'd have looked for adventure. And where else could he be? If he'd been anywhere in the house, he wouldn't have been able to resist the food on the kitchen floor. "He's out there. We just have to find him. Flynn, get another spoonful of lentil stew."

We stepped into the chilly mudroom. It was 3:53 by the oven clock. Flynn dumped the stew on the straw, and I breathed, "Cah! Cah, Cah, Cah!"

Martha twitched.

We froze.

This was the most dangerous thing I'd ever done in my life. Entering Martha's lair—in the dark—with no armor?

What were we *thinking*?

My body shook. Sweat dripped down my neck. I didn't dare wipe it.

It went against all my instincts to take my eyes off Martha, but I stared at the food. *Come on, Cah,* I thought. *I know you smell the food. Come feast.*

The minutes ticked away. 3:58, 3:59.

*Cah. Cah. Cah.*

The heat lamp clicked on, flooding the mudroom with warm, yellow light. Ivan jumped, but stayed quiet.

I glanced at Martha.

One of his beady eyes opened. Then the other. His head swiveled. He saw us.

"COCK-A-DOO-ARGH-ACK-ECK-EH!"

With squawks and fluttering, the chickens startled

awake. They flapped from their roosts to the ground. In a burst of feathers, Martha, enraged, launched himself at us—

And there he was! There was Cah! Scuttling madly toward the stew!

"CAH!" I yelled.

"COCK-A-DOO-ARGH-ACK-ECK-EH!" yelled Martha.

I lunged, but Martha was faster. He held Cah in his beak.

MARTHA EYED ME. "Let him go," I pleaded. "Please. I'll hunt you other cockroaches."

I hoped Cah didn't understand me.

"Nice Martha—sweet Martha—"

Martha took one step backward on his pickled legs.

It was a lost cause. He had never liked me.

My eyes filled with tears as he took two more steps back. Cah, frozen in his beak, was drawn farther and farther away.

And then Ivan strode forward. He flung his arms wide. Martha, startled, stared at him. His chubby arms quivering, Ivan yelled, "EAT IVAN!"

"Ivan!" I said. "No!"

"EAT IVAN INSTEAD!"

"Don't sacrifice yourself! It isn't worth it!"

"BABY!"

"Get Cah!" Flynn hissed to me. "Get him while Martha's distracted!"

I hesitated. "But—"

"TASTY BABY!"

Martha poked his head forward, his wattle swinging, his beak within inches of Ivan's soft arm.

I dove for Cah, and I plucked him from the jaws of death.

Martha, furious, wheeled around. "COCK-A-DOO-ARGH-ACK-ECK-EH!" he howled. He flew at me. I stumbled away, raising an elbow to protect my eyes, cupping Cah in my hands.

"Inside!" yelled Flynn, fumbling with the doorknob.

The three of us fell into the kitchen. Flynn slammed the door. Martha threw himself against it, but the glass held.

I slowly opened my palms.

"Are you okay?" I murmured.

Cah waved his antennae.

"Don't let him escape again," said Flynn.

"Oh," I said, depositing Cah into his habitat, "I doubt he'll want to escape anytime soon."

Cah flopped onto his sun rock.

"After all," I told Cah, "it's not every day that three heroes will step in to save your life."

"Tasty baby," whispered Ivan.

"We did it," said Flynn.

Ivan stuck out his right hand to me. It took me a second to figure out that he wanted to shake. I don't know where he got the idea, probably from a movie, but we shook hands.

He turned to Flynn, and they shook hands.

He looked at the two of us.

Flynn and I couldn't have avoided it if we'd wanted to,

and, you know, I don't think we did. We were awkward, like we were aliens who'd seen humans do this weird hand-rubbing sign of peace and wanted to try it out for ourselves, but we did it. We shook hands.

It loosened something inside me. I smiled at Flynn. He smiled back. "You know," I said, "you're actually—"

Footsteps thundered on the stairs.

# CHAPTER FORTY-EIGHT

THE LECTURE WAS not fun. Mom and Dad tag-teamed it, so as soon as one of them ran out of steam, the other reared up. Sometimes I think they must rehearse those things.

They told us they'd need time to figure out appropriate consequences, so we were sent to bed. About five minutes later, we had to wake up. Dad drove us to school since it was negative fourteen and we were hauling the fish tank and the science-fair board. "And remember, boys," he hollered out the door, "behave today, *or else*! You're skating on thin ice!"

"Ooh," I heard from behind me. "What'd you do?"

I spun around. Purple glasses, brown braids sticking out of a red wool cap—

Alex.

We nodded at each other, but it was too cold to stay outside, or even talk outside. Opening your mouth made your spit get all gummy and your teeth hurt like you'd bitten into an ice cream cone. In the too-warm entrance hall, radiators hissing overtime, I said, "Whoa. Hi. I didn't know you'd be here so early. Did you guys leave at two a.m.?"

"We stayed overnight with my aunt in Effie."

"Oh. Nice."

"ALEX!" I heard someone say.

Not someone. Three someones. The triplets hurried over.

"Andrezejczaks!" squealed Alex. "It's so good to see you!"

She was so high-pitched I almost thought she was faking it, but Olivia flung her arms around Alex's neck. Lila and Tabitha weren't the hugging types, but they were beaming too.

Flynn nudged me with the science-fair board.

"Who's that?" he said.

"Alex Harris. My best friend." She and the triplets had formed a tight little clump. "Well, she was my best friend until she moved."

"Is that who you're always video-chatting?"

"Yeah. Until a few weeks ago."

"Are you guys fighting or something?"

I shifted my weight. The fish tank was getting heavy, and I couldn't take off my mittens until I put it down. "Let's go to homeroom."

"Okay."

I turned to Alex. "Um, see you later, I guess? Are you here all day?"

"I have a visitor's badge. I can stay as long as I want

and I'm supposed to text my mom when I want her to pick me up."

"You have a phone? When'd you get a phone?"

"A couple of weeks ago." She flashed it. "There's a lot you miss when you don't talk to me."

"You're the one who wasn't talking to *me*!"

"Come on, girls." She linked arms with Lila and Tabitha, leaving Olivia to trail behind. "We need to find a private place to catch up."

"And we need to find Ruth!" said Lila.

I trudged to homeroom. Flynn followed me. He didn't say anything, which was nice. Ms. Hutchins's classroom was already crammed with projects, boards and plants and things built of Popsicle sticks. Flynn slid our board into a safe spot behind the begonia, and I checked to make sure Cah and Croach had survived the journey.

"Yes," I said to Flynn, "is the answer."

"Huh?"

"To whether we're fighting. Me and Alex. I guess we are, anyway. She has new friends. This girl at her school, and the triplets here. She barely knew the triplets before she moved."

"Well, you have new friends too," said Flynn.

"I do?"

Jéro ran up to us. "I saw Alex out there. Anything you want to tell me before tonight, Soren?"

"Uh, no."

"Come on. One little hint for your buddy Jéro? Your

favorite bookie? I won't tell anyone, I promise. They could torture me and I wouldn't tell."

Flynn eyed me. "Are you *planning* something?"

"No! I told you! I retired!"

"Because I worked really hard on this science-fair project."

"So did I! So did everyone!"

"Hmm," said Jéro. Flynn wasn't as obvious, but I could tell he wasn't sure either.

"After all the excitement last night," I said, "the last thing I want is chaos at science fair. I want everything to be peaceful and calm."

Jéro gaped. He turned to Flynn. "Did he really say that?"

Flynn started laughing. "I wish I'd gotten that on video. That's the weirdest thing that's happened all year."

THE RULE IS if it's negative degrees, we have to have recess in our homeroom teacher's classroom.

"G. Grandin versus E. Garcia." The class tournament of paper-clip badminton was up and running and hugely popular, and Jéro was reading off the day's matches. "J. Johnson versus T. Tyler. R. Grant versus F. Skaar."

"Flynn's playing?" Soup asked me.

"Yeah, he joined last-minute. Today, actually."

I'd asked him if he'd wanted to play during math that morning, and he'd gotten this look of utter joy and said, "Me? *Yes!*"

"Rats," Soup groaned.

"No, it's okay, he's actually cool—"

"Nah, I just mean, he's going to win. If he's half as good at badminton as he is at soccer, he'll flatten us all."

Alex came over. "Want to play?" I said.

Soup said, "It's the All-Class Paper-Clip Badminton Open. We're the tournament directors. It'd be a late registration, but we could get you in—"

"No thanks. I'm teaching the triplets the basics of paper dolls." Alex tilted her head at me. "If you know what I mean."

"Wait. What *do* you mean?"

"You want to join us?"

What *did* she mean?

I glanced at the triplets. They were already snipping at colored paper. I couldn't decide whether to be suspicious.

"Come on, Soren. It's not the same without you."

The three badminton matches were already under way, and the rest of the class was gathered around the competition desks, chanting and clapping. "We've got to help keep stats," Soup reminded me. "And do crowd control, ref any close calls . . ."

He was right. I was needed. "Sorry," I told Alex. "Maybe later?"

She shrugged. "Sure. Maybe."

# CHAPTER FORTY-NINE

FOR AN EARLY dinner before science fair, Dad heated up some leftover lasagna.

"You look nice, Soren," said Mom. "Very unusual."

"SOREN GROOM!" chimed in Ivan. He had a coloring book about royal weddings, and he thought wearing a tie meant you were getting married.

"Never," I told him.

"Aren't you excited to present your project?" said Mom.

"Yeah."

"You don't sound very excited. Nervous?"

"I guess so," I said. *Bothered* was more like it. *Preoccupied.* What was going on with Alex and the triplets and the paper dolls?

Flynn came downstairs. He was wearing blood-red dress pants, a shiny gray shirt, and a silver bow tie. "Wow," said Mom. "Very, um, different."

"Thanks!" said Flynn.

"DODGE, SOREN!" yelled Dad.

Fortunately, I have the self-protective instincts of a gazelle on the savanna. I ducked, and a clump of lasagna sailed over my head. Ivan chortled. "I'll run you guys over to school," said Mom, glancing between Ivan and my crisp white shirt.

"I'll come early too," said Ruth, pulling on her backpack.

"The audience doesn't need to be there for another hour," Mom said. "You don't want to stay here with Dad and Ivan?"

"Nah," said Ruth. "I'll be a sixth grader someday. I want to watch them set up so I can start thinking about my own project."

Dad stood and applauded. "What forethought!" he cried. "What a stand against procrastination! I hope you're taking notes, Soren."

Ruth was a bigger procrastinator than anyone. Unless Dad made her, she never started projects until the night before. She didn't even *think* about Christmas presents until December 24. Sometimes stores were already closed and she had to wrap stuff from her junk drawer.

She was up to something.

"Ready?" said Mom.

"Ready," said Ruth and Flynn.

"Yeah," I said, "I'm ready too."


"I FORGOT ALEX WAS VISITING!" said Mom in the school lobby. "Did you see her at school today?"

"Yep." She was with the triplets again. I waved, but they didn't see me.

"I wonder how long they're staying," said Mom. "We should have her and her mom over for dinner. And the Andrezejczaks, too."

"Mm-hmm."

"Let's go set up," Flynn told me.

"Yeah," I said, not taking my eyes off Alex and the triplets. Ruth had joined them. They were in a tight circle. All you could see was ponytails and backpacks.

Okay. It was official. They were definitely up to something.

"Come on, Soren," said Flynn. "We have to get everything ready before the judges arrive."

We set up our board and fish tank in the zoology section of the gym. The triplets came in to set up their projects. Alex and Ruth followed. I kept an eye on them. Over in chemistry, Ms. Hutchins was yelling at Freddy, who was sheepishly rubbing a towel over a large puddle of what smelled like gasoline. In psychology, Lila and Jéro were fighting over the angle of their board. "Come check out our ballista," Tabitha called to me from engineering. It was ten feet long.

"In a sec," I said.

"It works so well that Chloe's dad wants to buy it off us for deer season," said Billiam.

I'd lost track of Alex and Ruth. Ms. Hutchins opened the doors, and the parents and siblings and judges streamed in. "I'll be right back," I said to Flynn.

"You can't leave!" he said. "Our first judge is coming!"

"But—I'm worried—"

"Focus!" hissed Flynn. "Here she is!"

I straightened my tie. Dr. Adams approached. She's been my pediatrician all my life. "Why, hello, Soren," she said in the exact tone she uses when I'm naked and wrapped in paper on the exam table. "And you are . . ."

"Flynn. Flynn Skaar. I'm Soren's cousin."

"It's a pleasure. Now, tell me about your experiment."

We hadn't practiced, but it went well. "Would you do anything differently," said Dr. Adams, "if you were doing this experiment again?"

"I'd love to have more cockroaches!" I said. Flynn jabbed me. "Ouch—what? I *like* cockroaches. They make great pets. And the more the merrier, right?"

Dr. Adams made some marks on her clipboard. When she left, Flynn said, "Did you have to mention the biggest problem with our experiment?"

"What do you mean?"

"The fact that we only had two cockroaches. Sample sets of one. It's a huge flaw. I was hoping she wouldn't notice."

"Oh."

"So when our other judge comes, how about you don't point that out?"

Parents were milling around the gym. Judges were peering at clipboards. Kids in ties and dresses were gesturing at graphs. *Some* kids.

Some kids, it seemed, were missing.

"I have to check on something," I said.

"You still can't leave!"

"I'll be back in five seconds." Before he could protest more, I wove through the crowd to psychology. "Jéro!" I said. "Where's Lila?"

"I don't know. Bathroom, maybe? It's awesome. She told me I wasn't allowed to speak when the judges came around, but hey, she wasn't here, so—"

I was gone, ducking and dodging my way to earth science. "Tori!" I said. She and Olivia had done something about the hardness of rocks. "Do you know where Olivia went?"

Tori rolled her eyes. "She had to nervous-pee. If you'd ever been in a play with her, you'd remember that every time—"

I sprinted off. Engineering was my last stop. If Tabitha wasn't there, I'd know.

"Billiam!" I panted. "Where's Tabitha?"

He gave me a slow look. "Why do you want to know?"

"Just tell me!"

Billiam can be kind of a jerk. If you want something fast, he takes his time. Finally, he said, "I don't know."

"Thanks, so helpful—"

"She went out that door. A while ago now. Fifteen minutes, maybe."

AHHH! Fifteen minutes? You could do a lot in fifteen minutes. "Okay. Thanks."

I ran back to zoology, getting a lot of dirty looks from parents and judges along the way. "Flynn," I said, "I've got to step out."

"But we have another judge coming any minute now!"

"I'll be back as soon as I can."

"You're leaving me to defend our project alone?"

"I know. I'm really sorry. But it's an emergency."

Images flashed through my head: Ruth on the video chat with Alex. Ruth following the triplets up their driveway after school. The five of them hunched together, the murmurs, the backpacks . . .

Flynn's eyes narrowed. "You're trying to prank science fair, aren't you?"

"No!"

"I'm supposed to believe that?"

"Flynn." I stared into his eyes. "Please. I know you don't trust me—but please. Believe me. Give me a chance. I'm not trying to prank science fair. I'm trying to *save* science fair."

He looked at me for a long, excruciating moment. "Fine. Go."

"Wait. What? You really—"

"Go. I don't know why I trust you, but I do. I'll cover for you. Go."

# CHAPTER FIFTY

I HAD A detailed digestive excuse all ready, but no teacher intercepted me as I dashed out of the gym and into the empty corridors of the school.

Where had those girls gone?

I rattled the doorknobs of the kindergarten rooms. Locked, all locked. I turned down the next hallway, tried the first-grade doors . . .

*Think,* Soren.

I leaned against a first-grade bulletin board (HOW DID WE CHOOSE KIND TODAY?). I took deep breaths and thought.

They would have already planned the prank. The video chats, the after-school meetings, the huddles today—the planning stage was over. So if they'd all snuck out together, it was because they needed a launchpad. They needed a place to prepare supplies before their massive prank.

A private place, but a place they could get into.

I started running again. I skidded to a halt outside the tiled entrance to the two bathrooms.

The boys' was empty. Of course. I shouldn't have wasted time checking.

I paused outside the girls'. Did I dare? I'd never gone into a girls' bathroom, and I had hoped I never would.

I set a foot inside, and then I pulled it out. I couldn't do it. "Hello?" I called. "Is anyone in there?"

Goldie's mom popped out, shaking wet hands in the air. "Soren! May I help you? Did you want paper towels for the boys' room? Because they're out in the girls', too. . . ."

"Um," I said, "actually, I was looking for, um, my sister? My mom told me to find her because they need to go home early—she just got a phone call with, uh, test results, and Ruth is *very* ill, strep throat, I think, and it's so contagious that she needs to be quarantined immediately—"

"Oh!" said Mrs. Grandin, taken aback. Darn. As usual, I'd tried to lie and ended up babbling. "Goodness gracious. I didn't think anyone was in there, but let me take a look."

I waited. She came out. "Looked under all the stalls," she reported, "and it's empty as a bird's nest in winter!"

"Okay, thanks, bye!" I took off down the hall.

"Give your sister my best wishes for a speedy recovery!" she called after me. "I'll be sure to spread the word about the strep outbreak!"

Great.

I took the stairs, swinging on the banister to make the turn. On the first floor, I'd been able to hear faint noise from the gym, but the second floor was eerily quiet. I grabbed a few doorknobs just to make sure, but the classrooms were locked up here, too. If they weren't in the second-floor bathrooms, I didn't know where they'd be. I doubted I'd be able to find them in time to stop whatever they were planning to do.

I slowed as I approached the bathrooms. There was a yellow plastic sign propped on the floor: RESTROOMS CLOSED FOR CLEANING.

Hmm.

I tiptoed into the boys' room. It was clear, as I'd expected.

I hovered outside the girls' room.

There was definitely water running. It could be a janitor.

But then I heard a familiar sound. A very familiar sound. A giggle I'd been hearing for over nine years now.

I burst in.

"The girls' bathroom has a *mirror*?" I said.

And the five girls who were gathered around the sinks, who were pulling water balloons onto the faucets, and tying them, and throwing them into a tall, deep laundry hamper, which was almost full of colorful blobs—they all jumped. They shouted, "SOREN!"

# CHAPTER FIFTY-ONE

"THIS IS THE GIRLS' BATHROOM," said Ruth. "You're not supposed to be in here."

"Didn't you see the sign?" said Lila. "This restroom is closed for cleaning."

"Oh, you're cleaning?" I said.

"How did you find us?" said Tabitha.

I shrugged. "I knew something was up. You didn't cover your tracks very well."

That got to Alex, I could tell. She finished the knot on her balloon with a sharp snap. "We weren't trying to hide our tracks from *you*."

"You sure were secretive, then."

"You retired. We weren't about to blab all the details to someone who'd retired."

It kind of made sense. But then I saw Alex worrying the earpiece of her glasses. She was lying. I babble; she plays with her glasses. It's like the sunrise. Couldn't stop it if you tried.

"Oh," I said, realizing what was going on. "You're still mad at me."

"Maybe I am," said Alex. "So?"

"So you left me out."

"Now you know what it feels like," said Ruth.

"No offense, Soren, but you wanted to be left out," said Tabitha. "You literally told us you were done with pranks."

But being left out stinks. Even when you've chosen it.

"Let's keep going," said Alex, checking her phone. "We only have ten minutes to finish filling these balloons. We've got to get the laundry hamper to the catwalk before the awards presentation starts."

"What about him?" asked Lila.

"I'm not going anywhere," I said.

"At this point, he'll just have to help," said Alex. "Congratulations. We're un-leaving you out."

"No, I—"

"Here's the plan. You know that catwalk above the stage? The door's only a few yards down from this bathroom." She jingled something in her pocket. "And I got the key."

"How?" I said.

"That's classified. Anyway. We fill the rest of these balloons. Then we all pull this huge hamper to the catwalk. It's going to be really heavy. Then you and the triplets go back to science fair. Ruth stands lookout, and I'll be on the catwalk by myself. The instant Ms. Hutchins starts the awards, wahoo! Look out below!"

"But everyone'll know where the balloons are coming from," I said. "You'll get caught so fast."

"I can throw a lot of water balloons in the time it takes Principal Leary to get up a flight of stairs."

"You'll get in so much trouble."

"What are they going to do?" said Alex. "Expel me?"

In the past, we'd always had one major constraint: we couldn't get caught. Suspicion and detentions, fine. Evidence and suspensions, no thanks.

But now . . .

"Leary'll tell your mom," I said.

"And I'll tell her it's her fault," said Alex. "If she hadn't made us move, I'd still be doing nice, normal pranks with you."

She had a point.

"Now let's get a move on with these water balloons."

"It's going to be out of control," I said. Hundreds of bright bulbs hurtling down from nowhere, like God had given up on locusts and decided to send a plague of water balloons instead. "It'll be chaos."

"It'll be amazing," said Alex. "Probably our best prank ever." She checked her phone again. "Enough talking. Soren, can you tie? Our fingers hurt."

I took up position next to Tabitha's sink. I tied a balloon.

This wasn't what I'd intended.

But the prank was simple. It was glorious. I was a lifelong prankster, and this was the prank of a lifetime. Saying no to this prank would be like an ice cream connoisseur saying no to the best ice cream in the world just because he was full from dinner. And water balloons were harmless. I'd tell Alex to take aim far from the science-fair projects so none of the boards would be ruined. People would get wet, sure, but people can dry.

This was the true Dream Team. This was my chance to prank with Alex and the triplets and Ruth, the five most devilishly clever people I knew. Besides, *I* wouldn't get in trouble. I'd return to the gym, and when Flynn said, "Did you save us?" I'd say, "I hope so. I tried. I did my best." And if something happened anyway, well, I'd be as shocked and angry as he was.

I tied another balloon and tossed it into the hamper. It landed with a wet plop. I wiped my hands on my dress pants. "I can't do this," I said.

"Tying water balloons is hard," said Olivia sympathetically.

"No. *This.* I can't do this prank." I thought of Flynn saying he trusted me. I thought of Dad telling me he believed in me, how he thought I could figure it out, this pranking thing, and I thought of Mom telling me to act like the person I wanted to be. "It's not fair," I said. "It's not fair to ruin science fair for everyone."

"Nobody'll get hurt," said Tabitha. "They'll just get wet."

Sometimes, wet was bad enough. "You guys don't know what it's like," I said. The spelling bee had been my fault, and I'd learned my lesson. "You don't know how guilty and awful you'll feel. I'm telling you, it's not worth it—"

"Leave," said Alex.

She stared me down. She'd left a water balloon attached to a spigot, and it bobbled around in the sink as it filled.

"Leave now," she said. "You were never here. You didn't see a thing."

"I can't let you do this prank," I said.

"You think you can stop us?"

I stood in front of the hamper and crossed my arms. "I'm going to try."

"No, you're not," said Alex. "You wouldn't do that to me. Because I've been waiting for this day for months, Soren. This is the only happy thing in my life right now. Moving ruined everything—"

"That's not even true!" I said. "That's just what you keep telling yourself! Alex, you *like* Minneapolis! You like paper dolls! You like Ol' Bu—you like *Sophia!*"

Alex's fists clenched. I made sure I'd squarely blocked the hamper. "Don't try to tell me the move was a good thing."

"I'm not! But it wasn't a bad thing, either. Some parts are bad, yeah—I miss pranking with you, Alex—I miss *you*, I really do—but some parts are good. You wouldn't be friends with Sophia if you hadn't moved. You wouldn't be friends with the triplets."

"You wouldn't even be talking to me," pointed out Ruth.

"I can't *believe* you're happy I moved," said Alex.

I opened my mouth to protest, but she lunged forward and shoved me. I fell back—

—butt-first—

—right into the deep laundry hamper.

"AHHH!"

It didn't hurt, because it was full of water balloons. But half of them burst and I sank way down. I was doubled up in a V shape, getting more waterlogged by the second.

"Help! Get me out!"

A pair of people hurtled into the bathroom.

Ms. Hutchins and Principal Leary.

"Uh-oh," said Ruth.

It was at that exact moment that the water pressure got to be too much for Alex's balloon, which had been bobbling around on the faucet. It exploded off. It bounced around in the sink, spraying water all the way up to the ceiling.

For the first time ever, Ms. Hutchins and Principal Leary were speechless.

# CHAPTER FIFTY-TWO

FINALLY, MS. HUTCHINS got her voice back. "What in the *world*?"

The balloon in the sink sputtered merrily along. I was stuck in the hamper, trying not to move. I was worried that if I struggled, it'd tip over.

"The judges asked us why so many students were missing their partners," Ms. Hutchins told us. "So we thought we'd take a quick look around the school. And—well. Look at this."

"More sabotage," said Principal Leary. His lips were a thin line. "The rash of pranks that have marred our fine school this fall . . . I'd hoped it was over. But no. Not if you had your way."

The girls looked intensely guilty, all staring at the floor and turning red. I lurched a little deeper in the hamper. The water was still leaking out of balloons that had split when I'd landed.

"Trying to destroy science fair," said Leary, shaking his

294

head. "It's hard to believe you'd have so little respect for all the hard work that's gone into this event."

What was hard to believe was that Leary was saying basically the same thing I'd just said. It made me worry I'd grow up to be a principal.

"We're sorry," said Tabitha.

"No," I heard myself say. It was a total impulse. "*I'm* sorry. *You* had nothing to do with it."

"What?" said Leary.

I swallowed. I reminded myself, *Don't babble.* "It was only me," I said. "I was acting alone. They were trying to stop me."

"Soren—" said Tabitha.

I cut her off. "That's how I ended up in here," I said, gesturing at the hamper. A balloon popped at the movement, and I sank another inch. I was so folded up that my legs almost touched my face. "They shoved me down. They didn't want to resort to violence, but they had no other choice. I was about to take the balloons to the"—but I couldn't give away that Alex had the key to the catwalk—"to, um, downstairs."

Leary nodded slowly. "And these young ladies—these heroes—stopped you?"

"Right!" Oops. I couldn't sound too happy about it. I glared at the girls. "I had such a good plan, too. But they must have been tipped off. Maybe I left some evidence lying around at home, a water-balloon receipt, maybe, or . . ." *Don't babble!* "I was an idiot."

"That's not true!" said Ruth. "It was all of us! It was everyone *but* him!"

"Don't try to save me," I said. "Besides, nobody's going to believe it was you."

"Ruth, honey," said Ms. Hutchins, "I'm a little sister too, and I know it's hard to see your big brother in trouble. But you don't need to take responsibility for his actions."

"We do admire your loyalty, however," said Leary.

He whispered something in Ms. Hutchins's ear. I took the opportunity to give Ruth a threatening look. *Don't,* I mouthed.

"Nobody move," Leary told us. "The floor's very wet and slippery. We'll be right back. Your parents need to be here for this conversation."

They left the bathroom. The girls waited ten seconds, and then they turned on me. "Soren!" said Ruth, almost in tears. "You can't do this!"

"It makes sense," I said. "I get in trouble all the time. I'm known for it. But you guys, you have perfect reputations. You don't want to ruin them." I smiled, but it was shaky. I'd begun to think about what Mom and Dad would do to me when they found out. Taking the blame *did* make sense. I knew it. But I needed to remind myself why. "You'll be way more useful for future pranks if you remain above suspicion," I said.

"But it wasn't your fault," said Tabitha.

"Well. I've done a bunch of things I didn't get caught for. So it's only fair I get caught for something I didn't do."

Olivia tearfully twisted her hands together. "We've been working with you all fall," she said. "We're just as bad."

"But the spelling bee going so wrong, that was my fault. You didn't know that Ruth and Flynn would care so much."

"What about me?" said Alex. It was the first thing she'd said since they'd found us. "It should be me, Soren. It was my idea. And I was always going to get caught. That was the plan."

I met Alex's eyes and gave her a smile, as big a smile as possible for someone who's soaking wet and stuck in a hamper with their knees around their ears. "Nope," I said. "I've been waiting for this."

"What do you mean?" said Ruth.

"This one's mine," I said.

Alex shook her head. "This is so much worse than a few plastic ants."

"Then throw in that catwalk key."

"Soren—"

"Alex."

We locked eyes. Slowly, she began to grin. "Deal."

"Your moving away," I told her, "is about the hardest thing that's ever happened to me. I'm just trying to get okay with it."

"I know," she said. "Me too."

Lila stamped her foot. "This is *stupid*, Soren. We're not letting you take the blame."

"Let me," I said. "Please."

She faced me, her hands on her hips. Lila's bossy, but

I'm stubborn. I was feeling good again, and I knew I was in the home stretch. If I could convince them before the teachers came back, they wouldn't stop me—and I wouldn't stop myself—from doing the first truly nice thing I'd done for a very long time.

"If you don't let me," I said sweetly, "I'll call up your big brother. Ethan, right? I'll tell him all about what you've been up to this school year. Alarm clocks, Jim Bob, water balloons—oh, it'll be blackmail for *years*."

She twitched. "No! Don't!"

"Then keep your mouth shut."

She subsided. She tried to glare at me, but I saw the smile tickling the corners of her mouth.

"I'm only asking for one thing in return," I said.

"Anything," said Tabitha.

A water balloon popped. I sank an inch deeper. "Help me out of this laundry hamper?"

# CHAPTER FIFTY-THREE

RUMORS ARE AMAZING. By the time we made it downstairs, everyone knew that I had tried to destroy science fair with a hundred water balloons. By the time Ms. Hutchins took the stage for the awards, it was a thousand, and at the end of the night, Jéro said, "I heard you built an automatic water-balloon launcher. Like a catapult, except with a motor and a robotic arm for reloading."

"Um, not quite."

"That's so cool that I'm not even mad you didn't tell me. I'm just impressed."

"Well, I didn't—"

"Sticking to your story even now, huh?" He clapped me on the back. "You're a pro."

Principal Leary had come back to the bathroom alone. He'd told us to return to the gym, because Ms. Hutchins needed to announce the awards and it was getting late. "I've already told your parents what you did, Soren," he said. "You and I will meet with them tomorrow to discuss consequences." It'd be a painful meeting, I could already tell, but honestly, right now, I was glowing.

I joined Flynn at the board. Luckily my pants were black so it didn't look like I'd had an accident. "How was the second judge?" I said.

"Not bad. He asked me about the sample-size thing, though. He said, 'Wouldn't your results mean more if you had more than one cockroach in each kind of habitat?'"

"Oh."

"But he was impressed by our detailed data." Flynn shrugged. "So we'll see." He looked me up and down. "Soup and Freddy told me you were caught with a bunch of water balloons."

"I was."

"Were you lying to me?"

"No."

"Then," said Flynn, "I won't ask you anything else." He knelt to peer into the fish tank. "The second judge said Cah and Croach were the best-tended cockroaches he's ever seen."

I puffed up with pride. "It's all in the desserts. Cockroaches are happiest when they get dessert with all three meals."

"I think I'll add Cah and Croach to my mural."

"About that," I said. "How come you have a mural of me looking stupid?"

"Huh?"

"Every time I'm embarrassed, you draw it on your wall."

Flynn still looked confused. "No. I draw happy things.

Things I like about Camelot. They cheer me up when I'm feeling cruddy."

"You drew the time I sat on poop play dough!"

"No, I drew the first time Ivan acted like he liked me."

"What about everyone ignoring me at the block party?"

"You mean everyone wanting me to take piglet pics of them?"

I fell silent. Had I missed the whole point of the mural?

"Okay. What about Ms. Hutchins telling the class about the anonymous tip? Explain *that*."

"That's just a picture of science class."

"Then why is she holding a piece of paper?"

"Because she's a teacher!"

"Oh," I said.

"Are we cool, then?"

"We're cool."

Flynn stood. He squinched the knot of his silver tie tighter. "Hey. Thanks."

"For what?"

"You know." He gave me the kind of smile he usually flashes at gross food or an especially pleasing banjo chord. "For saving us."

I HADN'T NOTICED Principal Leary's necktie earlier. I'd had other things on my mind. As he stepped up to the stage, I saw that it was patterned with test tubes.

He tapped the mike. For once, it worked on the first try. "Good evening, and thank you for attending the Camelot Elementary School science fair!"

After some stuff about young minds and STEM and the curiosity inherent to human nature, blah blah, he turned the mike over to Ms. Hutchins. She started with the list of projects that received Superior, the highest designation. "Please," said Flynn under his breath, "please, please, please . . ."

Goldie and Kiyana got it, what a surprise, for *Does a Watched Pot Boil? A Scientific Investigation.*

And Soup and Evelyn got it, which actually *was* a surprise, for *What's Faster at Crawling: A Stinkbug or a Human Child?*

Flynn's shoulders sagged as the last Superior was applauded, Emily and Jeremiah's *Can People Do Math Problems Better in Peace, or While Listening to Heavy Metal and Being Poked with a Fork?*

"It was the sample-size thing," Flynn said heavily.

"That's my fault! I told Dr. Adams!"

"She'd have noticed it anyway, and the other judge saw it himself. It's all my fault. I designed the experiment."

"It's half my fault," I said.

Then we got Excellent, which was second best. Flynn cheered up considerably. "Excellent!" he said, admiring our certificate. "You know what? I'll take it."

I plastered the certificate against the fish tank to show Cah and Croach.

MOM AND DAD came over as we were packing up. "Where's Ivan?" I asked.

"He's with a few girls from your class," said Mom. "They think he's very cute."

"They aren't letting him near the engineering section, are they?"

"Well, as a matter of fact—"

I dropped the board and sprinted to Tabitha and Billiam's huge ballista. Sure enough, Ivan was toddling toward the lever, a giant grin on his face. He had already loaded the bucket with what looked to be an entire box of pre-chewed graham crackers.

"STOP HIM!" I panted.

"Oh, Soren," said Emily. "He's just a baby!"

Ivan stomped on the lever the moment before I reached him. The spring released. The spitty wad of graham crackers sailed up, up, up—

Everyone in the gym swiveled to watch as it soared through the air.

It hit the basketball hoop's backboard, rebounded, fell through, and landed on Ms. Hutchins's head.

She looked more surprised than upset as she reached up to investigate. "Oh," she said. She swiped another clod off her hair, and then gave a queenly wave to the gym of people staring at her in horror. "I'm fine!" she called. "Just another reason I'll be glad when this evening's over!"

Everyone broke into raucous applause.

"Let's see if the ballista's strong enough to shoot *him*," I said, delivering Ivan back to my parents.

"IVAN FLY!" he yelled.

We were in the parking lot on the way to our car when Mrs. Grandin ran up. "I'm so glad I caught you!" she said to Mom. "How *is* she? Sleeping, I hope?"

Ruth was carrying our board. I motioned to her, and she lifted it up to cover her face.

"Who?" said Mom. "What?"

"Your wonderful son told me about poor Ruthie's illness," Mrs. Grandin said. "Earlier tonight, when he was looking for her in the bathroom."

"Earlier tonight," said Mom. "Really."

"I was on my way out—that first-floor bathroom is so ridiculous for adults; it's kindergarten-sized, of course, the toilets about eight inches from the floor—and Soren said you'd sent him to find her. What a kind brother."

"The first-floor bathroom," said Dad. *"Really."*

"You were searching for her in quite a tizzy, weren't you, Soren?"

"Quite," I said.

"Do tell me she's being treated," said Mrs. Grandin.

"I'm sure she'll be fine," said Mom. "Thanks for asking, Gardenia."

# CHAPTER FIFTY-FOUR

MOM AND DAD totally knew what had happened. I got two days of in-school suspension from Principal Leary, but they didn't punish me extra at all, and either they forgave Flynn and me for being out of bed at four a.m. or they forgot. For obvious reasons, I couldn't ask.

The one tricky thing about the meeting was when Principal Leary said, "So. I have to wonder, Soren. The alarm clocks? The piglet? Were those you, too?"

I don't know what I'd have done if Dad's lawyer half hadn't firmly collided with his protective papa-bear half.

"Ex*cuse* me," Dad said. "Are you suggesting that confessing to one crime is tantamount to confessing to *all* crimes?"

"No—er—"

"Because the fallacies therein, sir, are not only manifold but also problematic, vide Federal Rules of Evidence 404(b), and I, for one, would take serious umbrage—"

"I just—uh—"

Dad eyed him. "Yes?"

"It was just a passing thought," said Leary. "Let's move on, shall we?"

On the way out of the meeting, Dad said to me, "This confession. I assume you know what you're doing."

"Yup," I said.

"Well, don't ever do this again. But I'm proud."

"Me too," said Mom. "Soren, do you remember when Alex first left? And I told you, 'Keep doing what you like to do'?"

"Yeah . . ."

"If you're going to retire from pranking," said Mom, "you should Michael Phelps–style retire."

I hoped that didn't involve the butterfly, because whenever I try that stroke I swallow a gallon of lake water and spend the rest of the day with algae-flavored burps. "What do you mean?"

Mom put her arm around my shoulders. "Retire, and then make a triumphant comeback in a few months."

"Agreed," said Dad, putting *his* arm around my shoulders, and for a minute we stumbled down the hallway like that, giggling as our legs got tangled up. Then I saw Tabitha at the water fountain, and I squirmed out of their arms. You don't exactly want a girl in your grade to see you in a parent sandwich.

FLYNN HAD PLANNED to spend winter break in Brooklyn, but he asked his mom to come to Camelot instead. "I like it here," he told us.

"Really?" I said. "Don't you miss the green tea? The vintage trunk shop?"

"Soren," warned Mom.

"My mom will replenish my supply of green tea," Flynn said. "And you can only own so many vintage trunks."

This was undeniably true.

"Plus," said Flynn, "everything I care about is right here in Camelot—"

"That's so sweet," said Dad.

"My banjo, my rhyming dictionary . . ."

"Right," said Dad.

"In fact, I've written one last song for my concept album. Would you like to hear it?"

"We wouldn't miss it for the world," said Mom.

Flynn strummed. "A remix of 'Winter Wonderland'!" he cried, and began to sing.

> *"Oh, the climate is dismal,*
> *And the coffee's abysmal.*
> *The nearest Thai food's two hours removed.*
> *Exiled to a small-town wonderland.*
>
> *"But the crops here are top-flight.*
> *There's no traffic, one stoplight.*
> *And what is more posh than prize-winning squash?*
> *Living in a small-town wonderland!*
>
> *"Back in Brooklyn, I was on my lonesome,*
> *And when I got here, I kept calling out,*

*'Don't you want to hear of where I've flown from?'*
*'Not at all,' you said, 'but let's hang out!'*

*"Now I've learned that I cheer up*
*At the taste of corn syrup.*
*My dear country folk, let's share a Coke,*
*Living in our hometown wonderland!"*

"Is that supposed to be a subtle hint?" said Dad. He went to the garage and came back with a twelve-pack of Coke.

"That's two each," said Ruth.

"Not so fast, young lady," said Mom. "You and Soren may split a can to start."

"Speaking of sharing," said Flynn, "I've been thinking. What if Soren moves back into my room?"

"You're the guest," I said. "I don't mind another semester being crammed in with Ruth and Ivan."

"I think it'd be fun," said Flynn.

"Me too." I thought for a second. "Can we keep Cah and Croach on the windowsill? They prefer natural light."

Flynn grimaced. "I suppose."

"Don't worry," I said. "They'll never escape again."

Ivan came running into the kitchen with a present from under the tree. It was the one he was the most curious about, a package that was long and skinny and weirdly light. "IVAN OPEN!"

"Not till Christmas, sweetie," said Dad.

"If that's what I think it is," I said, "I might move out."

"Ivan's fencing instructor says he has some real talent," said Dad. "It's only right that we let him develop it."

ON THE FIRST day back to school, Ms. Hutchins was humming with excitement. "This semester, we continue our mission to think like a scientist," she said. "And you've proven you can handle advanced scientific tools!"

She whipped a sheet off a table of equipment.

"Bunsen burners!" she said.

Oh, *heck* yes.

Comeback, here I come.

Ms. Hutchins began to review safety procedures, but all I could see was the steady blue flame.

When you're *allowed* to play with fire at school—

When playing with fire is actually *the assignment*—

The possibilities were endless.

Flynn took notes. The triplets looked about as happy as I felt. "Psst!" said Tabitha. "Want to plot during recess?"

"You bet."

"Only after our badminton tournament's over," said Jéro.

I paid careful attention as Ms. Hutchins explained how to work the Bunsen burners. I didn't know yet what we'd do, but I was starting to get a few ideas.

# ACKNOWLEDGMENTS

I am deeply grateful to the people whom I lived among as I wrote this book. You are the lights of my life, and very chuffing besides. Thank you, Henry, Peter, Rebecca, Emma, Lucy, Derek, and Spencer. Thank you, Mom and Dad. Thank you, Phil. Thank you, Abbey, Allison, Ariel, Desi, Ken, Liz, Nate, Peter, Rita, Rita's vomiting rooster, Sarah, and Sasha.

Erin Clarke, thank you for having faith in this book when it was only three chapters and a synopsis that was heavily centered on the Bayeux Tapestry. It has truly been an honor to work with you again. Uwe Stender, I am, as ever, grateful for your insight, hard work, and good cheer. Many thanks also to Leslie Mechanic, Karen Sherman, Artie Bennett, Alison Kolani, Kelly Delaney, and the whole team at Random House.

I cannot express the depth of my gratitude; I am fortunate to be able to try. Thank you.

# KATE HATTEMER

is a native of Cincinnati, but now writes, reads, runs, and teaches high school Latin in the D.C. metro area. She is the author of two novels for young adults: *The Vigilante Poets of Selwyn Academy,* which received five starred reviews and was named a best book of the year by the American Library Association, *Kirkus Reviews,* and *Bustle,* and *The Land of 10,000 Madonnas.* Learn more about Kate on her website at KateHattemer.com.